PU[illegible]

HORRID[illegible]

Payal Kapadia grew up rea[illegible] get her hands on; writing poetry for a captive a[illegible], and presiding over a club called the Stupendous Six, wh[illegible]endous amount of nothing.

Her critically acclaimed debut, [illegible]ozzariter, won the Crossword Book Award 2013 for Children's Writing. Payal writes full-time now (if you don't count the time spent getting her two daughters to eat faster, please). She has authored *Colonel Hathi Loses His Brigade, Puffin Lives: B.R. Ambedkar* and *Washed Up!*, a reader for Australian, British and American schools. *Horrid High: Back to School* is the eagerly awaited follow-up to her bestselling school adventure, *Horrid High*.

Payal has travelled to the Jaipur Literature Festival, Bookaroo, the Sharjah Children's Reading Festival and the Kala Ghoda Festival. She reads to children at schools all over the country where she refuses to be taken seriously.

Find her at www.payalkapadia.com or www.horridhigh.com

Other books in Puffin by Payal Kapadia

Wisha Wozzariter

Puffin Lives: B.R. Ambedkar

Horrid High

HORRID HIGH

BACK TO SCHOOL

PAYAL KAPADIA

Illustrations by Roger Dahl

PUFFIN BOOKS

An imprint of Penguin Random House

PUFFIN BOOKS

USA | Canada | UK | Ireland | Australia
New Zealand | India | South Africa | China

Puffin Books is part of the Penguin Random House group of companies whose addresses can be found at global.penguinrandomhouse.com

Published by Penguin Random House India Pvt. Ltd
4th Floor, Capital Tower 1, MG Road,
Gurugram 122 002, Haryana, India

First published in Puffin by Penguin Books India 2015

10 9 8 7 6 5 4 3 2

This is a work of fiction. Names, characters, places and incidents are either the product of the author's imagination or are used fictitiously and any resemblance to any actual person, living or dead, events or locales is entirely coincidental.

ISBN 9780143333180

Typeset in Crimson Text by R. Ajith Kumar, New Delhi

Printed at Repro India Limited

www.penguin.co.in

For my darling girls Keya and Nyla, who eagerly devoured this book, chapter by chapter, hot off the mind-press, and did without me for days on end when I was away at Horrid High.

For Kunal, for letting me figure this book out all by myself. How very Granny Grit of you!

For Roger Dahl—you are a true artist! You make producing masterpieces look easy.

For my editor, Niyati Dhuldhoya, for leading me out of the Get Lost Forever Woods where my plot and I would have languished till the end of time. This book is yours as much as mine.

And for all the enthusiastic readers of Book One who asked the question I love most: 'What happens next?' Now you know.

HORRID HIGH
GET LOST FOREVER WOODS
ABANDONED FACTORY
DUCK LAKE
DEAD END STATION
TO HH
POST OFFICE
OLDY MOLDY'S CHEESES
FLOG SHOP
HORRID HIGH

CHAPTER 1

If twelve-year-old Ferg Gottin had been bought from a store, his parents would have returned him and demanded a refund. Instead, Mr and Mrs Gottin sent their son to Horrid High and took off for a vacation in the Bahamas.

Mrs Gottin hadn't stepped out of her air-conditioned room because she was certain that the heat would curl up her hair. Mr Gottin hadn't stepped into his room because he was certain that sweating it out on the patio would make him thinner. But they were happy—as it is expected that any parent on a holiday without children would be.

Mrs Gottin was reading the *Daily Post* online: *Happy High is actually Horrid High: Tammy Telltale tells all.* She stiffened. 'Darling!' she called out, a tremor in her voice. 'D'you think they'll send him back to us, now that Horrid High is no longer horrid?'

Mrs Gottin felt her hair curl at the thought and she cursed the tropics. Mr Gottin felt his holiday mood curdle and he cursed his wife.

Halfway across the world, another head was bent over the same headlines. This was an exceptionally ugly head, an extraordinarily hideous head, an eminently objectionable head. This head was infested with horrid ideas. They swam around like germs; they whispered horrid things; they seethed to be let loose like snakes in a pit.

The hair on this head was practically fried to a crisp by all the horrid activity underneath. There were large welts of angry skin where the hair had fallen clean off. What hair remained was frizzled and grizzled, like it had been left on a barbecue and forgotten. If you were to run a hand through that hair—and no one except its owner had ever dared do that—you would find that it *sizzled.*

On the left of this eminently objectionable head, square on its owner's right shoulder, sat a bamboo lemur.

'It can't be,' the head muttered, and the shoulders dropped so abruptly, the lemur jumped. 'It can't BE!' And now the owner of the head crumpled the newspaper into a large ball and lobbed it across the room, knocking the lemur clean off.

'Stupid monkey!' he snarled, even though the stupidity was entirely his to mistake a lemur for a monkey. The lemur skittered away, which was a sensible thing to do because it was the last of its kind left on earth.

The extraordinarily hideous head was on the phone now. It did not waste time with niceties like 'Hello?' or 'Would this be a good time to speak?' It came to the point right away. 'Find the Grand Plan—and fast! Or our deal is off!'

'What about her?' said the faint voice on the other end. 'She'll only be in the way!'

The hairless patches on the back of that head got redder. 'Leave her to me!'

The head made one more call. 'Stir up some trouble in the Amazon, cut down some forest, choke up a river or two but enough about how Happy High is actually Horrid High! Give the papers a new story, will you?'

Somewhere between the Gottins and the lemur owner, a better-looking head was bent over the same newspaper in a school that had once been horrid. The hair on this head was a gleaming silver. *This* head was brimful of the sort of rock-solid ideas that save the planet and make children everywhere feel loved.

The owner of this head was also disturbed by the headlines because she knew that there were more ways in the world to destroy something than to save it. Over twenty years ago, she had left this school to start the Grit Movement. It was a worldwide movement now, fighting politicians and business barons hell-bent on plundering the planet for their own gains, and saving animals from the brink of extinction. Last year, she'd returned to find that the happy school she'd left behind was on the brink of extinction too. It was a horrid school now, possibly the world's most horrid school.

Granny Grit's face brightened as she remembered how the children and she had pitted their wits against Principal Perverse. How they'd busted the Grand Party he'd thrown for a thousand horrid teachers before he could announce his hideous Grand Plan. Even though they had no idea what the Grand Plan was or where it had vanished, Horrid High was in safe hands now. Why waste newspaper space on it? It was the rest of the world Granny Grit was worried about.

'Oh dear, thousands of refugees have fled Burma with nowhere to go,' said Granny Grit, narrowing her chocolate brown eyes. 'And *this* makes front page news?'

The children of Horrid High were huddled over the *Daily Post.* They had been cut off from the world earlier, but Granny Grit always began her classes with news time. They read the papers together, they circled the stories that made them think and they discussed why some of the smallest stories were often the most important. Immy read the story out loud from the newspaper, even though all the children knew it inside out. They had, after all, lived it.

> *'An unruly celebration attended by 1000 horrid teachers turned into a police crackdown after five clever children at Happy High shot a video and took photographs as proof that their school was far from happy.*
>
> *'"Happy High is really Horrid High!" says Tammy Telltale, a student and author of the bestselling The Tales of Horrid High. "It is the world's most horrid school!"*

'In a shocking revelation, Miss Telltale told this paper that her school masqueraded as a happy orphanage in order to receive a generous government grant. "Principal Perverse was a horrid man!" says Miss Telltale. "He dragged me to the Tower of Torture once for no fault of mine!"'

Immy couldn't help but stop to mutter under her breath, in a perfect impression of Tammy's nasal voice, *'For no fault of mine!'* That certainly wasn't how she remembered it! Tammy had been threatening to tattle on them. But instead, she'd ended up in the dark, windowless tower where Principal Perverse liked to punish his students. It served her right, it did!

'Go on, Immy!' said the class, giggling because the school's most talented mimic had muttered loud enough for everyone to hear. Immy pulled a face, drew a long breath and resumed reading.

'It now appears that this horrid school was a training ground for horrid teachers everywhere. The principal and his teachers are in jail now, but no one at school, not even Miss Telltale, will divulge the names of those clever children. Nor does anyone seem to know what a thousand horrid teachers were celebrating that day. It probably doesn't matter. It is the children of Horrid High who should be celebrating, now that their school is horrid no more.'

The kids drummed their desks with their hands and stomped their feet. In Granny Grit's classroom, it was perfectly all right to express joy—even if they were a little too loud about it! When the jubilation had subsided, Granny Grit spoke again.

'The Grand Party has come and gone,' she said, brushing away a stray white lock of hair. 'Can you find other stories on the back pages that should have been out front today?'

This was no ordinary classroom and Granny's style of teaching took some getting used to. There were a few orphans here but mostly, the children were runaways and rejects for whom the school was home. Like Phil Fingersmith, legendary lock-picker whose parents had moved to Somalia without leaving a forwarding address. And Immy Tate, mimic beyond compare, who escaped the circus after her folks abandoned her. Like Fermina Filch, pickpocket par excellence, whose parents had so many children that the novelty had worn off. And Ferg Gottin, with a remarkable memory for the tiniest of details, who ended up at Horrid High so that his mom and dad could forget *their* tiny detail: him.

Most of the children had ended up at Horrid High because this was a school where you could dump your kids and forget about them. Now, orphans, runaways and rejects are scarcely Most Wanted—unless they've committed a crime. But Granny Grit made it a point to make the children feel Most Wanted—to ask how they were, to mark their birthdays, to note what books they enjoyed, and yes, even to seek their opinions on the day's news.

'Tammy looks good in this photo,' said Fermina grudgingly.

Then she asked the question that was on everyone's mind. 'Will she be back at school?'

There was a pause as everyone who had known Tammy secretly prayed that she wouldn't. You see, Tammy Telltale was an incurable snitch and an intolerable snoop. Back when Horrid High had been horrid, she had made life miserable for the other children by swooping down on secrets and eavesdropping on conversations that she had no business listening to. Tammy couldn't resist a good story, especially if telling that story landed someone in trouble. A horrid school full of horrid teachers set right by five children—*what a scoop!*

Granny Grit grimaced as she thought of Mrs Telltale, who called her every two weeks. 'We're at a bookstore in the mountains now, Grandma Grit, and the entire village has trekked up to hear my Tammy read!' she said in a voice that set Granny's teeth on edge, and not only because Mrs Telltale insisted on calling her Grandma! 'My Tammy's been practically mobbed by fans and the queue for her readings stretches all the way down two streets!'

Both mother and daughter were having too much fun being famous. Granny Grit was certain that school was a distant thought for them. 'I don't think she'll be back any time soon,' she said, marking that it had been thirteen whole days since Mrs Telltale's last annoying call. Thirteen blissful days.

Calls! Granny glanced at her watch. They were only halfway through an exciting lesson, but now she would have to tear herself away from the classroom and attend to calls. She sighed. Being principal wasn't even half as much fun as teaching.

'There's an oil spill in Alaska on page twelve that deserves to be on the front page,' said Phil wryly. 'Another leaky ship that forgot to clean up after itself!'

'You'll have to wait your turn,' said an impish girl on the middle bench, making everyone laugh because of the imperious way in which she said it. 'There's a fantastic library about to be demolished because no one will cough up the money to preserve it! Page fourteen!'

'And what about the last page, just ahead of the sports section?' said Ferg. 'Children dying of starvation when there's enough food to go around!'

The children broke into a heated discussion until a tall boy at the back raised his hand. 'Let's do this in an orderly way, boys and girls,' he said. 'Yes, Immy, what do you have to say?'

Granny heaved a sigh of relief. Her class could manage without her, at least for a half hour. 'Could I be excused?' she asked. 'It'll be time for lunch soon, and we have a new cook. Highly recommended, too, by the way!'

The class promised not to be noisy—OK, not *too* noisy—and Granny Grit hurried out, smiling. Horrid High was certainly a happier place with Tammy away, with Principal Perverse in jail and with every last horrid teacher rounded up by the long arm of the law.

Every last horrid teacher. That thought slowed Granny Grit down. Could Horrid High put its horrid past behind it at last? Just then, a loud clatter of dishes from the kitchen made her start. The new cook! Food had been a nasty business for the old cook. Chef Gretta Gross had delighted in making the sort of food that no one could eat. Merely the memory of her Maggoty Pizza and Fermented Fish Soup made Granny's hair stand on end, and she decided to go downstairs to the dining room. A small detour to see what Chef Gretta's replacement was up to couldn't hurt.

She walked a little faster past the Great Hall on the ground floor. That was where Principal Perverse's whip lay, in a glass case, like the ridiculous red velvet chair he had sat on while hatching his wicked plot to spread horridness everywhere. The Throne. The whip and the chair always brought unpleasant thoughts like flies to a feast. It had been far too tempting to burn them, just as every copy of the *Book of Rules* had been burnt. Or to bury them or cart them to the farthest garbage dump on the planet, where no one would ever see them again. There! Horrid thoughts were taking hold, even though she'd looked away, but then the aroma of vanilla got into her nostrils.

Ah! It was the smell of freshly baked cake, of birthday parties and warm, loving families. It was as if the new cook had sent the aroma wafting out of the kitchen by way of introduction. And Granny Grit's mind switched from Chef Gretta to the lunch menu like it was the easiest thing in the world.

The new cook had his back to her. He was leaning over a large pot of something that smelt delicious and bubbled wickedly. He turned quickly, even before Granny had spoken, as though he'd sensed that Granny was behind him. He was so tall, his head knocked against a pan hanging from above.

'Don't mind me, I'm only sneaking a peek,' said Granny, when the cook put out a large veined hand to shake hers. It dripped egg yolk and milk—or was that milk?

'It's custard,' said the cook, reading her mind. 'For lunch.'

He was a bulldozer of a man, a misfit in the kitchen, dwarfing even the enormous oven to toy size. He was almost doubled over the stove, and every time he moved, his elbows or his head struck something. His hair was pulled back in a topknot, slicked into place.

He was all sinew and muscle, more the sort of person who should be doing push-ups in an army camp than cooking for a school full of children. But his smile was playful and his mouth twitched at the edges, like it would break out into a laugh anytime, anywhere. And if the aromas in his kitchen were any indication, he knew what he was doing and he had fun doing it.

'I'm just leaving,' Granny Grit said, taking in the mess, the eggshells and the empty packets waiting to be binned. It wasn't easy cooking for so many children, Granny knew—she had done this every day since the police had carted Chef Gretta off to jail.

She stuck her head back in as an afterthought, or maybe

because another whiff of that heavenly, creamy dessert would send her floating upstairs without a care in the world. 'What are you making?'

'Crème brawlay,' he said with a small smile.

It was only when Granny Grit returned to her desk and reached for the phone that she gave the cook's reply a moment's consideration. 'Crème brawlay,' he had said. Now, Granny was well travelled and loved crème brûlée. She also knew that B-R-Û-L-É-E is pronounced 'brulay', not 'brawlay'. She chuckled to herself; the poor man had a problem with his French, that was all.

CHAPTER 2

A yellow blob of egg yolk landed on Tammy Telltale's face, turning the caption under her photograph into a black mush. As Cook Fedro Fracas spread the day's paper over the kitchen counter, he giggled. It was rather an odd little sound issuing from someone this large and it made him sound like a schoolkid, but the good cook couldn't be bothered to produce a more aggressive snigger. There was something about food on face, *any* face, that tickled his funny bone.

Why, the first time Cook Fracas got food on *his* face, he'd only just been born. His arrival had produced a cry of joy from his mother, a whoop of delight from his father and a fresh flurry of activity from the doctor. But outside the hospital window, down in the streets of Ivrea, it made no difference to anyone.

You see, in this small northern Italian city that you needed good eyesight to find on a map, a battle was underway. It was nothing terrible, really—no blood, no guns—just a crowd of madcaps in medieval costume pelting each other with oranges. Yes, oranges. It's an annual tradition.

Now, *bambino* Fedro had only just taken his first breath. The doctor had slapped his bottom, the nurse had pinched the goo out of his nose and he had taken a pee that made him feel wet and cold. None of this helped his mood any. So when a segment of orange came flying through the window and landed splat on his head, he bawled lustily.

In the years to come, that war-worn orange had an unexpected effect on young Fedro's personality. Why else would he take such delight in flinging carrot puree at his parents from his high chair? Or pitching peas at his classmates? Or, worst of all, lobbing a ketchup-soaked French fry at his principal that got him a suspension from school?

Many suspensions later, Cook Fracas applied for the post of army cook because he assumed that an army mess was a place where it was perfectly all right to make a mess. If only someone had told him that an army mess is just the word for an army kitchen!

He threw tomatoes at some soldiers and one landed straight on the general's face. At this point, you should know that a general is the army's version of a school principal. Neither have been known to possess a sense of humour, especially when it comes to flying food. The flying tomato was the end of Fedro's army career.

Now, Cook Fracas was beating a hundred eggs in the Horrid High kitchen. A French dessert was on the menu—crème brawlay! The cook giggled again. The real reason Cook Fracas called his cream dish a 'brawlay' was because it *wasn't* a 'brûlée', which means 'burnt cream'. It was the cook's own invention, inspired by the English word 'brawl'.

From what Cook Fracas had been told about Horrid High, the cook before him had been a real meanie. Now, Cook Fracas was no meanie, but he certainly made a mean dessert. He rubbed his hands gleefully. He'd leave the kids at Horrid High licking their fingers. And wiping their faces. And mopping the floor. In other words, Cook Fracas's crème brawlay was an unholy excuse for a rumpus, a scuffle, a right and proper food fight.

He noted, with pleasure, that the yolk on that day's paper had spread outwards, making a spongy mess of Tammy in her Sunday best. Served her right, whoever she was.

Upstairs in her office, Granny Grit was listening closely to the police inspector on the other end of the telephone. 'We haven't found every last horrid teacher, Principal Grit, but we will,' he was saying.

Granny sighed—the whole sticky matter was giving her a headache. She'd been away from school for a long time, too long, leading the Grit Movement. If she had dreamt, even for one moment, that the happy school she'd left behind would turn into a horrid school . . .

She pinched her eyebrows with her fingers to dull the pain. And somewhere above her right brow, she found a smidge of custard that came off on her fingers. She should have washed in the basin but it would be rude to put the busy inspector on hold. Without another thought, Granny Grit licked the custard off. And even though licking food off your hands isn't the best way to get them clean, principals have been known to do it. The custard was so heavenly, it made Granny feel like singing.

'We still haven't been able to get to the bottom of things, why the principal needed to throw this mad bash and call every horrid teacher,' the inspector was saying. 'We haven't had any leads on the Grand Plan. Perhaps it's best forgotten for now?'

'As long as we don't forget forever, Inspector,' said Granny Grit as she rung off. *History will not repeat itself as long as we remember,* she thought to herself. Wasn't that why the whip and the Throne were preserved for everyone to see? Wasn't that why she'd insisted that the school should still be known as Horrid High?

But only in name. The old sign, the one that said *There will always be consequences* had been trashed. The new sign on the gate put it quite well: *There will always be a home here.* But turning a school around wasn't as easy as just changing the sign on the gate—Granny knew that.

The school was a little smaller for now. Some of the old children had left, those with distant relatives or parents who'd had a change of heart after reading the newspapers and been horrified enough to come claim them. Granny Grit thought of Mesmer Martin, the dark-haired girl with hypnotic skills,

and smiled. Mesmer was home with her father now and there was no better place for a child than home.

Granny hoped that Horrid High would be a home, too, for the kids who weren't as lucky as Mesmer. Certainly, she'd done everything to make it happier. The old insulting dorm names—Lowlife, Scumbag, Nincompoop and Dimwit—had been swapped for new houses named after mythical creatures. They sounded heroic and exciting—Centaur, Sphinx, Pegasus and Dragon. The children now had real beds to sleep in; there was hot, fresh food in the dining room; the unkempt schoolyard had been transformed into a lush green playground; and the tadpole-infested tank had been replaced by a real swimming pool.

The locks on the front gate had been removed and the Tower of Torture had been turned into the Tower Library. A reading nook perched high above the ground, the Tower Library had books, a slowly growing news archive and a cosy corner filled with bright, plump cushions.

In Granny's classroom downstairs, the heated discussion of the day's news would have petered out by now. But just as Granny Grit rose to leave, the phone on her desk rang again. Abella! It had been ages! This young Spanish animal lover had been with the Grit Movement for five years now. But Abella was saying something that made Granny's smile flicker and fade. Her eyebrows shot up, worry lines appeared on her forehead and in a choked voice, she gasped, 'Oh dear!'

It was a quick conversation—the connection from Puerto Maldonado in Peru was a weak one. 'Terrible things going on in the Amazon . . .' and then phone static. 'I'm going undercover . . . something very dangerous . . .' More static. 'Some cunning plans are afoot.' And although Granny shouted 'Be careful!' more than once, she was drowned out by a fresh burst of static and then they were cut off. There was so much horridness in the world . . . but then Granny smiled weakly as she remembered her children in the classroom downstairs. At long last, there was one tiny place on earth that was horrid-proof.

Granny Grit lingered near the telephone for a few more minutes, just in case Abella called back. The list of new teachers caught her eye. Dr Bloom was coming in to teach 'hands-on science,' she'd said over the phone when Granny Grit interviewed her, 'the sort of science that gets under your fingernails—plenty of experiments and field trips!' Granny Grit loved the idea. Education didn't make sense if you were caged in a classroom all day, reading in books what you could see, smell and touch for yourself outside.

Nita Nottynuf would take maths and although she was still a little rough around the edges, Granny Grit knew Miss Nottynuf would settle in. It was never easy growing up being told that you were less than everyone else, and what Miss Nottynuf needed was time to heal.

Colonel Craven, the new sports teacher, was an army hero with many medals to his credit and he'd recommended Cook Fracas too. Granny had a good feeling about the colonel. His right eyebrow twitched several times without reason and his left arm jerked up without cause but those were nervous tics, that was all. If you'd escaped from an enemy camp after months of captivity, you'd be nervous too.

The phone rang again. Abella—it had to be! Granny Grit grabbed it on the first ring but the voice on the other end was a tremulous one. Granny knew it only too well. 'Mrs Telltale!' said Granny, wishing that Mrs Telltale would go someplace far away with a poor phone connection. Someplace like Puerto Maldonado, Peru.

But oh no, Mrs Telltale was threatening to do quite the opposite. 'Grandma Grit,' she started, making Granny grimace. 'Tammy and I thought we'd drop into school for a few days, Tammy so misses her friends!'

What friends? It was an ungracious thought for a school principal, but principals have been known to have those too.

'Just a quick catch-up, you know,' Mrs Telltale was saying, 'before we go off on book tour again? We could pencil it into our diary?'

But Granny Grit leaned across her desk to make a red circle on her calendar two weeks down. *Mrs Telltale's next call!* she scribbled next to it. *Avoid at all cost!*

Mrs Telltale was still talking. 'Tammy's on a TV show . . .'

The lunch bell rang. Not the wailing sound that had heralded the hour at the old school but a cheerful chime that was music to hungry ears.

Alas, Mrs Telltale's tall tale had no end in sight. Granny felt a weariness take hold of her. She felt grateful all of a sudden for the large man in the kitchen downstairs. Being principal *and* cooking for a hundred hungry children was too much, even for her.

CHAPTER 3

A hundred hungry tummies rumbled when the lunch bell rang. For Phil, the thought of food drove away all other concerns. The day's news was old and had already been chewed on. Lunch, on the other hand, was fresh and tasted much better.

Ferg and Fermina were in the middle of a heated discussion about a news story on page twenty-two. 'What makes you think that this doesn't deserve to be on the front page?' Fermina demanded.

'The fact that there are at least three other stories that deserve it more?' Ferg said. 'Let's just agree to disagree, shall we?'

Fermina gave a tight nod, flinging her braids from front to back and pretending that disagreement was fine with her. In truth, though, her feathers were a little ruffled. These days, Ferg was being positively annoying!

Ferg tried hard not to laugh. Fermina looked so funny when she was in a huff! 'Come on, Ferm, don't take it personally—ouch!' Phil had pinched Ferg's arm. 'What did you do that for?'

'To remind you that there's more pain coming if we don't go to lunch this instant!' said Phil.

'I'll tell Granny Grit that you held us up, Ferm and you!' added Immy, her dimples flashing to indicate that she was only half serious.

Fermina collapsed into giggles at that, forgetting her sullen mood of a moment ago. 'Let's go, quick, before Immy turns into Tammy!' she cried, slapping Ferg on the back a little harder than she needed to and quite enjoying it.

Upstairs, Tammy's mother was on the verge of delivering her 173rd sentence in five breaths flat when she stopped. Had she finally run out of air—or words? Granny didn't waste a minute to consider this. She had been given a glorious opportunity to cut in—ah, and the perfect excuse! There was a car pulling in at the school gates. 'I must go, Mrs Telltale,' Granny cried. 'We have unexpected visitors!'

As she rung off, Granny's heart exulted. The school hadn't had any visitors in a while, and they couldn't have come at a better time! They drove a fancy red convertible, the sort where the roof slides back and you can drive with the wind tugging at your hair. Oddly, though, the roof was down, the windows were up and the occupants seemed quite unaware of what a beautiful day it was. As a man and a woman got out of the car, it became evident why.

They were squabbling, their voices loud enough to be carried on the breeze, though Granny could not catch what they were saying. The man slammed his door. The woman slammed hers. The man was dragging a young boy out of the backseat. The woman was dragging another one out. The man was shaking his fist at the woman. The woman was shaking her fist right back. They were slugging it out, point for point, like kids in a schoolyard scuffle. The two boys who trailed behind them were behaving more grown-up, wearing the sort of expression indulgent parents do when their children misbehave.

If the four visitors had bothered to look up at the school, they might have wondered how Horrid High could ever have been horrid, with its sparkling red roof and spanking white walls. They might have noticed the green window from which an old lady was staring down at them, looking incredibly sad that there were parents in this world who had no qualms about fighting in front of their children.

The warring parents were so busy trading insults, they hurried past Ferg and his friends in the hallway without lowering their voices. 'It was your idea to have them!' the man was saying.

'And I suppose it's a bad idea just because it's mine?' countered the woman.

'Not one, but *two*!' said the father, heading for the stairs with a renewed burst of speed as though he wanted to get away from his family. 'What is it with you and pairs?'

'You make it sound like I *miscounted*!' It was the mother's turn now. She matched him, step for step, propelled by her anger. 'Hurry up, boys!'

Why were they talking about their kids like this, plain enough for everyone to hear? Ferg's cheeks were burning. The visitors reminded him of his own mom and dad, as clearly as if he had held up a family photograph. 'Should have got a dog instead, I told you,' the man was muttering as they clattered up the stairs.

The newcomers had dampened everyone's mood. The kids couldn't help feeling sorry for the boys. Fermina dug her little hands deep into her pockets and shuffled faster towards the dining room. Immy picked at her cornrows and ran her tongue over her new braces. Phil kept his face expressionless, but it bothered him, too, and made his heart beat a little faster. Parents! Who could understand them?

One welcoming look from Granny Grit pottering about the kitchen would have driven away every last dark thought. Granny Grit was not in but the aroma greeting the children made up for it quite well. The children stopped short, they had quite forgotten! Hadn't Granny mentioned that there was a try-out this week for the job of school chef?

Perhaps they had imagined someone like Granny, lean and spry, with twinkling eyes and a ready laugh. The new cook was a good deal taller, his chef's hat grazing the doorframe. With massive shoulders, a neck as solid as a block of wood and a hard, square chin from which a patch of dark hair was sprouting, he looked like he could be standing beside a battering ram on some medieval battlefield, giving a war cry.

Only, there was no castle to attack and no walls to be breached—just a humongous pot full of something that smelt heavenly, sealed off on top with a dark-brown crust. 'That's a crème brawlay!' Cook Fracas was saying as the children entered. 'The only thing that lies between you and that creamy custard is the burnt sugar on top! Mmmmmmmm!' And here he stooped low to take a huge whiff. 'It smells delightful, doesn't it?'

The children nodded mutely. You see, it's physically impossible to inhale and speak at the same time, try it and see. And at this moment, the children were inhaling huge lungfuls of the heady aroma. It sailed into their mouths and settled in their stomachs.

As if reading their thoughts, Cook Fracas held up a large kitchen hammer.

'Who'll have first go?'

Confounded looks were exchanged—first go at what? 'Go on, shatter the crust if you want what's below!' said Cook Fracas, pointing at the pot. 'Who'll go first?' and now his eyes wandered around the room, settling tentatively on one face, then another. 'You?'

The children turned at their tables, tracing a line from the cook to the person he was looking at, all the way to the back of the dining room. To the very last table where a large girl sat alone. As she always did. Volumina Butt.

'Yes, you!' the cook nodded, tapping the palm of his hand with his hammer as though he were keeping time.

Volumina glowered at the cook and kept sitting.

'Come on up here!' Cook Fracas persisted. 'You look capable of doing the job!'

Volumina narrowed her eyes and glared at the cook, rising slowly. 'Are you calling me *fat*?'

A tremor passed through the room, from child to child, like a ripple in a pond. No one would call Volumina fat! Not because she wasn't but because no child would like 'You're fat!' to be his last words. Volumina could sit on any child at Horrid High and snap him like a twig. She didn't need to be told she was fat—she knew.

'I'm calling you *strong*,' said the cook gently. His words disarmed her a little.

'I don't feel like it!' she mumbled, 'I can't!' And she promptly sat down, hard enough to make the bench shudder.

'Why not?' Cook Fracas persisted. The girl winced and shook her head.

'I'm waiting,' said the cook, and now his solemn mouth melted into a gleeful smile. 'Come on, try, it'll be *fun*!'

All eyes were on Volumina now. She could have sat on the cook and flattened him if she wanted to—she was still the school bully, even if her bottom hadn't settled on anyone this term because there were no new kids yet. But hadn't the cook promised that this would be fun?

The bench groaned as Volumina rose again and everyone watched, curious and confused, as she lumbered slowly to the centre of the room. She peered into the dish. The golden brown crust glistened. It was rather an odd request. Why go to the trouble of shattering something that looked so flawless?

But Cook Fracas was giving her a nod now and issuing a battle cry: 'BREACH THE BRAWLAY!' The hammer was heavy but Volumina swung it easily.

Kerrrrchanggggg! The sugar crust came apart like the ground during an earthquake. 'BREACH THE BRAWLAY!' Volumina swung again. *Kerrrrchanggggg!* The crust ripped like a shirt caught in a doornail, top to bottom, and shards of sugar went flying. 'Ooooooh!' groaned a girl where the crust had grazed her cheek. 'BREACH THE BRAWLAY!' *Kerrrrchanggggg!* Now the jagged, sticky sugar projectiles were flying like arrows, splintering against chairs, ricochetting off walls. The children dived for cover (or to taste the sweet slivers where they had landed on the floor, sparkling like ice). *Kerrrrchanggggg! Kerrrrchanggggg!* It was *snowing* sugar now!

'It's stuck to my hair,' a girl cried, trying to pry bits of sugar loose. 'It got me on the forehead!' exclaimed a boy who hadn't ducked in time.

'Bravo!' shouted Cook Fracas, bringing his hands together like a monkey crashing cymbals. 'Bowls and spoons, kids, for the custard! Dig in! I've kept some sandwiches out on the counter too!'

Volumina didn't need to be told twice; she treated herself to an extra-large helping of everything. All that hammer-swinging had only whetted her appetite.

A clamour of kids edged closer to the brawlay pot, plucking up the courage to move in after Volumina had finished. Moods were a little on edge, tempers frayed, and a few kids elbowed each other for a long-delayed lunch. At the corners of the room, minor spats had broken out. A few fragments of caramelized sugar were hanging from the ceiling now, like a chandelier. The ground was a sticky trap. Cook Fracas brought his hands to his lips, blew kisses everywhere and trilled, '*Benissimo! Sopraffino!*'

Ferg had no idea what '*benissimo*' meant, or '*sopraffino*'—he wasn't Italian, after all—but the English translations of these words popped in his head like fireworks on New Year's Eve. Excellent! Marvellous! Incredible! Were there any other words to describe how wonderful Cook Fracas's brawlay tasted?

'Here! Under the table!' he hissed, calling Fermina over and tugging at Phil's trouser leg as he made his way through the sugary mess, bowl in hand. 'New seating arrangements?' panted Immy, ducking and sliding next to Ferg to make place for the others. 'Too much sugar flying!' said Fermina, squeezing in and cringing as a pair of sandals skidded on sugar, their owner flailing in the air before crashing to the ground. 'I've never seen anything like this,' sputtered Phil between mouthfuls of smoked salmon sandwich. 'The new cook is mental!'

The mess and the madness overhead faded into silence as the children ate. None of them had dined in fancy French restaurants, but you don't have to be an expert on food to know when something tastes good. This brawlay was *beyond* good. The sandwiches weren't bad either. They certainly beat Chef Gretta's rat-tail ratatouille! And although Granny Grit's cooking had the wholesome flavour of anything prepared with love, the children knew that Granny couldn't be running the kitchen forever. As principal of Horrid High, she had more on her plate than just food.

During that particular lunch hour, what Granny had instead of a plateful of food was an office full of unannounced guests—two squabbling parents, two sulking children—oh, and four chihuahuas in panic mode. You see, Mr Brace had knocked imperiously on the door mid-rant. Granny's 'Come in!' had interrupted him as he enumerated to Mrs Brace the many ways in which dogs are better than children. So when he pushed open the door and his foot narrowly missed a chihuahua—'THERE! That's what we should have had!'—he triggered a chihuahua crisis.

Hider, the shy one, skittered about and collided into Teacup, who had had a narrow brush with death under Mr Brace's giant foot and was feeling jittery anyway. Bella disliked loud voices and Mr Brace had raised his voice on 'THERE', making her jump. The three of them stood up on their hind legs and looked longingly at the pink, polka-dotted bag on Granny's desk. Tortilla was a canny survivor who knew that there was safety in numbers and joined right in. They matched howl for howl and yowl for yowl till Granny lowered her handbag to the ground. The bag juddered as they all disappeared inside it, and Granny Grit set her mouth in a thin line and said, 'Now, how can I help you?'

Her question released a torrent of words, Mr and Mrs Brace

both speaking at once in great agitation. Now, Granny Grit had had more than her day's share of ravers and ramblers. She turned to the two miserable boys, her face softening—'Would you please wait outside while I speak to your parents? If you're lucky, you'll meet our school pet. He's a darling little white mouse called Saltpetre, I'm sure you'll love him. He's scuttling about in the hallway somewhere.'

As soon as the boys had left the room, Granny Grit instructed Mr and Mrs Brace like insolent children who had spoken out of turn. 'Start again, please, from the beginning, and speak one after the other.' They had a long list of complaints against each other and against their boys, which now took twice as long because they weren't speaking in unison.

When Mr Brace was halfway done, Granny glanced at the clock. 'Have your sons eaten?' The Braces exchanged puzzled looks. 'Wha . . . Didn't you feed them?' cried Mrs Brace. 'You didn't tell me to!' retaliated Mr Brace. Amidst all the finger-pointing, Granny popped out to tell the boys, 'Why don't you head down those stairs to the dining room? If you're lucky, there'll still be some lunch left over. We have a new cook.'

The new cook was whistling *Funiculi Funicula,* which is a popular Italian song about a funicular that once chugged its way up Mount Vesuvius. The cook's crème brawlay had done as much damage to the kitchen as the volcanic eruption on Mount Vesuvius that ultimately destroyed the funicular. But this was a jaunty song and it was putting Cook Fracas in a jaunty mood. Even if the poor kids who had to clean up that afternoon didn't feel as, well, jaunty.

Fermina was on all fours, teasing a stubborn crust of sugar off the floor with her fingernails. 'I wouldn't have eaten so much if I'd remembered that I was on duty today!' she groaned. Ferg grunted in agreement. He had been swabbing the same sticky patch for ten minutes to no avail.

Fermina bit her lip thoughtfully. She felt bad whining about cleaning up. The kitchen was in a shambles but their bellies were full of good food. That had to count for something.

'Well, hello!' said Cook Fracas, 'You've missed all the fun!'

The children looked up. The boys were standing at the door of the dining room, looking perplexed.

'We have some brawlay left over if you're hungry,' said Cook Fracas, smiling broadly. 'Your principal has missed lunch—I'll take some of this up to her as well.'

The boys eagerly fell upon the two bowls of brawlay, eating as though they had been starving for days. Ferg shot Fermina a meaningful look. It wasn't that far back in time that they'd been famished like this.

The boys looked so alike, Ferg found himself staring and rubbing his eyes, just to check that this wasn't a case of double vision. They were tall and wiry, with clear faces, eyes that turned up at the corners and bushy brows. A thick lock of their dark hair flopped down over one eye, giving them a mysterious look. They were dressed the same, too, down

to the last detail. When the boys looked up and caught Ferg staring, one introduced himself.

'Mallus!' he said, raising his left hand in a small wave. 'And he's Malo, short for Malcovich!' His twin scratched his right cheek in a sheepish gesture.

'Are you both staying?' asked Fermina, suddenly conscious of the pimple growing on her chin. She tried to hide the eagerness in her voice. Everyone was missing Mesmer and their gang could use two more friends, that was all.

The twins shrugged together in a well-timed gesture: 'We'd like to!'

When Cook Fracas returned, he didn't look pleased to see Ferg and Fermina taking an unscheduled break. 'Back to work, kids, it'll be time for class soon!' he said. 'Boys, are you on clean-up too?'

Malo and Mallus shook their heads. 'Oh, you're the *new* boys!' cried the cook, remembering the noisy guests in Granny's office. 'Off you go then—out, you're wanted back upstairs!'

The twins threw small smiles at Ferg and Fermina as they left. 'I hope they stay!' said Fermina, staring after them. Ferg returned to the stubborn stain with renewed energy. His ears were tingling, as they normally did when something was about to go wrong. Now where was that tissue box? There! Ferg blew his nose and his ears popped. He felt relieved. It was only a cold, that was all.

CHAPTER 4

Granny Grit closed her eyes and blessed Cook Fracas. The delicious crème brûlée had warmed her up inside. She'd have liked to eat it slowly. She'd never understood why some people treated food like it had legs and would get away if they weren't fast enough to grab it. Food was meant to be savoured.

But a car door slammed downstairs. The Braces had come to Horrid High with their minds made up. They were only too eager to unload both suitcases and children so that they could speed off into the horizon to freedom at last!

'Get a dog . . .' Mr Brace had said, his eyes lighting up at the hopeful thought. 'Get a life . . .' Mrs Brace had said, glaring at Mr Brace.

Granny Grit exhaled slowly. When the twins came up, she would have to break the news to them. Their parents had bolted without waiting to say goodbye. The phone rang a few more times and stopped. It was likely Abella from Peru, trying to get through. She glanced at the clock—it was too late to resume that lesson she'd left halfway. There was so much to teach the children, she feared she was falling behind. But the children were probably in Miss Nottynuf's maths class by now.

Fractions were making everyone feel rather fractious. Cross, in other words, and irritable. How could 3/6 and 4/8 be the same thing? Yet, if Miss Nottynuf was to be believed, they were!

'Oh dear, I've not been very good at explaining this, have I?' Miss Nottynuf hunched her shoulders, swept her fine hair back from her face and turned to the board.

3/6 = 4/8 = 5/10.

Her hair was so soft and straight, it sprang loose again. She blinked hard at the class through her thick spectacles. 'Do you see a pattern in these numbers?'

It was obvious to nobody but Phil. He grinned from ear to ear. 'All these fractions are different ways of expressing a half!'

Miss Nottynuf shot him a wan smile. But as her eyes swept over the puzzled faces in the room, her smile faded and a shadow crossed her face. 'Yes, no matter how you express half, it's a miserable little fraction, isn't it? Half and not whole.'

She walked to the window for a moment, deep in thought. Her shoulders sagged as she remembered her parents and how they had always made her feel half as good as any other child. 'It's not good to be half, you know.'

'I'm not sure I understand any more!' said Phil, dismayed.

No one did. How could fractions have feelings? This was a maths class, and Miss Nottynuf did not seem to be sticking to the subject.

'Oh, yes!' she said, looking at Phil with a sad light in her eyes. 'No one cares about you if you're not whole. There was

a little girl whose life was measured in fractions . . . Let's call her Nita, shall we?'

Miss Nottynuf wrung her hands. 'Nita was half as beautiful as her mother, half as clever as her father and half as athletic as her brother!'

The maths teacher stopped again, hugging her narrow shoulders and shivering.

Phil opened his mouth to interrupt Miss Nottynuf when Immy nudged him. Sad people needed their silences—Immy knew that much. She remembered her father's long silences during his ventriloquist shows at the circus and how they made the audience restless. 'Go on, will you?' they'd shout. Phil would just have to be more patient. Miss Nottynuf was giving 'half' a whole new meaning by telling them her own sad story.

'What happened, then, Miss Nottynuf?' blurted a scruffy boy in the middle row with a runny nose.

'Well, Nita's heart broke in half with all that scoring, and she walked around forever with a hole inside her, right in the middle, like a big zero! It was the missing bit of Nita, the one without which she would never be whole.'

Miss Nottynuf was blinking back tears now and there was an awkward silence as everyone pretended not to notice that the maths teacher was crying.

'I'm sure the class wasn't good enough and I'm so sorry about it!' she said, sounding choked up as the bell rang. With a last smothered sob, she was gone.

Later that night, the children met in the common room of Ferg's dorm. It used to be called Scumbag but these days, it was known as Sphinx House.

Things had changed so much for the better. These had only been empty spaces earlier, but now, all the kids flocked to their common rooms when classes were over. The common rooms were home, even though most of the kids at Horrid High were a bit foggy about what home meant.

'I'll get you started,' Granny Grit had told each house, throwing in comfortable sofas, a few beanbags, large floor lamps, a bright rug and an enormous bookshelf to transform each common room into an inviting place. 'The rest,' she said, 'is up to you!'

The children were given a house allowance to spend at one go, or slowly. Sphinx House had splurged on a games corner; Dragon House had an art wall that they redesigned every three months; Centaur House prided itself on having wangled a small refrigerator stocked with midnight snacks; and Pegasus House was still mulling over what to spend its allowance on.

Ferg, Fermina and Phil were sitting on beanbags in one corner. Fermina was wondering where Immy was, when she burst in, giggling. 'The new boys are in my house!' she said, popping back out and pushing the twins in.

The twins were painfully shy. Dressed in identical checked pyjamas, they stood awkwardly just inside the doorway. Immy could barely contain her enthusiasm and prodded them from behind. 'Go on, they're my best friends here!' she urged the twins. 'Ferg, Fermina and Phil!'

'We've met,' said Fermina with a solemn nod although she wanted to jump for joy. New friends—and they were pretty cute too! Phil moved over, plumping the throw-cushions and restoring them to fullness. 'How are you settling in?'

'Just fine,' mumbled Malo, massaging his right eyebrow with his finger.

'Thanks!' interjected Mallus, tugging at his left ear.

Ferg, who hadn't spent any time around twins, couldn't take his eyes off the boys. They smiled very little, he noticed, and their conversation skills were poor. He recalled their squabbling parents—it was no surprise the twins weren't comfortable around new people. Hadn't he been the same way, all but invisible, till he got to Horrid High and made friends? It wasn't easy having parents who treated you like a giant mistake.

'I wonder where Saltpetre is!' said Immy brightly as though she sensed what everyone was thinking and wanted to change the subject.

'Our school pet is not allowed into class, you see,' explained Phil to the twins, 'and he misses us terribly!'

'Not today, though!' said Fermina, laughing in an exaggeratedly high voice. 'Maybe he's found better company!'

Ferg frowned. Fermina was behaving a little daft around the twins. She was beginning to remind him of those giggly girls at his old school who made his hair stand on end.

'It must have been wonderful growing up as twins,' said Immy. 'Tell me, are you absolutely and totally identical?'

'We are!' the twins cried, a little quickly. 'Our mother always liked identical pairs!'

'She must have adored you!' gushed Fermina.

The twins' voices dropped. 'She did, until she found us a little disappointing . . .'

If the twins had divulged more, if the children had pressed further, the story of Mrs Brace's love for twos would have emerged. Mrs Brace loved things that came in pairs, especially *identical* pairs. It was silly, how Mrs Brace bought two copies of the same book or two blouses of the same colour, or how she always knocked on wood, twice, for good luck. Mr Brace was in love with Mrs Brace then, and when grown-ups are in love, even silly things are forgiven.

Mrs B had no way of knowing that she would have twins, or else she would have skipped (two steps at a time, mind you) for all nine months. But right before the twins were born, Mrs Brace was possessed by a sudden craving for Chinese food. Perhaps it was the thought of those identical chopsticks—we will never know—but off they went, Mr and Mrs B, to the best Chinese restaurant in town. After dessert, when Mrs B bit into her second fortune cookie, she gasped. For the message inside both cookies was the same: *Good things come in pairs.* This could mean only one thing, and Mrs Brace was sure of it. 'Twins!'

She would have given them the same names, but that

would have been rather silly, even for Mrs Brace. So instead, she named them Mallus and Malo, and she dressed them so that they couldn't be told apart. 'My two peas in a pod!' she told everyone proudly. She read them the same story every night: *Noah's Ark*. '*Two elephants, two zebras, two hippos went into the ark . . .*'

When the twins were in their terrible twos, Mr Brace bought them their first set of crayons. Two identical sets. And to Mrs Brace's utter dismay, she discovered that her precious boys weren't identical. *Almost* identical. But *almost* wasn't good enough for Mrs Brace. Just as it hadn't been good enough for the Nottynufs.

Mrs Brace fell out of love with her twins just as fast as she'd fallen in love with them. She stopped reading them *Noah's Ark*. She stopped telling everyone about her two peas in a pod. That is, perhaps, where all the twin trouble began. And Mrs Brace concluded that you can never trust a cheap fortune cookie to reliably tell your future. Good things most certainly do not come in pairs!

But of course, Ferg and his friends heard nothing of this twosome tale because just then, a boy with long hair found *Funiculi Funicula* on the radio.

'That's the tune Cook Fracas was whistling this afternoon!' Ferg leapt up, pulling Fermina to her feet. 'Let's dance!'

'I won't be caught dead dancing with a boy!' said Fermina, whirling about the room with him nonetheless, her braids flying.

'I have two partners now,' cried Immy, pulling the twins to their feet. 'Phil, can you manage?'

But Phil wasn't the dancing sort. He sat back, head against his hands, and guffawed. Dinner had been carrot soup, olive bread and piping-hot samosas. His friends were crashing about the room like baboons. The twins were laughing now because Immy was teaching them to jive. His heart felt as full as his stomach. All was well, apart from the brouhaha over the brawlay, of course—and they would tell Granny Grit all about it. But not today. Today was for new friends, new teachers, a new school and new experiences. Today was about being happier than all of them had been in a long, long time.

CHAPTER 5

'Are you sure it was a go—?' Immy was laughing so hard, she couldn't finish her sentence. 'You say you saw a go—?' Fermina was having as little luck completing hers when she erupted into giggles. Phil slapped Ferg on his back and added, 'Are we getting your go—?' before doubling up, his shoulders shaking and his eyes streaming.

'Goat!' Ferg shouted, pretending to be angrier than he really was. 'Goat!' After all, a horned ruminant had no business being at Horrid High and Ferg was certain he had seen one from the window, right after his shower that morning. Of course, his friends didn't believe him. They hadn't said so in so many words, but their loud hoots of laughter and the sight of Phil rolling about on the floor got the message across plain and clear.

'So I'm the butt of all your jokes this morning, am I?' said Ferg, arms folded across his chest, trying to look as miffed as possible.

'*Butt* of all our jokes?' screamed Fermina, covering her mouth now and rocking back and forth. 'Good one, Ferg!'

Ferg tapped his foot impatiently and rolled his eyes. *Getting your goat. Butt of all our jokes.* Would the goat jokes never cease? 'I'm heading down for breakfast,' he said. 'You clowns can follow once you're done laughing your heads off!'

The four friends clattered down the stairs. 'We won't be BA-A-A-A-A-AD any more,' Phil bleated, sending Fermina into a fresh fit of giggles. Poor Immy, red in the face from laughing so hard, was trying to change the subject for Ferg's sake. 'Didn't see Saltpetre all day yesterday, why, even this morning . . .'

She broke off, not to laugh this time, but to gape. Fermina and Phil had their mouths wide open, too, the way your mouth drops down when you're taken by surprise.

'A go—' said Immy, pointing at the caramel-coloured, four-legged grazer who was nibbling at a head of cabbage in Cook Fracas's kitchen.

'Goat!' Ferg shouted for the third time that morning. He was getting really tired of this routine of half-completed sentences but now it was his turn to laugh.

The goat in question had a chef's hat on and a pancake in her mouth as she trotted out into the dining room. 'Good, isn't it, Gypsy?' Cook Fracas was saying. Both Mallus and Malo—no one could tell who was who!—looked quite amused. Shedding their shyness for the first time, they flashed lopsided smiles of recognition at Fermina and her friends. But before the kids could help themselves to pancakes, Granny Grit took one look at the guest goat and said, 'OUT!' Gypsy gave Granny Grit a measured stare and chewed on her pancake slowly.

'We can't have your goat in the kitchen, Cook Fracas,' said Granny.

But Gypsy had other plans. There was a clatter and a crash as she bolted back into the kitchen, emerging with a saucepan on her head and a sprig of parsley in her mouth. She ambled past Fermina, pausing briefly to tug at one of her hair ribbons.

'OUT!' yelled Granny and this time, Gypsy understood. She raced out the door, Cook Fracas pelting after her. 'Gypsy, you forgot your pancake!'

That did it. The dining room erupted into peals of laughter. 'The poor animal was rescued by Cook Fracas,' said Granny Grit when she had caught her breath. 'Was going to get thrown off a church roof and caught in a canvas sheet by the crowd below.'

'Thrown?' the children cried. The thought of a goat being flung off a roof was even more unthinkable than the sight of it in the school kitchen. 'Yes,' said Granny, wiping her eyes with the edge of a lacy handkerchief. 'Some silly custom in Zamora in Spain, but Cook Fracas saved Gypsy and they've been inseparable ever since. Isn't that true, Colonel?'

The children turned. A strong, sturdy man was standing in the doorway, his back upright, his feet firmly planted. The colonel gave a sharp, swift nod, a barely perceptible flick of the head. 'It is,' he said, his words crisp and clear, 'though I doubt the cook will catch up with Gypsy. That's one fit goat!'

Granny Grit broke into a smile, the sort that made her eyes

crinkle and light up. 'In that case, Colonel, I think you and I will have to serve the pancakes!'

'But of course!' said Colonel Craven, marching in, his long legs covering the room in a few large strides. Deftly, he dropped two pancakes into each plate and Granny Grit slathered them with syrup. 'Good food is a must!' he boomed. 'Followed by good exercise!'

'Meet your new sports teacher, kids,' said Granny Grit, serving herself now. 'The colonel spent many years in the army and I'm sure you have lots to learn from him!'

As soon as breakfast was done, the colonel had the children form a single file and march into the playground. It was a windy day, and the children held on to their hair and their flapping tees while the colonel raised his voice to outshout the wind. His own hair, cropped close to his head, did not move at all. Nor did his shirt, tucked in tightly, or his well-pressed trousers.

'Not the best day to build a fire,' the colonel said, looking up at the sky. 'But people don't get lost after checking the weather bulletin, do they?' He chortled at the thought. It was hard not to like a man with a sense of humour and the children chuckled with him. Their last coach had been anything but funny. 'If we can build a fire in bad weather,' Colonel Craven was saying now, 'we can build a fire anytime! Tinder, please, and kindling!'

Colonel Craven split them up house-wise. 'Look for dry pine needles, moss, twigs and small pieces of wood!' he urged.

'Any fool can light a fire but making it last, making it produce more heat—ah, that takes special knowledge!'

Pegasus House collected the most tinder; Centaur the most kindling; and Sphinx House had the fire going merrily in a matter of minutes. The Dragons didn't have much luck with anything but the colonel laughed at their disappointment.

'You've already survived so much horridness together!' said the colonel to the muddy children once they were done. 'If you know how to make a fire, you can survive anything, I promise!'

The bell had gone—there was barely enough time for a quick wash-up before science class.

'Can't wait to see what our new teacher is like!' said Immy.

'Look!' said Phil as they passed Cook Fracas in the hallway, looking beaten and bruised. 'I don't think he's had much luck feeding his goat!'

The poor cook was scratching his chin where a few pancake crumbs hung off his chin hair, trembling. The sight of chin hair set Fermina off again.

'Isn't that called a go—' she collapsed into laughter as they scurried to science class.

'A goatee?' guessed Immy, joining in the laughter.

'More goat jokes?' cried Ferg, shaking his head in disbelief. 'I'm not laughing any more!'

'It's funny, I'll give you that!' said a melodious voice as the children tumbled into class. The new science teacher was long and sinuous. Her hair was drawn away from her face, shiny and strong. Her smooth skin was pulled tight over cheekbones sharp as blades.

How did she know what Ferg and his friends were laughing about? As it turned out, she didn't. It was the green potted plant she had brought with her to class that was putting her in such a cheerful mood. She tilted her head so that you could see her hair, coiled like a fat worm on the top. Golden brown with dark roots.

'Like perfect pitchers, aren't they?' she said, stroking the leaves as though the plant were a house cat.

The leaves were certainly odd, curled up like cups, pink near the mouth and green at the base, each one tethered to the plant by a delicate tendril. The science teacher ran a slim finger around the ribbed mouth of the pitcher leaf and chuckled at some inside joke. 'Meet *Nepenthes bicalcarata*,' she said, smiling. Large, white teeth revealed themselves, perfectly even but with dark slivers of space in-between.

'That's our teacher's name, right?' Immy whispered to the others.

'I seriously doubt it!' replied Fermina. But someone else at the back had had the same notion.

'Miss Nepinti . . .' said a scrawny girl. 'I mean, Miss Bykillata . . .'

The science teacher tittered. Her nose was so sharp you could have cut an apple on the bridge of it. 'Oh, dear me, no! Surely, you don't think that *I* am Miss Nepenthes Bicalcarata. It's what this plant from the jungles of Borneo is called!'

SYMBIOTIC
Nepenthes Bicalcarata

She laughed and the hesitant children joined her, Immy laughing loudest of all—'Foolish guess on my part,' she leaned in to tell Fermina.

'Bloom!' the science teacher said, pointing a svelte arm in the direction of the girl who had mistaken her for a plant. 'I'm Dr Bloom! Gather around, children, you haven't seen the funniest bit yet.'

And as the curious kids collected around the desk, Dr Bloom took two glass bottles out of her worn leather satchel. The first bottle was full of little spiders. Some of the children drew back in horror—'Yeeooooouu!'—but Ferg leaned in, he couldn't look away. Dr Bloom was giggling uncontrollably as she pulled three spiders out of the bottle with a pair of tweezers.

'Little Miss Muffets,' she sang between half-suppressed snickers, 'sat on tuffets!'—and now she placed the three spiders on the rim of a pitcher leaf. The spiders scuttled along the rim. 'It's the sweet nectar inside the pitcher leaf that makes our spiders go "yum",' said Dr Bloom, her voice dropping to a whisper now. 'But someone else will be going "yum" very soon, just you see!'

Ferg's ears were tingling now—that cold was really coming on strong. No sniffles yet, or coughing, just that hard tingling. Could it be a bad feeling about the spiders? Were they about to . . . and as Ferg watched them slip and slide along the swollen, red rim of the pitcher leaf, his heart sank. The spiders were about to fall in! Just as the idea occurred to him, one spider toppled backwards into the pitcher, flailing its flimsy legs in vain. Ferg gasped as it disappeared into the cup of the leaf. Down, down it went, into the darkness! Dr Bloom began singing:

'Our little Miss Muffets,
They sat on some tuffets,
Dreaming of nectary whey!
But there was a hitch-a,
They fell in a pitcher,
And soon became liquid-ey prey!'

Dr Bloom had barely finished her little number when the second spider fell in. '*Nepenthes bicalcarata* is a carnivorous plant. It lures unsuspecting creepy-crawlies to its slippery-sweet rim, only to have them fall in. Clever, isn't it?'

Only one spider was left, edging its way warily around the rim, hoping to meet a better fate than its friends, perhaps.

'Hurry up, foolish little spider!' exclaimed Dr Bloom with a little shiver.

Some of the children were feeling sorry for the spiders. 'Can't we save the last one?' they asked.

'What? And spoil all the fun?' tittered Dr Bloom. 'That last spider will dissolve in the acidic potion at the bottom of these cups, just like its friends!'

Her eyes shone brightly now and in spite of his own unease, Ferg couldn't help feeling fascinated. Who would have thought that a plant could be carnivorous?

'What's in the other bottle, Dr Bloom?' he asked finally, unable to bear the suspense any more.

Dr Bloom unscrewed the cap of the second bottle, pulling out five, six, seven wriggling ants and placing them carefully on the rim of another pitcher leaf.

'Why'd you ask her?' cried Fermina in dismay. 'Now those poor ants will fall in too!'

But no, the ants weren't falling in or struggling to keep their balance on the slippery rim. They were walking deftly around it. When one dived in, a boy at the back yelped. 'It's gone!'

'Don't worry, these are no ordinary ants,' grinned Dr Bloom. 'They're killer ants. They dive into the pitcher plant and feed on leftovers!' Sure enough, the killer ant scurried back up only a few minutes later, dragging something else out.

'Look what our killer ant has caught!' cried Dr Bloom, and she ran her tongue around the gaps in her teeth. Her tongue gleamed, pink and fleshy. 'It's a mosquito larva! The pitcher plant's digestive juices can't dissolve it. If it weren't for our killer ant here, this pesky larva would end up eating all the other insects that fall in!'

It made the children squeamish but they couldn't help feeling a grudging admiration for the whole arrangement. It was awfully clever. 'The pitcher plant and the killer ants make great partners!' said Dr Bloom. 'Do you know what it's called when two organisms are in a relationship that benefits them both?' She stopped to write S-Y-M-B-I-O-T-I-C on the blackboard. 'We're in a symbiotic relationship too, aren't we? You get to learn from me, and in return, I get to learn something too.'

The last spider was scuttling to stay in place but Dr Bloom was staring out of the window now, as though she were weighing the thought. 'I've always loved the woods.'

'Not these woods!' said an ashen boy who'd been at Horrid High for many years. 'An orphan disappeared into these woods once and she hasn't returned since.'

Dr Bloom shuddered with the rest of the class. 'So I've heard.' She clapped her hands again. 'But enough of these morbid thoughts! I almost forgot to tell you, the killer ants drop their poop into the pitcher plant too!'

Someone went 'yuck!' at the back of the class. 'Dee-li-cious if you ask me!' said Dr Bloom, doubling up with laughter. Ferg couldn't help noticing that when Dr Bloom laughed, her cheekbones disappeared and her face looked softer. 'Poop full of mosquito larvae is yummy, nutritious and packed with protein!'

For a brief moment, the children remembered their old school chef, Gretta Gross, and shuddered. This was just the sort of thing she would say! But of course, Dr Bloom was only making a scientific observation.

The bell rang. It had been a creepy and exciting class. 'Time to go, kids!' said Dr Bloom, sweeping up the plant in both her arms with unexpected strength for someone so willowy. Her eyes fell upon the last spider, still fighting to stay alive. 'Oh, well . . .' she said. There was an odd expression in her eyes. With the slightest flick of her finger, she sent it flying into the pitcher. 'The end!' she trilled, flashing one last toothy grin as she sailed out.

CHAPTER 6

'I know you've met your new classmates already,' said Granny Grit as she peeked into the classroom.

'We have!' the children chorused.

'But I would love to formally introduce them,' laughed Granny, gesturing to the Brace boys to come out in front with a friendly wave of her hand.

One of the boys tugged at his left ear, and the other ducked his head and averted his eyes.

'The poor fellows have probably never received so much attention in their lives,' Fermina whispered. Ferg only nodded. He knew what it was like to feel rejected by your parents.

'I had to leave the breakfast table early,' said Granny, 'Too much to do! This is what happens when you start the day with too many go—'

'Goats?' interrupted Fermina, who still hadn't had her fill of goat jokes. Besides, this was the only class in which an interruption was not frowned upon.

Granny threw her head back and laughed with the rest of the class. 'I meant to say "goals", not "goats", but yes, a certain goat took matters quite into its own, well, mouth, shall we say? We've had enough *caprine* business for one day, haven't we?'

Granny Grit looked around to see if 'caprine' had registered. 'Aha! A new word hangs in the air!' she exclaimed, her eyes twinkling. 'Who knows what "caprine" means?'

Ferg shot his hand up proudly. '"Caprine" comes from the Latin word "caper" and is an adjective used to describe a goat or anything that resembles one.'

'Gabba gabba yay!' bellowed Granny, her face lighting up with delight as she used her favourite expression for joy, or pride, or simply to say, 'Well done!'

'But look at how far we've wandered,' Granny slapped her forehead good-naturedly. 'Meet the Brace boys, and yes, as you can see, they're twins!'

The Brace boys looked sheepish for all the attention, but one raised his right hand. 'I'm Malo,' he said. 'Short for Malcovich!'

'And I'm Mallus,' another hand went up.

'Welcome to Horrid High,' said Granny Grit, patting their shoulders. 'But we're nowhere near as horrid as we used to be!'

Fresh peals of laughter ensued but Granny held up a hand for silence. She rarely did that, so the effect was magical and an almost audible hush fell upon the room.

'Boarding schools can be lonely places for newcomers,' said Granny slowly. 'I wanted someone to show the twins around, to be a friend to them here.'

Ferg felt a movement beside him. Fermina was squirming in her seat. 'Me!' she shouted, jumping up, her eyes shining.

Granny's face softened some more. 'Oh, Fermina, I'm sure

you can do a great job but I'm afraid I've already found the perfect person.'

Fermina's face fell. Suddenly, she felt sheepish. The children looked about the room—who was going to be given the enviable job of looking after two new students? *Maybe it's Ferg,* thought Fermina, *and that won't be so bad.*

Maybe it's Phil, thought Immy, *and wouldn't that be fun?*

Maybe it's me, thought every other kid in class. But one.

The student already knew. Granny had taken her aside that morning and spoken to her. It had been a long time since *anyone* had spoken to her.

Volumina rose slowly as Granny looked directly at her, smiling. It was probably a rude thing to do but the entire class gasped. Volumina Butt? The school bully? The one who sat on newcomers and flattened them? How could she possibly be trusted to look after the twins?

Ferg bit his lip in bewilderment. Volumina had been staring at the twins all morning with ill-disguised glee. Hadn't she looked flushed with excitement? How could Granny Grit let this happen?

Granny's mind was made up. She turned a deaf ear to the gasps of disbelief. 'Mallus and Malo,' she said, 'you'll be in good hands with Volumina!'

Immy and Phil exchanged a grimace. Granny Grit had shuffled the classes after she took over as principal, and it was bad enough that Volumina was in their class now. But to be put in charge of the twins, it was simply awful!

The poor twins didn't know better. They sat down beside Volumina, flashing lopsided grins at her that made Fermina feel a little wobbly. Did she have a crush on them? The thought bothered her. She twisted her braids uneasily and wondered why Volumina looked so stony-faced. The twins were beaming at Volumina and asking her something, but Volumina mumbled a quick reply and looked away.

'It doesn't make sense,' muttered poor Fermina under her breath, feeling utterly miserable. 'She doesn't even look happy!'

The children were clearly in a mutinous mood but Granny gracefully sidestepped them.

'Now let me see how much you remember about the Romans,' she said. 'Who founded the city of Rome?'

The children had studied Rome with Granny for five classes now and there was nothing they didn't know. A forest of hands shot up. Granny threw more questions, in rapid-fire style, and the classroom erupted as everyone vied to answer.

The Brace boys had their hands up too. One of them knew all about Remus and Romulus and the other told everyone how the Romans were fabulous architects, not just warriors. Granny looked pleased—the new boys were clever and eager to fit in.

'Favourite Romans—come on!' Granny goaded them. '*Everyone* has a favourite Roman!'

Everyone in class certainly did. 'Trajan!' said a girl with jet-black hair and an overgrown fringe. 'Nero!' chuckled Phil, chuckling louder as Granny raised her eyebrows in horror.

Granny had told them how Nero, according to some historical accounts, sang as he watched Rome burn in the Great Fire.

A floppy-haired boy spoke hesitantly, as if making a confession, 'Cleopatra, she's beautiful!'

'Beautiful but Egyptian, not Roman!' shouted a voice from the middle rows, and the class exploded in laughter.

'Caesar!' said Fermina, depositing her braids from back to front as if the question had been settled once and for all.

'My favourite Roman is much less known,' said Granny finally. 'Gaius Plinius Secundus, better known as Pliny the Elder, who was a writer and a thinker, also a naval and army commander. A man of ideas and action! What a great combination!'

Granny paused and clasped her hands under her chin, her eyes moving slowly across the room. The signs were obvious. Granny was about to tell them a story. The class settled down.

'He gave us the world's first encyclopaedia,' said Granny, 'and this became the model for every encyclopaedia that followed!'

Phil leaned in: 'Miss Verbose would have loved him!' Immy poked Phil sharply in the forearm. She didn't want to miss anything Granny was saying.

'It's also very likely that Pliny the Elder was the first person to make invisible ink,' Granny was saying. 'From the milk of the tithymalus plant—he talks of it in his encyclopaedia.'

Invisible ink! Immy shivered. *What a fascinating idea!* 'You mean he wrote things that couldn't be seen?' she interjected.

'Yes,' said Granny, smiling at Immy's excitement. 'In wartime, messages to allies were written in invisible ink, or in code, so that they wouldn't be understood by the enemy. Maybe Colonel Craven could tell you more about that sometime—he's an army hero, you know.'

'But if you write in invisible ink and it can't be seen, what's the point?' asked Immy, a little puzzled.

'Oh but it *can* be seen,' said Granny, 'but only by someone who knows *how* to see it. And how do you make invisible ink if you don't have a tithymalus plant handy?'

'Lemon juice!' shouted Ferg. 'I read about it in a mystery novel!'

Granny nodded. 'That's right, and also bodily fluids like saliva . . .'

There was a round of 'Yuuuuuurrrrrkkk!' from the class. Someone had managed to produce a gurgling, spitty sound that was most annoying.

'. . . or sweat!' cried Granny, quite enjoying the reaction she was getting. 'Even pee!' and now Granny threw her head back and laughed as the class ignited in a collective 'Yeeeeeeoooooooohhhhh!'

'Pipe down now!' protested Granny, as a boy at the back of the class made gagging sounds at the thought of urine being used as ink. 'Maybe Ferg can tell us how a letter written in lime juice got deciphered in the book he read?'

Ferg stood up, feeling rather proud to share information with the rest of the class. His ears were still tingling and he

tugged at them. 'They exposed the letter to a flame and the lettering showed up brown!'

'That's good,' said Granny. 'Ever wondered why it shows up brown? It's because lime juice and sweat are organic ink. Organic ink changes the structure of the paper it's used on. The part of the paper that has organic ink on it burns faster, turning brown when exposed to heat. Like when you hold it near a light bulb, or . . .'

Suddenly, Granny Grit's eyebrows came together in a frown and her sentence trailed off into nothingness. 'Shhhhhh!' she said, craning her neck as though she were listening for something and holding up her hand for the second time that day. This time, the class fell silent more reluctantly.

'It's a phone ringing,' Ferg said, and all eyes turned towards Granny's pink, polka-dotted bag. Granny never brought her phone to class—she must have been expecting an important call. She was fumbling frantically in the bag now and by the time she had fished out her phone, it had fallen silent. Granny Grit stared at it and a shadow passed across her face—only a flicker that went unnoticed by everyone but Ferg. And then her phone buzzed again, but once, only once.

A message. Granny Grit glanced at it, her face expressionless. 'Something's come up. Why don't you tromp up to the Tower Library and find something else on Pliny the Elder, hmmm?'

'Should we come back downstairs for Miss Nottynuf's class?' the children asked, a little surprised to be let off so early.

Granny Grit looked preoccupied. 'Oh no, don't! I'm afraid

I'll be calling a teachers' meeting right now, and Miss Nottynuf will be held up. How about I get her to call you down when we're done?'

Granny Grit picked up her handbag and strode to the door, where she hesitated briefly before leaving. 'I feel terrible, kids, but I've got to go.'

Go. Fermina would have cracked one last goat joke—Granny Grit had given her the perfect opening, after all—but something stopped her. It was the same something that made Ferg's ears tingle harder than before. And this time, he was sure that it was more than just a cold coming on.

CHAPTER 7

Up in the Tower Library, Fermina had settled on a book about the foundation of Rome. 'Do you think Romulus killed Remus because of sibling rivalry?'

'I don't believe twins can be rivals!' exclaimed Immy. 'I'd imagine the Brace boys get along famously!'

Fermina sat up a little at the mention of them. 'Where are they?' she said, trying to sound casual but craning her neck a little to see if she could spot them among all the books.

But they were nowhere to be seen. Volumina was missing too.

'Do you think they're OK?' said Fermina, rising now, too distracted to read further. 'I mean, Volumina won't be *sitting* on them somewhere, will she? It baffles me—why would Granny ask Volumina to look after them?'

Ferg's voice floated up from the newspaper aisle. 'Get over your disappointment, Ferm! Come look at this!'

Fermina flicked her braids from front to back. 'Hmmph! Who says I'm disappointed? Wow, isn't that just—'

What Fermina said next was 'incredible' but her nose was buried too deep in Ferg's newspaper for the last word to be heard clearly.

'The world's smallest water lily, just half an inch in size,' Ferg marvelled at the photograph. 'Got nicked from the Botanical Gardens on Valentine's Day last month and no sign of it yet!'

'Was it edible?' asked Phil, feeling hungry all of a sudden.

Fermina folded her arms and glared at him. 'It was a flower on the edge of extinction, Phil—'

'The last of its kind on the planet, actually,' Ferg read aloud.

'And look at that!' said Immy, running her finger along the words. 'Scooped neat out of the mud where it was planted in broad daylight! They're calling it a plant crime!'

Phil simply wasn't getting it. 'I'm stealing a pancake from the kitchen if we don't have lunch soon!' he muttered. '*Food crime*, that's what they'll call it in the papers!'

But Phil didn't have to commit a food crime that day. The kids were called down early to lunch because all the teachers were in a meeting. Immy nudged Fermina. 'I take back what I said earlier because it certainly looks like the twins are competing for Volumina's attention!'

Fermina winced. Immy was right. The Brace boys were sitting on either side of Volumina, talking animatedly. She was chewing slowly for a change, and nodding between mouthfuls, but their own food was untouched. She looked a little ruffled by all the attention but the boys seemed to have a lot to say to her, as if their lives depended on it.

Fermina knit her brows together. One of the twins had his arm around Volumina now. She was shaking her head and smiling reluctantly. Funny, nobody at Horrid High had ever seen Volumina smile.

'The twins are so likeable,' muttered Fermina, more to herself than to Immy. 'Even Volumina seems to be warming up to them.'

The group hurried to class but they needn't have. Miss Nottynuf was late. 'We have *half* a maths class left!' Phil quipped, horsing around as always. Even though this was an exaggeration, there were appreciative sniggers from the others, abruptly cut short by Miss Nottynuf's entry.

'Sorry, I'm terribly sorry!' she said, fidgeting at her hair and rambling. 'Principal Grit needed to have a word with me, with all of us, really, and it couldn't wait! *She* couldn't wait! Really, the *flight* couldn't wait! Three hours to make it to the city and fly out, what with packing and figuring out who will run this place while she's away—'

She would have gone on if Fermina hadn't interrupted her: 'Please, Miss Nottynuf, is Granny Grit going somewhere?'

Miss Nottynuf looked mystified, like she'd been woken up in the middle of a bout of sleepwalking. 'Wha . . . ? You mean . . . ? Didn't she tell you she was going?'

Going? Well, of course, to be perfectly accurate here, Granny had certainly told the children she was going. But they had assumed she was going to her office, going off to attend to the sort of work she'd been busy with as school principal. How were they to imagine she was going *away*?

Fermina frowned. 'Granny would never go away!'

'And not without saying goodbye!' said Phil, his voice sounding more certain than he really felt. After all, hadn't Granny come into their lives unannounced, right at the moment when they were losing all hope that Horrid High would ever be a happy place? Now, when they were only starting to forget all that horridness, could she be leaving again, just as suddenly?

Miss Nottynuf's hands flew to her face in shock, her handkerchief fluttering between her fingers as it made the same journey. 'Oh no, I'm not explaining myself well. I've never been very good at talking to children—I told Granny Grit just as much when she asked me to run the school while she was gone. There are many good reasons I couldn't look after this school in her absence, even if it's just for a week—'

'A week!' shouted Phil in relief. He wanted to shake Miss Nottynuf out of her self-pitying mood. 'Is Granny away only for a week, then?'

Miss Nottynuf nodded many times, as though her head was bobbing on a faulty spring mechanism. 'Isn't that what I've been saying? Colonel Craven will be standing in for Granny Grit while she's away, it's better that way.'

Relief washed over the classroom like a warm wave and all the children relaxed visibly. Granny Grit was going away for only seven days! Although this would have seemed long enough in ordinary circumstances, it felt like a very short time indeed now that every child had weighed the frightening prospect of Granny going away forever.

'Dr Bloom was very keen to step in and help, but Granny Grit settled on the colonel after I said no, I'm sure he'll do a better job than I could dream of!' Miss Nottynuf was saying when Immy broke in: 'Where's Granny gone?'

Miss Nottynuf tottered like a bowling pin. 'Ah! Gone? Yes! To the Amazon—at least I'm pretty sure that's what she said!'

The children reeled. They thought of everything Granny Grit had told them about the Amazon: tall trees reaching up to the sky and blocking the sun; the second-longest river after the Nile snaking through the rainforest; and the impossible varieties of birds and fish and animals. The very thought of the enormous Amazon had a shrinking effect on them. Suddenly they felt small, their classroom felt light years away from where Granny was going.

'Do you think you could come up with equivalent fractions for half today? Anyone?' said Miss Nottynuf, her eyes anxious behind her thick spectacles.

Phil and Immy were still in the Amazon, picturing Granny Grit threading her way through unforgiving jungle.

'Two upon four,' said Fermina, eager to go first.

'Four upon eight!' shouted a boy from the back.

'Yes?' said Miss Nottynuf, squinting through her spectacles at one of the Brace boys who had his arm raised.

'Er, no, I was just scratching my neck.'

Miss Nottynuf smiled. 'That's quite all right but why don't you have a try anyway?'

But the boy was scratching his cheek now and a red welt

was coming up where his hand had been a minute ago. 'Sorry, Miss Nottynuf!' he said, scratching his nose and then his neck again.

'Are you all right?' asked Miss Nottynuf. She turned to the other twin. 'What's wrong with your brother?'

But there was no reply. The second boy was scratching his back with one hand and his ankle with another.

'Are you two boys allergic to something?' Miss Nottynuf rushed over. 'Oh dear, you have red welts all over! What did you eat for lunch?'

'Fried rice,' said Phil, who was still nursing delightful memories of lunch. 'And noodles!'

Miss Nottynuf was wringing her hands now. 'What should I do, boys? You need a doctor!'

'Dr Bloom!' suggested Fermina.

Miss Nottynuf stopped short. 'You're right! She's *some* sort of doctor, I guess. Let me go get her! Now, I'm not sure if the boys are contagious, so I don't want anyone touching them while I'm gone! Volumina, would you move away, please?'

Volumina rose wordlessly, the bench heaving with relief behind her.

'She's quite the friend!' said Fermina, sounding bothered. 'Couldn't get away fast enough from the twins and their germs!'

Everyone in class was speaking at once when Dr Bloom swept in. The twins were scratching themselves furiously

now, and one of them had broken into a sweat. 'Ah, what do we have here? Let me see . . .'

'Well, we were studying fractions and the boys just started itching without stopping,' said Miss Nottynuf, twisting her handkerchief into a rope.

'Uhhhhmm,' said Dr Bloom, sounding thoughtful. 'It's certainly a rash,' she said, leaning closer to the boys. Her hair was done up in tight curls on the top of her head today. Like a swarm of eels.

One of the twins flinched as Dr Bloom ran a thin, long finger along the back of his neck. 'Hmm, I can feel small bumps here!'

The other was edging away from Dr Bloom. 'I'm fine,' he mumbled.

There was a small twitch in her jaw. 'Now, don't be afraid,' she said. 'I'll take care of this!'

And she knelt down and clasped his ankle with her hand. He started as though he had been jabbed by a needle. 'Easy, easy,' said Dr Bloom. She sounded so composed. 'I know it hurts now. The skin is all sore where you've scratched it and it burns when I touch it. But it'll burn more when it starts peeling off like paint.' And now she stood up and threw the boys a long, hard look. 'New skin can take *weeks* to grow!'

Miss Nottynuf gasped. 'What do you think we should do, Dr Bloom? What do you think it is?'

'Fever, chills, sores, it's a textbook case of rash,' said Dr Bloom. Her jaw twitched again. 'Nothing for the others to worry about! The boys probably touched something they weren't supposed to. *Am I right, boys?*'

Mallus and Malo nodded. One of them was shivering now. 'To the clinic! I have just the thing to get you up and about in a jiffy!'

Suddenly, the boys looked reluctant to leave. 'Go on,' said Miss Nottynuf, patting them on the shoulder. 'They'll get well soon, won't they, Dr Bloom?'

Dr Bloom giggled as she led the boys out. 'I'm sure they'll be up to mischief again in no time, Miss Nottynuf, don't you worry!'

The exceptionally ugly head was having a bad hair day. Huge tufts of hair had fallen off. The large welts of angry skin underneath looked angrier than ever. There was a revolting smell of burnt hair in the air.

Although the exceptionally ugly head didn't need any excuse to be in a foul mood, it didn't help that the voice on the other end of the phone sounded so calm and collected. It was downright annoying.

'Have you found the Grand Plan yet?' The hideous head didn't waste any time getting to the point.

'Haven't I told you to begin conversations with a "hello?"' said the calm, collected voice. 'Even a simple "How has your day been?" would work.'

The extraordinarily revolting head persisted: 'Tell me, have you found it?'

The voice on the other end did something even more annoying than sounding calm. It *laughed.*

The extraordinarily hideous head kicked his lemur. There! That felt better.

'I haven't found it yet,' said the calm voice after it had finished with the nasty business of laughing. 'But I will, soon enough. I have new allies now. Unexpected allies.'

'Well, hurry!' said the eminently objectionable head, flicking a few hairs off his lap. 'I'm running out of patience.'

The calm, collected voice hesitated. The owner of the eminently objectionable head was renowned for his tantrums. A sound spanking might have helped him in his younger days but it was too late for that now. 'Give me a few more days?' the calm voice said.

The ugly head rung off without another word. Now, where was that lemur? He needed to kick it again.

CHAPTER 8

It had been less than a day since Granny Grit left but the children were missing her already. As if the teachers sensed this, they went out of their way to be kinder.

Cook Fracas had outdone himself with breakfast. 'There is no child on earth who can say no to hot waffles drowning in melted butter and honey!' he said.

This was mostly true, except that on this day, there were two girls at Horrid High who were having some trouble getting through breakfast.

'He hasn't come in for his daily chocolate nibble!' Immy was distraught. 'What if he's in trouble? You haven't seen him in Sphinx House, have you?'

Fermina looked preoccupied. 'Wha . . .? Who? Malo? Or Mallus?' she said, her eyes darting towards the door as though she expected the twins to materialize any minute now.

Immy gave Fermina a steely look. 'I was speaking of Saltpetre, actually.'

Fermina averted her eyes guiltily. Of course, she cared about the mouse too! But did anyone care about the twins, if their rash was better and whether they'd be down for breakfast? Volumina certainly didn't! She was wolfing down two waffles at once.

'Maybe I'll ask if I could take breakfast upstairs for the twins?' she said, wandering off in the direction of Cook Fracas.

Cook Fracas was feeding Gypsy grapes. The goat was back in the kitchen and didn't appear to be missing Granny Grit one bit.

Phil smothered a chuckle. 'Gypsy's not that different from a Roman emperor at a feast,' he said under his breath but Fermina shushed him. She didn't want to offend the cook, not when she had a favour to ask.

'Of course you may take waffles up to the twins!' said the cook, grape juice running down his hands. 'The boys are lucky to have a friend like you!'

Fermina blushed, and then she blushed again at the thought of blushing. Phil was giving her a strange look, which she pretended not to notice. She'd barely slipped the waffles into a paper bag when Dr Bloom entered the dining room, the twins behind her.

'I hear the twins were down with a terrible rash?' said Cook Fracas.

Dr Bloom inclined her head gently. 'Some plants don't agree with them, isn't it, Malo?'

'Mallus,' muttered the twin she was looking at.

Cook Fracas nodded at Fermina. 'This young lady was planning to take food upstairs for the boys.'

'They're hale and hearty now, aren't you, Mallus?' Dr Bloom continued.

'Malo!'

'Twins! Who can tell them apart?' said Dr Bloom with a small laugh and a wave of her hand. 'What matters is, you're well and you have at least *some* good friends.'

She threw Volumina a long, hard look, but the twins perked up at the sight of their friend. They waved to her excitedly but Volumina lowered her eyes and continued eating.

'You forgot your waffles,' called Fermina after them, her voice dropping away as they rushed to Volumina's table.

'That's what you get for your trouble?' hissed Immy, glowering at their backs. 'Saltpetre would have been more grateful!'

But Fermina shrugged. 'It's nothing.'

The Brace boys were whispering in Volumina's ears, one from each side. They broke off when Fermina approached, the waffles piled up on two plates. 'Thanks!' they chimed in unison, turning their attention to Volumina again. 'Would you like an extra waffle? They smell amazing!' Volumina mumbled no, her eyes trained on Fermina.

'I'm glad to see you're better now,' said Fermina brightly to the boys. 'Say, did you find out what that rash was?'

But before the twins could speak, Volumina broke in. 'It was—' and a few waffle crumbs went flying.

'Wasn't asking you,' Fermina cut her off, flicking a waffle crumb off her shoulder in the most obvious way. 'I'd like to hear it from *them*, really!'

The twins shrugged. 'It was an allergy,' they said together in that disconcerting manner they had of being completely in sync. 'Don't know to what!'

'Some plant, that's what Dr Bloom said, isn't it?' nodded Fermina. The twins shifted in their seats. 'You still look a little pale, eat up and feel stronger!'

'I think—' Volumina said, but her mouth was still full and Fermina stopped her. 'I don't think you should be talking with food in your mouth, Volumina!'

Pushing the bench back so hard that it shook, Volumina rose, breathing heavily now. 'Do you have a problem with me, Fermina?'

'Why, will you *sit* on me if I do?' Fermina retorted, flinging her braids from front to back, gearing up for a fight.

Immy's eyes widened in terror. 'Ferm, let's go!' she said, tugging at her sleeve, but Fermina was transfixed to the spot. The twins put an arm each around Volumina. 'Come, there's nothing to argue about!' they said so amiably that Fermina backed away.

'I agree,' she said, tears stinging her eyes, 'there isn't!' She turned on her heel, feeling Volumina's fiery gaze drilling a hole into her back.

'Are you crazy?' said Phil as they hurried to class right after. 'Picking a fight with the school bully!'

'She wouldn't even let them *speak*!' said Fermina through her teeth. 'Aarrgh, how will I ever get through the day feeling so mad!'

But Fermina's anger dissolved by the third class of the day as Miss Nottynuf walked in, her face all but hidden by the boxes she carried in her arms.

'Pizza!' she said, doing a little skip. The children perked up at the word. 'Forty-eight slices of thin and crispy margherita! Help yourselves, come along!'

What did pizza have to do with mathematics? This question would have been considered with the seriousness it deserved if Miss Nottynuf hadn't thrown open the boxes and the smell of warm, freshly baked dough and melted cheese hadn't poured out.

Chairs were being shoved back and desks were being rocked as the children shot up and out of their seats, following their noses. Miss Nottynuf had already turned to the board, speaking aloud as she wrote: 'Express the number of slices of pizza you eat as a fraction of the total number of pizza slices.'

Miss Nottynuf sounded more confident now. Her hair fell over her face, but with a decided shake of her head, she said, 'We'll also look at what we ate as an entire class and express that as a fraction. Then, we'll look at what remains!'

The pizza was delicious and the slices were disappearing so fast, it didn't seem that *anything* would remain.

'Oh, don't open that last box yet!' she told one of the Brace boys. 'That's chocolate cake, for later!'

Chocolate cake! A thrill went through the classroom. And even though they wouldn't have believed it possible, two slices of pizza were left over. 'Any takers?' Miss Nottynuf asked repeatedly but even Volumina didn't budge.

Miss Nottynuf called them to the blackboard one by one. 'Write down what you've eaten, in fraction form!'

2/48, wrote Ferg, who had only managed to polish off two slices. *5/48,* wrote Phil with a silly grin on his face as the class poked fun at his appetite. 'Where did all that pizza go, Phil?' Miss Nottynuf laughed, taking in Phil's lean, wiry frame.

'Can I go next?' 'Hey, what about me?' All the children wanted to go up to the blackboard. Ferg looked around the class in disbelief. Could maths be such fun? The twins raised their hands at the same time, as if they were perfectly in sync. It was interesting, thought Ferg, how one Brace boy had his right hand raised and the other his left. Could the twins be using different hands? That hardly seemed likely! The twin with his left hand up was nudging the right-handed one good-naturedly. Ferg chuckled.

There were a few more titters from the class. Everyone else was laughing at a boy with thick eyebrows who'd forgotten how many slices he'd eaten. Miss Nottynuf was urging the boy to remember when Ferg's eyes fell on the twins again. Both of them had their left hands up in the air now. Ferg shook his head. Maybe he'd imagined it!

'Yes, you!' said Miss Nottynuf, picking out one of the Brace boys.

And then there was a flash of white, the slightest flurry of movement at the corner of Ferg's eye. 'Saltpetre! You weren't supposed to come out now!'

PIZZA FRACTIONS
Ferg
2/48
Phil
5/48

Fermina's ears perked up! Who'd said that? *Volumina?* It didn't matter, not at that moment when the sudden appearance of the white mouse that had been in hiding for two days mattered so much more. Not least of all because the school pet had landed square upon the chocolate cake! The cake was so soft, it was caving in under the rodent's weight, Saltpetre's small legs scrabbling to get a hold on the quicksand of chocolate icing he suddenly found himself in.

'A mouse!' yelled the Brace boy near the blackboard, which was a rather silly thing to say because everyone could plainly see that this was a mouse. In fact, it was quite clear that although the mouse had planned to eat chocolate cake, it was a case of cake consuming mouse instead!

Saltpetre was squeaking in alarm as his wriggling body sank into the chocolate but you could only tell this from the fact that his mouth was half open. His squeaks had no chance of being heard over the din of Miss Nottynuf shrieking, 'Oh dear, I've never been good enough with animals and certainly not mice!' and the Brace boy near the blackboard shouting 'A mouse! A mouse!' again and again like he'd made a most startling discovery.

'Stop, Saltpetre! Don't!' Volumina was shouting, and 'Saltpetre, where have you been all these days?' Immy was crying. The other Brace boy had jumped up now and picked up the cake box. He was shaking it frantically till, with one last desperate thrust, the mouse went flying.

'Saltpeeeeeeeeeeeeetre!' screamed Fermina, but her worries

were unfounded and Saltpetre landed on his feet unhurt.

'Here, Saltpetre, this instant, here!' urged Volumina through gritted teeth. 'Here!' begged Immy.

'Come to me!' said Fermina, throwing a burning look at Volumina. How dare she!

Saltpetre scurried this way, then that, confused, his whiskers twitching. With a final mad lunge, he scooted out the door, leaving a trail of small chocolate footprints behind.

'Catch him, somebody,' cried Immy, who had missed Saltpetre more than anyone else, 'before he disappears again!'

'SIT!' said Miss Nottynuf in her highest voice, her composure blown to bits by all the chaos and by a certain chocolate-covered mouse.

Ferg tugged at Immy's hand, forcing her into her chair. 'He'll be back, Immy,' he said. But Immy was shaking her head now, tearful. 'It's not like Saltpetre to do this!'

'SIT!' said Miss Nottynuf one final time and, as everyone settled, there was a squelching, squishing sound followed by an 'Oh no!' Actually, two 'Oh nos'. The Brace boys were staring at Volumina. One of them was pointing at her with his right hand. Ferg frowned. So it was not a fluke! The other was covering his mouth with his left hand. The boys did use different hands! Ferg couldn't help feeling a little pleased that he could tell the twins apart—who would have thought of that?

'It's *under* her!' the Brace boys said together. Ferg was lost in his own thoughts. Could the left-handed twin have nudged the right-handed twin because—'NO!' shouted poor Immy, fearing the worst. A little mouse would not make a great landing pad for Volumina's enormous behind!

'Hush,' said Ferg and Fermina glared at him. Sometimes he could be so insensitive! But Ferg had been thinking of something else before Immy had cried out. If only he could remember *what* that was!

'Saltpetre isn't under her, Immy!' whispered Fermina. 'He ran out in the hallway, didn't he?'

If the chocolate-covered mouse was not under Volumina Butt, *who* was? Or *what?*

Volumina rose slowly, as if to provide the answer to that question. The seat of her jeans was a brown, sticky mess. The chocolate cake was smeared across it. The colour was slowly rising in her face, and were those tears Ferg saw in her eyes? But Volumina blinked hard and squared her jaw.

Miss Nottynuf's voice was tight now, strained. 'How did you manage to sit on that cake?' she asked. Volumina swivelled around to look at her jeans in dismay. 'I don't know, it wasn't there a minute ago . . .' and then she saw the disbelief on Miss Nottynuf's face and her voice trailed off. 'You don't believe me?'

'You're dripping chocolate, Volumina!' broke in one of the Brace boys. 'Here, let me help you!' said the other twin who'd run out and returned with a box of tissues.

'Thanks,' said Volumina, looking a little embarrassed. 'But I didn't . . .'

One of the twins had dropped to the floor already and was mopping up dark splotches of chocolate. The other was scrubbing the bench. 'I didn't . . . I mean, I don't . . .' and Volumina couldn't get any further. Her ears were bright pink now. She bent down slowly to help the twins.

Miss Nottynuf's eyes looked hard and knobbly now. 'Never mind helping those poor boys, they're almost done! Go get yourself cleaned up!'

Volumina was breathing heavily now, like she did when she was angry. She shuffled out without so much as an apology, only pausing to throw the Brace boys a look of utter confusion.

'Decent of them to clean Volumina's mess!' hissed Fermina as the school bell sounded, her tiny hands curled up into fists.

Immy had darted out already, shouting for Saltpetre in the hallway with such a plaintive note in her voice, it made Phil's insides twist.

'Just when Miss Nottynuf was starting to feel more sure of herself!' muttered Ferg. He thought of the much-loved mouse that had been frightened into hiding; new students who were wasting their kindness on a remorseless bully; and a plane that was taking off very soon for the Amazon.

An interesting idea had occurred to him but only a whiff of it. What had it been? Ferg would have liked to think harder but Immy was stumbling back into class, crying, 'Saltpetre's gone again!' and he had to set aside his tingling ears and his thoughts for another time.

CHAPTER 9

'Who brought Salt Eater to class?'

It was Saltpetre, everyone knew that, and Immy would have been the first to howl with laughter at the misnomer but Colonel Craven's question only brought another sort of howling from her, the one that comes with tears.

The hubbub in the classroom had brought the colonel running. 'Trouble?' he asked Miss Nottynuf. 'Do we have trouble?'

And even though Miss Nottynuf tried to play it down, the smears of chocolate all over the front bench told another story. Now the colonel was pacing up and down and he seemed very different from the man who had slapped his thigh and laughed uproariously during their class that morning.

'It was only a harmless prank,' said Miss Nottynuf, throwing the children a sympathetic look. 'Children will be children, Colonel!'

'That's true! I must admit I'm more used to dealing with army cadets than with kids! But discipline is essential, isn't it? What do *you* suppose we should do?'

Now, while the colonel was not used to dealing with children, Miss Nottynuf was not used to being asked for advice, especially by army colonels and school principals. 'Er . . . I don't know . . .' she stuttered. 'Give them a warning and let them off, perhaps?'

The colonel straightened up. 'That's a good idea but this was once a horrid school, don't forget! We might have to be stricter. Now, who brought Salt Eater to class?'

The children were all looking pointedly at Volumina, but she stared at the ground and said nothing. Her nose was red like she had been crying.

'Crocodile tears,' mumbled Fermina. 'She has the twins completely fooled. See how worried they're looking? They don't want Volumina to get into trouble.'

Ferg shook his head. 'Maybe they're worried for themselves? I think they've just discovered Volumina's reputation for being the school bully—some kids were telling them about it when Volumina went off to get herself cleaned up.'

Phil nudged the two of them into silence. The colonel was speaking again. 'If no one owns up, I'm afraid all of you will be in trouble!' he said.

The children threw nervous glances in Volumina's direction. *Please own up!* But Volumina's eyes flashed angrily and she said nothing to save the others.

'Suit yourself, then,' said the colonel, folding his arms across his chest and puffing it up like a car tyre. 'Hit the ground, cadets! Give me 500!'

Five hundred *what*? 'Go on!' said the colonel, glaring at his watch. 'We don't have all day!'

'Aren't 500 push-ups too harsh, Colonel?' said Miss Nottynuf, sounding braver than she felt.

'Harsh?' said the colonel, sounding baffled. 'Not at all. In the army, we did 500 push-ups while brushing our teeth! Sit-ups, if you prefer? Or crunches? Jumping jacks, perhaps?'

Miss Nottynuf looked aghast. 'Ah, well, you're right, they're only children!' Colonel Craven exclaimed, throwing up his hands. 'Off to bed without dinner, everyone!'

Someone groaned. 'WHO WAS THAT?' barked the colonel. A hand went up slowly. It was Phil's. He couldn't imagine going without dinner.

The colonel approached Phil with slow, sure steps, bringing his face up close. 'Would you like to groan again?' Phil gulped.

Without warning, the colonel's left arm flew up into the air. Phil ducked, Ferg winced, and there was a sharp intake of breath from everyone. But the colonel didn't intend to strike Phil. His arm, it seemed, had moved up of its own accord.

'It's a nervous tic,' said the colonel, turning to Miss Nottynuf. 'Like my eyebrow. All the noise and the mess of war, Miss Nottynuf, it's made my left arm and my right eyebrow awfully jumpy, not to mention the rest of me! Mind you, all the shouting and screaming from your classroom seems to have had the same effect!'

He turned to Phil and pronounced his punishment. 'Two hundred jumping jacks the next time we have class!' The punishment was groan-worthy, but no one groaned now.

'And YOU!' said the colonel, looking directly at Volumina. 'You *squashed* the cake, yes?'

Volumina shook her head.

'Ah, I see. You *squished* it, then?' the colonel asked.

Volumina's mouth was set in a stubborn line that made her look defiant.

The colonel bounced on his feet. He was getting impatient. 'Did she *squish* the cake or *squash* the cake, Miss Nottynuf, which was it now?'

Fermina couldn't keep silent any more. No one else needed to be punished for Volumina's mistakes! She stood up and pointed at Volumina. 'She squished the cake—er, and she squashed it, too, Colonel, and she brought poor Saltpetre to class!'

'Sit down, Ferm, what're you doing?' hissed Phil. Immy tugged at Fermina's shirt sleeve. 'Sit!'

But Fermina's mind was made up. She glared at Volumina, eyes blazing. 'We've been looking for Saltpetre everywhere, Colonel, and my friend Immy is half sick with worry. You see, we haven't seen him for days! And then I heard her say it: "Saltpetre! You weren't supposed to come out now!"'

'She doesn't like me one bit!' Volumina burst out, pointing a finger at Fermina. 'No one does! She's lying to get me in trouble!'

The colonel frowned at Fermina. 'Are you sure about this? Making a false allegation against somebody is a very serious matter.'

Now Ferg's head was reeling. He doubted that Volumina would pick on small animals—she much preferred children. But Fermina was no liar either! He rose slowly. 'That's what Volumina said, I heard it too.'

There! It was done. Everyone gasped. The battle lines were drawn and while there was no one on Volumina's side, only a few children could imagine standing up to her.

'It's settled, then,' said the colonel, turning to Volumina with a severe expression on his face. 'Two hundred jumping jacks for you too!'

Miss Nottynuf was looking distinctly dismayed now. But the colonel wasn't finished. 'Now, who brought the cake to class?'

'Me,' said a tiny little voice emanating from Miss Nottynuf. The colonel marched up to her and peered at her so hard, he might have dissolved her with his gaze. His left arm flew up again, but Miss Nottynuf sidestepped it smartly.

'*Chocolate*, Miss Nottynuf? No self-respecting army school allows its cadets to eat candy or chocolate.'

'I was only trying to cheer them up,' said Miss Nottynuf, 'given the *circumstances*.'

And because of the way she'd said it, it was amply clear that by 'circumstances' she meant the sudden departure of Granny Grit. The colonel's right eyebrow was twitching now and there was another chest-bursting inhalation. 'As was I, Miss Nottynuf, as was I! I thought that these children needed some good-natured fun, but it appears that this school is no different from an army school. Cadets, children, they're all the same. They need RULES, they need DISCIPLINE!'

'It was a harmless prank, that's all,' said Miss Nottynuf.

'Ah, but that's where you're wrong, Miss Nottynuf,' said the colonel as they left the classroom together.

As they retreated down the hallway, the colonel's voice could still be heard. 'I won't have one prank, as you call it, plunging this school back into horridness. There will be no more chocolate till that Salt Eater mouse is found!'

Immy choked back a sob for the misnamed mouse. Where in the world was he?

Spirits were low in the dorms that night. The radio in the Sphinx House common room had been unplugged, a few children were flipping listlessly through the books on the shelf, and Phil was sitting in one corner, eating a bag of chips with a glum look on his face.

'I'll never make it without dinner!' he told Fermina, clutching his stomach. 'If you find me cold and dead in the morning, will you give me a decent funeral?'

But Fermina was in no mood for jokes. 'Cut it out, Phil, Immy's worse off than you are right now.'

Phil straightened up. 'I'm sorry, you're right—should we go to Centaur House and get her?'

Ferg shook his head. 'She needs some time on her own, leave her be!'

It was only a few minutes before lights-out when Immy appeared. Her eyes were puffy and red. 'He'll turn up,' Ferg said kindly, 'don't worry!'

But Immy shook her head, disconsolate. 'It isn't like Saltpetre to stay away. What if Volumina's keeping him locked up somewhere without food?'

'Did you get a chance to talk to the twins about this, just in case they know something?' asked Ferg.

'They haven't left Volumina's side once all evening,' said Immy, casting a careful look at Fermina as she spoke. 'They made a card for her, and there was something funny inside it because it made her laugh. They also wangled a snack from the Centaur larder, gift wrapped it and gave it to her. Cheered her up somewhat, I'm sure!'

'What does she need to be cheered up for?' said Fermina sullenly. 'She brought this on herself!'

The others fell silent. Fermina was right. Volumina didn't deserve so much kindness.

'Say, Immy,' said Ferg, breaking the silence as Immy got up to go. 'Didn't you once mention that the circus you grew up in had a pair of twin clowns?'

'Yes, they were a real riot! Why?'

Ferg shrugged. 'Did they both use the same hand to do things? Juggle balls, clown around, you know what I mean.'

Immy picked at her braces. 'I never gave it much thought!

I imagine they did, they were identical twins, after all!'

'One of the Brace boys is right-handed and the other is not,' said Ferg. 'I wasn't sure at first but I feel fairly certain now. It's fascinating, really!'

Immy shot him an unhappy look. 'Oh, Ferg, I can't seem to care about anything right now but where Saltpetre has disappeared to!'

'I feel the same way,' muttered Fermina, feeling ungracious as she said it. 'Who cares which hand the boys use? What I want to know is why they want to be friends with a bully like Volumina!'

Phil groaned and patted his stomach. 'Let's keep this utterly fascinating discussion on twins for another day, when we're all well fed, shall we? And if my tummy rumbles and keeps you awake tonight, Ferg, I apologize in advance for it!'

CHAPTER 10

'Breakfast in bed!' cried Colonel Craven the next morning, surprising the children bright and early with a loud rap on the dorm doors. 'Brought eggs, toast and chocolate milk upstairs because I figured you'd all be famished after skipping dinner last night!'

There was an excited clamour as the children bolted out to quickly wash up. The thought of a hot breakfast going cold gave them a new sense of urgency. 'I must admit I felt a little bad sending you to bed hungry,' the colonel told Ferg's dorm-mates as they helped themselves, 'but no more monkey business! Is that understood?'

The children nodded gratefully, wolfing down enough breakfast to make up for last night's lack of dinner. 'By the way, Cook Fracas talked me into letting him take sports class,' said the colonel, snorting in amusement. 'He's an old army buddy of mine so I couldn't say no. He said something about many pairs of hands being needed to prepare lunch today.'

The children hurried outside to find Cook Fracas standing in-between two large pyramids of shiny, red apples. He looked triumphant, like he had just raided an orchard.

'Apple tumble on the menu today!' he said, his mouth

twitching like a joke were about to escape it any minute.

'He means apple crumble,' said Ferg. 'One of Granny's favourites!'

'No, he doesn't,' said Fermina, her eyes firmly fixed on the two empty straw baskets set up under a tree and the two apple piles carefully balanced on the edge of the gravel path that dropped down to the gates of Horrid High.

'Bruised apples make the best apple tumble,' chuckled the cook. 'Now form a line behind each apple pile. Centaur and Pegasus to one side, Dragon and Sphinx to the other! When I say "go", we'll roll the apples down the hill, and the team that retrieves them and piles them into the straw baskets there first, wins!'

It was the strangest way to prepare lunch that the children had heard of but it sounded more entertaining than a regular sports class. The colonel had his doubts. He raised an eyebrow. 'Are you sure you want to do this, Fedro?'

Cook Fracas nodded. 'Sure as can be, Colonel!'

'Keep it simple, Fedro! One apple at a time, mind you!' cried the colonel. 'Fall in line, troops!' As the children formed queues, the cook whistled a tune under his breath. A *familiar* tune. If any of the children had heard the opening notes of *Funiculi Funicula,* they might have deduced that a fruit fray was coming up soon.

But Cook Fracas's jubilant song was interrupted when he shouted, '*AHIA! AHIA! AHIA!*' This is how Italian people say 'Ouch!' Three times. He clutched his right leg with both hands, hopping on his left. What could have produced this triple cry of pain from him?

As if to answer that question, an apple whizzed through the air. It hit Cook Fracas on his topknot, knocking it straight off its perch, a cascade of dark hair tumbling down his face.

With admirable fielding skills, Cook Fracas caught the apple on a bounce. The children ducked, which was mighty sensible of them. You see, someone was throwing apples at the cook and flying apples are very painful. Besides, an angry cook blinded by his own hair, maddened by pain and in possession of an apple could only be planning one thing—revenge!

But Cook Fracas was a precise man and he didn't see the point of flinging his apple without a guarantee that it would find its target. He groped in his apron pocket and pulled out a catapult like it was the most normal thing to carry around. He snagged the apple around the elastic band. Letting loose a stream of Italian words that no child should hear, he prepared to let loose the apple.

He pirouetted towards the half-open window on the first floor, from where the apple had evidently come. Now a pirouette is best achieved by ballet dancers. You see, it's a delicate movement that involves spinning around on your feet in one spot.

But Cook Fracas was no ballerina. Each of his feet were the size of a medium pizza. A pirouette only caught him off balance. To make matters worse, Colonel Craven chose this unfortunate moment to spring upon the cook's back, shouting

'Mission abort! Mission abort!' which is what army types say when there's been a change of plan.

The plan certainly changed. The cook's clumsy pirouette turned into a swan dive, and his foot caught in another foot. As the other foot in question was not his own but belonged to a boy standing near him, both took a tumble.

Cook and child cartwheeled downward, and the apple pile assigned to Centaur and Pegasus took off too. The cook's other foot, the un-entangled one, triggered the apple pile assigned to Dragon and Sphinx. All the apples were off like runners in a race.

'My apples!' shouted the cook mid-tumble. 'After them!'

The children in front wore confused expressions but those at the back surged forward, carrying the undecided ones with them. The effect was that of a pile of cards crashing. A pile of rather heavy cards. There was a rumble and a roar as the hapless children tumbled after the apples. The downward slope of the hill made a compelling argument to keep running downward. Soon, the children were bouncing, tossing and jouncing to their grassy end at the bottom of the hill.

'Bruised apples make the best apple tumble,' the cook had said. But what about bruised children? No one gave this much thought because what ensued was a right and proper rough-and-tumble. A long-legged boy had run ahead of the apples in his enthusiasm. When the apples caught up with him, they knocked about his ankles and tripped him up. Just a little behind him, a girl was lying on her back, winded, as

apples and muddy feet rained around her. Another tiny girl with long hair was doing cartwheels without quite meaning to.

A scuffed shoe joined the flood of apples, a pair of spectacles twisted out of shape and even a milk tooth skimmed the slope (though that didn't bounce very far). The grass came up in clumps, mud was flying and the air was filled with groans and cries of surprise. The long-legged boy who had made it to the bottom of the slope first scooped up a few apples and dived for cover as the others came tumbling down after him.

'Bring them up! Hurry!' The cook had climbed back up the slope now. He waved his arms in wild excitement as bruised children brought their bruised apples up the path. 'Into the baskets!' he cried. The long tumble down had taken the edge off his anger and he sounded like he was enjoying himself.

The children certainly weren't. Like all things globular, apples are happiest rolling about, and the children weren't very good at dissuading them. Several apples broke loose and made another bid for freedom. 'After them! Don't let them get away!' Cook Fracas yelled.

'How much lonGAAAAAAH!' yelled Ferg as he raced down the slope after an errant apple, only to fall over a girl who was crouched in the grass looking for her glasses. 'Just the last PHEW!' said Immy, who meant to say 'few' but tripped over an apple mid-sentence and made a stomach landing. She spat out blades of grass that tasted like apple juice. Fermina's braid was caught in another girl's earring and they both climbed the path together, yelping in painful unison.

The children slowly scrambled to their feet, with scraped elbows and scraped knees. Cook Fracas was standing at the top of the slope, surveying the damage with a gleam in his eye. He brought his hands to his lips, blew kisses everywhere and whooped like a tribal chieftain.

'*Benissimo*! *Sopraffino*!' he trilled, and Ferg wiped the sweat off his forehead as one of the twins stooped to pick up his wristwatch. 'Got knocked clean off!' he said to Ferg. 'Thanks!' Ferg whispered, noticing how the boy rounded up a last runaway apple with his right hand and plunked it into the basket. 'It's interesting,' said Ferg, smiling, 'how you're right-handed and your twin isn't!'

The colour drained from the boy's face—what had Ferg said to unnerve him? 'No, you're mistaken,' he said, sounding hollow. 'We're both left-handed.' He made a show of strapping his watch on his right hand, the way someone *left-handed* would wear it. Ferg frowned after him, puzzled. Hadn't he picked up his wristwatch, too, with his *right* hand? A thought took root in his head. Just then, a loud cry blew the thought to smithereens.

Beeeee-eeeehhhh-ehhhhhhh-ehhhhh! No, this wasn't Italian—this was a bleat, and the animal that had produced it had just been hit by an apple! Gypsy was now running as fast as her four legs could carry her towards the gates of Horrid High.

'GYPSEEEEEEEEEE!' cried Cook Fracas now, pelting after the goat. Of course, he was only half as fast because he had only half as many legs. There was a stunned silence as the children watched cook and goat bolt out the school gates and down the road. They looked about in amazement for a cue from Colonel Craven—what should be done next?

But before they could locate Colonel Craven, Cook Fracas reappeared. Alone. No sign of Gypsy. His white apron was brown with mud, his hair hung loose and wild and his hand was curled around his catapult again, the other around an apple.

'NOW TO FIND THE PERSON WHO THREW APPLES AT MY GYPSY!' said the cook, his feet stomping out a war song.

'I'LL . . .' and Cook Fracas drew his giant arm back in a stupendous arc as though he had finally decided to back his threats up with some action. The elastic of the catapult strained against his fingers and the alarmed children ducked for the second time that day.

'STOP, FEDRO! I'VE GOT HER!' That was Colonel Craven's voice. The children whipped about. The colonel was dragging someone out of the school building and, by the look of it, a considerable effort was required to do so. 'She tried to get away but couldn't!'

Cook Fracas dropped his catapult and the children heaved a huge sigh of relief. A large figure emerged in the doorway, spitting and hissing like an angry cat. Her legs wobbled; tears ran down her cheeks; her stubborn feet scuffed the ground.

'Volumina!' shouted the Brace boys together, their faces crumpled with dismay. 'It's unforgivable!' the colonel

bellowed. 'This one is a real troublemaker. I found her in the classroom.'

Everyone gasped. Whatever had possessed Volumina to hurl apples at Cook Fracas's head and then throw up such a fuss when apprehended?

Volumina glowered at her captors and stayed mum. Her silence angered the colonel even more. 'Going without dinner didn't teach you anything!' he said, his left arm flying up and down now. 'I wonder if Miss Nottynuf will still think this is a *harmless prank!*'

Volumina blinked back angry tears but she bit her lip and said nothing.

'Back to class, troops!' Colonel Craven boomed, his voice louder now. He had Volumina's arm in a firm grip. 'We'll let this cadet cart all the apples into the kitchen as a punishment. *And* clean up after lunch!'

Cook Fracas had his head in his hands. 'My poor Gypsy!' he said, again and again. 'I wonder where she's run off to!'

'She's a clever goat, she'll turn up sooner or later,' said Colonel Craven.

The Brace boys lingered near Volumina, looking rueful. 'Don't!' she sputtered angrily when they opened their mouths as if to comfort her.

Fermina met Ferg's gaze and shook her head slowly, her mouth puckering like she'd tasted something sour. 'It's heart breaking, how the twins feel responsible for Volumina when it's entirely her fault!' she hissed.

Ferg's ears tingled painfully as he watched Immy ushering the twins into the school building. He recalled what a show one of the twins had made of being left-handed earlier that day, when it was so obvious he wasn't.

'It's a little suspicious, how they both insist they're left-handed,' Ferg started but Fermina cut him off. 'No more of your mysteries, Ferg! Hey, Immy, wait up!'

Ferg stared after Fermina as she brushed past him, trying not to feel peeved. 'Fermina isn't in the mood to listen,' said Phil, trying to mollify his friend. 'But what's certainly a mystery is why Volumina would play pranks of this sort.' Ferg didn't say anything. Phil had a point but Ferg was trying to chase down another mystery before it eluded him.

CHAPTER 11

Volumina pushed the sorry-looking dumpling around in her plate as if it was a football on a field. Meals were a mess with Gypsy gone, and Cook Fracas was faring no better himself. He alternated between hysterical sobbing bouts where he moaned for Gypsy, and wild mutterings about what he would do to Volumina for her part in this. 'I'll shoot her with carrot sticks! I'll squirt her with orange juice! I'll . . . I'll . . .'

Colonel Craven put an arm around him, 'Now, Fedro, after all that trouble in the army mess, you promised there'd be no more food fights!'

'Gypsy,' said the cook under his breath, peering out the window with a hopeful light in his eyes.

'Why don't you step outside and see if she's back?' urged the colonel.

Volumina kept her head down and said very little. After the apple tumble, she'd been sentenced to kitchen duty for a whole week. She broke her silence only once to say 'Thanks, Malo!' as the twins helped her clear the tables.

'Can you imagine, she ate *all* the dumplings in her plate?' marvelled Fermina. 'Even though they were inedible?'

'Drop it, Ferm!' said Immy. 'It must be hard being reminded

constantly of how fat you are and how much you eat.'

'Besides,' cut in Ferg. 'What's more interesting is that *she* can tell the twins apart!'

'What's that got to do with—' Fermina butted in but Ferg wasn't going to let Fermina stonewall him again. 'Volumina called Malo by name. Perhaps she's noticed too.'

'Noticed what?' asked Fermina, hands on her hips. 'That they're the only friends she has at Horrid High?'

Ferg took a deep breath and barrelled on. 'That Malo is right-handed and Mallus is left-handed!'

'Wow, you've managed to figure out which twin is which!' Phil was clearly impressed.

Fermina shook her head so vehemently, her braids swatted Ferg. 'Right hand, left hand, it doesn't matter!'

Before Ferg knew what he was doing, he'd grabbed Fermina by the shoulders and given her a good shaking. 'Well, if it doesn't matter, why do they pretend that they're both left-handed, Ferm? Wouldn't it be easier for everyone to tell them apart if they didn't keep it such a secret?'

'Let go of me, Ferg!' cried Ferm, her eyes flashing. 'You're so into secrets and mysteries and tingling ears, you sound no different from Tammy Telltale! And no one liked *her* very much.'

'Break it up, you two!' cried Immy in dismay. 'You're always at each other's throats these days.'

For once, Phil couldn't think of anything funny to say. Perhaps he'd noticed that Fermina wasn't the only one close to tears. 'Come on, off we go,' he said, patting Ferg on his back. 'I just saw Miss Nottynuf go into class!'

Later that afternoon, Colonel Craven handed out rucksacks to all the children. 'Carry them with you at all times! Basic dry food that lasts forever, clean drinking water and a few Band-Aids! Just in case of an emergency evacuation. And I've got a pair of army boots for each of you too!'

'Wish I could strap mine on right now and be out of here!' Phil grumbled. As the children ruefully shrugged on their rucksacks and wore their new shoes, they felt the same way. With Granny gone and the colonel so jittery, everyone felt like making a run for it—except that they had nowhere in the world to go.

'There's a storm coming.' Colonel Craven squinted up at the blue, cloudless sky and shuddered.

'It's in his head,' muttered Phil. 'Say, Ferg, do you think "storm" is military lingo for something? Hmmm?' He elbowed Ferg but Ferg was staring at Volumina.

'Phil, didn't you once say that it was a mystery why Volumina was playing all these pranks all of a sudden? It isn't her style, is it?'

Phil elbowed him again and raised his eyebrows in Fermina's direction. Ferg fell silent. Fermina was within earshot, and he certainly didn't want to risk setting her off again! Perhaps she was right. Imagining too many mysteries wasn't doing anyone any good.

'We have two possible escape routes!' Colonel Craven

squatted in the mud and drew a set of criss-cross lines with a twig. *Escape routes?*

'Yes!' Colonel Craven continued, pocketing the twig. 'We could run into the Get Lost Forever Woods but what good would that do us?' Here, he rummaged in his clothing for something. 'Ah! What's this?' he said, dislodging the twig he'd put into his pocket just a moment ago and staring at it as though he'd never seen it before. Tossing it over his shoulder, he fumbled some more. Now a key came flying out of his pocket and clattered to the ground. With a cry of discovery, he dived for it.

'This opens the back gate and we'll never need to use it!' he said, brandishing the key like a weapon. 'We'll go out the front gate, the way Gypsy did, wise girl that she is!'

And just as he mentioned Gypsy, a familiar white head with horns on top glimmered at the gates like an actor appearing on stage just in time to say her lines. Of course, Gypsy had only one line—*Beeeee-eeeehhhh-ehhhhhhh-ehhhhh!*—and she was in no position to deliver it because her mouth was full of leaves.

'The GO—!' blurted Immy, when Fermina broke in, 'At the GAY—' and Phil interrupted her with a 'Isn't that GU—?' And Ferg shouted, 'The goat is at the gate, isn't that good?' because he was tired of the effect Gypsy had on people's sentences.

'GE—!' shouted Colonel Craven before ducking low and scurrying in the direction of the gate. He had meant to say, 'Get down!' but the children were already crouching as though they realized that this was a delicate situation where the slightest movement would send Gypsy off again.

Colonel Craven was a man on a mission: Lure Gypsy in past the front gate, lock it firmly behind her, call Cook Fracas out and watch the tearful reunion of goat and master. What a fairy-tale ending it would be!

'Gypsy-wipsy!' cried the colonel, doing a little skip. Gypsy surveyed him mid-munch with admirable solemnity.

'Goatie-woatie!' cried the colonel, doing a little hop. Gypsy froze, mid-chew, looking mildly amused.

'Girlie-whirlie!' cried the colonel, doing a little tap dance. Perhaps it was the tap dance, which was so very bad. Perhaps it was the rhyming, which was not much better. It might have well been the colonel's twitching eyebrow, though one shouldn't make too much fun of people's tics.

But Gypsy gulped hard and took three steps back. One. Two. Three. She would have taken a fourth when she paused, her hoof mid-air. And then something made her take three steps forward. One. Two. Three.

The colonel broke into a grin. Would you believe it? The clever goat was dancing with him. He had always been quite the ladies' man, a whirlwind on the dance floor, a devil in dancing shoes . . . but a musical voice punctured his little daydream:

'Here, Gypsy, come here, lovie,
Wouldn't you like some poison ivy?'

As rhymes go, this one was terrible too. And Dr Bloom wasn't much better when it came to dancing. But what Gypsy was staring at with a new gleam in her eyes was the leafy branch in Dr Bloom's gloved hand.

'Lunchie munchie?' said Dr Bloom, her hair glistening in the sunlight.

Gypsy was drawn to Dr Bloom like an iron nail to a magnet. She crossed the front gate, and in a trice, Colonel Craven had jumped up and swung it shut behind her. Gypsy couldn't have cared less. She tugged at the leafy branch in Dr Bloom's hand and chewed it with relish. Then she cocked her head to one side and took a step forward as if to say, 'Is there more?' She nosed Dr Bloom's trouser pocket hopefully but the teacher held the bag backed away. The goat persisted, grabbing a lock of Dr Bloom's hair and tugging hard until the hair came loose.

'Now look what you've gone and done, you silly goat!' said Dr Bloom as Gypsy ambled off into the overgrowth, dejected. The science teacher threw her head back and laughed, her hair cascading down her back. Golden brown with dark roots. For a brief moment, her hearty laughter reminded the children of Granny Grit. 'Goats will eat anything, Colonel! she said. 'They're just dumb ruminants with nothing on their minds but food. But they have a special fondness for poison ivy.'

'Humph! Who'd have thought it?' said the colonel, beaming with pleasure. 'I'm very grateful, Dr Bloom, and I'm sure Fedro will be too! Come on, kids, inside. Let's give him the news!'

Just then, the bell rang. 'You might want to do that on your own, Colonel,' said Dr Bloom, smiling graciously. 'I have a class with them now, and you've given me an idea to keep the kids out a little while longer. This is no day to be cooped up in the classroom, is it?'

'Don't stay out too long, there's a storm coming,' said the colonel and, with a brisk nod, he was off.

Dr Bloom looked up at the sky—it was blue—and shrugged. 'Looks like a perfect summer day to me! I dare say the crows wouldn't be nesting up there if it weren't.' She threw a glance up at the tower.

The crows were wheeling around in tight circles, making a commotion. Fermina narrowed her eyes and watched them intently. 'They look like they're in a flap, don't they?'

'This is the time when their young are learning to fly,' said Dr Bloom. 'The older crows are keeping an eye out for danger, that's all!'

Phil guffawed. '*Colonel Craven* has an eye out for danger all the time these days!'

'Well, danger has a way of making things more *tantalizing*, doesn't it?' Dr Bloom's eyes roved towards the Get Lost Forever Woods. 'That giant "Keep Out" sign on the back gate only makes you want to go there all the more.'

'Oh no, the woods are bad news!' cried one of the children.

Dr Bloom's jaw twitched. 'You're right, they're probably bad news for *children* but if you were a botanist or an explorer, you'd *burn* with curiosity, wouldn't you? About those untouched woods, about rare plants and exotic trees that no one has ever seen . . .' She perked up suddenly. 'Speaking of untouched, there's something I'd like to show you that's best left that way!'

She rummaged in her trouser pocket eagerly. 'Draw closer, now!' With a gloved hand, she held up another branch of poison ivy. She pointed at the three leaves, two that branched off in opposite directions like a pair and a third one at the tip. 'Now be careful not to touch! These three little leaves will give you the most horrid rash, make your eyes swell up, even give you blisters—*oozy* ones!'

And as she said 'oozy', Ferg could have sworn that Dr Bloom's eyes rested on Mallus and Malo. Only for an instant. The twins looked uncomfortable but Dr Bloom seemed to enjoy the effect she was having upon them. 'Oozy!' she said again. 'Oooooooooo—'

The second part of 'oozy' never followed. Instead, there was a swooping and a sweeping of the air, a fluttering of multiple wings and a raucous bout of cawing. Before anyone could bat an eyelid, a black shadow of crows descended on Dr Bloom like a swarm of locusts on a rice field!

She cried out in alarm and ducked, shielding her head with her hands but the crows were not to be discouraged. They wheeled about her, sharp beaks and heavy wings, diving in to peck her, skimming the top of her head with their legs, black feathers shaken loose in the flurry.

'Run!' shouted Ferg, although the children had already turned tail and bolted towards the school building. Dr Bloom led the pack, her shining hair askew.

They were barely inside when the crows scattered, cawing in a disgruntled way. Inside, a current of shock ran through the baffled children:

'Where did the crows come—'

'Top of the tower—'

'They went straight for her!'

A *murder* of crows! Ferg's head was spinning now. It seemed like a lifetime ago . . . He remembered a teacher at another school somewhere telling him that a flock of crows was known as a murder. Hadn't they wheeled about in the sky the day he first came to Horrid High? He shuddered. Hadn't he seen them as the first horrid sign of things to come?

Who would have thought that the crows would attack a teacher, or anyone at that? Ferg tugged at his ears, although he knew that the tingling wouldn't stop.

'Did you know—'

'—that this was going to happen?'

'*She* couldn't have!'

Ferg's ears perked up. The Brace boys weren't talking about the crows like everyone else. They were standing well within hearing and whispering frantically.

'She couldn't have what?' he burst out, even though he'd been eavesdropping and he shouldn't have.

The Brace boys jumped. One scratched his left cheek as

he always did when he was embarrassed. Mallus! 'What, you heard us?'

'I told you, you were *too loud!*' said the other twin, nudging him with his right hand. Malo! Ferg's breath caught in his throat. An idea was forming again in his head, a shapeless, formless idea, like a wisp of smoke curling up from a chimney.

'Please!' Mallus begged and the idea in Ferg's head was gone, as easily as if it had been blown away by a gust of wind. 'She won't take it—'

'—kindly if she knows we told on her,' said Malo, completing his twin brother's thought.

Told on her! Ferg blanched as the thought hit him as hard as a stone being thrown at him. The twins were talking about Volumina! What couldn't she have done?

As though the twins had read his mind, they glanced around nervously, Ferg, too, all three of them appearing as guilty as thieves. But Dr Bloom had run up to her room and the children had scattered into small groups in the hallway. Volumina was nowhere to be seen.

'Tell me what happened,' Ferg pressed the twins. 'Please!'

'It's just a hunch,' said Mallus, twisting his mouth uneasily.

'We can't be certain,' said Malo.

'We did spot a fledgling crow this morning, though, didn't we?'

'Ah yes, yes of course! We did! It was learning to fly!'

'Fly? Right! She might have troubled it.'

'Yes, that's it, she troubled it!'

'Slow down,' said Ferg, confused by the speed with which the truth was being constructed now, words being thrown back and forth between the twins like a ball in a game. His ears rang as they told him what had happened, in half-formed sentences, with an anguished look in their eyes.

'It can't have been easy telling on the one girl at school they're so obviously fond of!' said Fermina, when Ferg told the others later that night. Her eyes flashed with anger.

'Pretty brave of them,' agreed Phil. 'It won't be fun when Volumina finds out that they've told on her!'

Immy's face darkened. 'First Saltpetre, now a little bird that can't fly away! I can't believe Volumina's cruelty!'

Ferg was quiet. Why was Volumina playing pranks and hurting animals? It seemed so out of character. And the twins had been whispering. *Too loudly.* If they really didn't want anyone to know, why did they confide in him? Was it because he'd overheard them? It would have been hard not to. Something was missing here. It was a crucial link, he felt sure of that, and the more intently he followed it, the further away from him it danced.

CHAPTER 12

Fermina's bleary eyes settled on the morning light streaming in through the window and the Tower Library beyond. She stretched and smiled—there was no better view to wake up to, and Saturdays were special. Alas! Her arms dropped as she remembered. This was no regular Saturday. With no library time, it just didn't feel like a Saturday . . .

After the attack on Dr Bloom the day before, Colonel Craven had flapped about more than the entire murder of crows put together. 'No one goes near the Tower Library till we can figure out why this happened!' he said, his left arm doing a march, his eyebrow all jumpy.

'Edgy!' said Phil. 'Though I wonder if there's a *military* term for such nervousness.'

'Overwrought,' muttered Immy.

'*Overreacting!*' mumbled Fermina, who was heartbroken over the indefinite suspension of library class.

The colonel wasn't the only one suffering from a case of nerves. Dr Bloom had been absent from dinner the night before and from breakfast this morning. 'She's very shaken up,' disclosed Miss Nottynuf, wringing her hands in dismay. 'Has a deep gash on her forehead, too, it's just awful! I hope it wasn't another prank, children? The colonel no longer believes these pranks are harmless and I don't either!'

Ferg and his friends flinched; Volumina had a hand in this and their secret weighed heavily on them.

'Volumina didn't sit with the twins at breakfast today!' said Immy as they walked to class. 'You think she's on to the twins, Ferg? Perhaps she's guessed that they've spilled the beans on her?'

'I don't think that's likely,' frowned Ferg. 'Wouldn't she teach them a lesson for squealing on her if she knew?'

'She *is* punishing them, don't you see?' cried Fermina, recalling the twins' long faces at breakfast, how they stole glances in Volumina's direction and whispered to each other.

Ferg snorted. 'That seems awfully *kind* for a school bully, Ferm, to give her victims the cold shoulder and little else? Isn't it more like Volumina to sit on the twins to teach them a lesson?'

'That's true,' admitted Fermina grudgingly. 'Instead, she seemed withdrawn and paid no attention to them.'

'Yet, when you told the twins to come sit with us, they hovered around her table.'

'And shook their heads hard like they couldn't imagine being friends with anyone but that girl!' muttered Fermina. She was still smarting from the rejection.

'The question is, do we tell the colonel what we know about the attack on Dr Bloom?' wondered Ferg aloud as they stepped outside into the sunshine.

'That's not a good idea,' said Phil, staring at the playground quizzically. 'I think the colonel has other things on his mind!'

Hands flew to half-open mouths, gasps were withheld, a few pairs of feet froze in their tracks. Who wouldn't be surprised? You see, the colonel was standing in the middle of the playground, half naked!

OK, not half naked if you counted the entire shrub's worth of leaves and branches that he had draped around his shoulders like a leafy cape, and the green stems that stuck out from behind his head like a verdant version of a hat. Or the leaf-print night-shorts he wore that ended just above his hairy knees!

'CAM—MOO—FLAGE!' the colonel shouted like they were the words of some ancient tribal song, the black streaks of paint on his cheeks making him look quite the chieftain. 'Camouflage makes you blend in like that cunning poison-ivy plant that caught your poor science teacher unawares!'

'It wasn't poison ivy, it was the crows!' Phil whispered in disbelief.

The colonel blustered on. 'I looked for that cursed plant everywhere. I'll uproot it before it attacks someone else, I thought! But it couldn't be found. Anyone knows why?'

The colonel teetered on the brink of his punchline, passing his expectant eyes over the children.

'CAM—MOO—FLAGE! That's why!'

Ppphttterkowwlggff! This was the sound of Immy laughing and trying not to laugh at the same time.

Phil rolled his eyes. 'The way he puts it, you'd think the

plant lay in wait for Dr Bloom and pounced upon her!'

Ferg's mind had galloped off in another direction. The colonel had looked for the poison ivy everywhere and he said it couldn't be found in the school. If it didn't grow at school—and now Ferg felt his pulse quicken—*Where did Dr Bloom get it from?*

'It was the crows that swooped down on Dr Bloom, Colonel!' said a long-haired boy who felt brave enough to correct the colonel's perception of things.

'They won't swoop down on me, cadet!' said the colonel, puffing up his chest as he took a deep breath. 'Not when I'm in—

'CAM—MOO—FLAGE!' butted in another voice.

The children turned—Colonel Craven's leafy outfit had been so grabbing, they hadn't even *noticed* Cook Fracas! He was standing proudly in the same spot where he'd stacked up the apples the day of the apple tumble. Except, in place of apples, there now stood a giant telescope!

'We're going to see stars!' gasped Immy without thinking.

'In the daytime?' retorted Fermina, frowning Immy into silence.

Cook Fracas leaned his considerable bulk against the telescope and swivelled it around to point out beyond the gates of Horrid High. 'She's ready to go. What shall we fire her at?'

Fire?

'It's a *cannon*, not a telescope!' murmured Ferg in amazement. How had it landed up at school?

'From my war days!' the colonel said, striding up to the

cannon. His chest billowed like the sail of a boat on a gusty day, the black streaks on his cheeks quivering from the effort. 'I've modified it slightly! For an emergency evac!'

'An "evac" is a quick escape,' started Ferg before trailing off. The gates of Horrid High had been shut since Gypsy's return. There was only one way a cannon could be used to evacuate people . . .

Immy was thinking along the same lines. An old, unpleasant memory came back from her childhood days in the circus. Her voice faltered: 'It's a—'

'*Human* cannon!' shouted Colonel Craven, his voice bursting with pride. 'I'll fire you all, one by one! Over the gates to safety at last!'

'We'll certainly see stars,' said Phil, a forced brightness in his voice. 'Just not the ones you had in mind, Immy!'

Immy was swaying like she'd been struck. The human cannonball was the most sensational—and dangerous—act in the circus. There was no other act that made the circus master so nervous. Every time a human cannonball was shot out of a cannon, a gazillion things could go wrong. And sometimes they did.

The colonel's eyes roved over them. 'Now, who wants to go first?'

Not a single hand went up. Colonel Craven, not to be discouraged by the children's lack of enthusiasm for his brilliant war toy, shouted, 'YOU!'

Immy gulped. Colonel Craven was looking directly at her!

Surely, there was someone else behind her. There had to be! She turned slowly and found herself looking into Gypsy's deep brown eyes! She knew from her circus days that what got fired out of a cannon was a human being, not a goat. There was no doubt about it, the 'You!' was meant for her!

Her legs trembling, her mouth quivering, Immy stepped forward. She knew that if she refused, the colonel would insist, or worse, press someone else to go in her place. Colonel Craven was saying something about how easy it all was, how all you had to do was step inside the barrel of the cannon, keeping your hands by your sides, and think of how birds fly . . .

Immy didn't hear a thing, of course, except for the sound of her blood pounding in her ears.

She had to ease herself into the narrow barrel, one leg at a time. Once inside, her arms were jammed so tightly to her sides, she couldn't wiggle a finger. Colonel Craven clambered up on the barrel and squeezed her shoulder. 'It'll be quite all right, you'll see!'

But Immy knew it wouldn't be. The human cannonball act took months of training and planning. Nets had to be placed in such a way that the human being shooting out of the cannon made a safe and soft landing. Immy's nose was tickling now. She sniffed. Gunpowder! Now, wait a minute! Did Colonel Craven even know that these cannons were not like real war cannons? That fireworks were used to create the noise and smoke that made them seem real? That these cannons used bungee springs—not gunpowder—specially designed to launch a person into the air?

'Shall I fire?' Cook Fracas shouted, like a child about to blow out the candles on a birthday cake.

Immy closed her eyes and gulped hard. This was it! The end.

'Wait!' Immy's eyes shot open. That was Ferg's voice. 'This cannon won't work!'

'How do we know that this contraption is safe, Colonel?' That was Fermina.

'Surely, we'd be better off simply running out the gates when an emergency comes up!' That was Phil.

Immy felt tears prick her eyes. Her friends were loyal and brave to stand up for her! It was of no use, of course. The colonel was beyond reasoning.

'Won't work? Won't *work*? You call this sophisticated piece of machinery a *contraption*? Get that girl out of the cannon!'

Immy couldn't believe it! She blinked back her tears as she was pulled out by the colonel's strong arms. In a trice, he had managed to squeeze his considerably larger body in. All that could be seen of him now were the green stems of his hat, shaking vigorously as he spoke: 'I won't have anyone doubting this cannon—in the old days, it shot—'

A pigeon alighted on the hat, mistaking it for a branch, and surveyed the odd proceedings with a tilt of its head. 'Off!' cried Colonel Craven, glaring at the pigeon. It was physically impossible to move his head enough to shake off its winged occupant. The pigeon was keenly aware of its position of advantage and glared right back as if to say, 'Why don't *you* take off first?'

'Shall I fire the cannon?' Cook Fracas shouted, quite beside himself with anticipation. He could almost imagine the colonel soaring across the sky like a bullet! Maybe the pigeon would go with him too. There was a faint 'Go on!' from inside the cannon.

Now, no one expects a cannon to go off in silence, whether it is firing a regular cannonball or a human one. The children stuck their fingers into their ears and cringed. Cook Fracas whistled *Funiculi Funicula* under his breath. He struck a match and lit the fuse. It burned all the way down.

There was no explosive sound, no smoke. Colonel Craven did not streak across the sky like a bullet. And the pigeon on his head did not so much as flap a wing. Instead, it groomed its feathers in a bored sort of way.

'It won't fire!' said Cook Fracas in utter dismay.

'What do you mean it won't fire!' said Colonel Craven, muttering a few curses under his breath and clambering out of the cannon.

'It won't fire!' repeated Cook Fracas because that's exactly what he meant. He had no more of a sense of how cannons work or don't than the pigeon roosting on the colonel's hat.

'I'll dive in and take a look,' said the colonel, conscious that all eyes were upon him now. He crawled inside the barrel head first and the pigeon resettled on the cannon's edge.

'Shall I fire the cannon?' Cook Fracas shouted again, bouncing on the balls of his feet. He hadn't fired anything in very long, not a popcorn slingshot or a French-fry gun. Not even a pickle missile.

Now, it isn't clear whether Colonel Craven found anything inside the cannon to explain why it wouldn't fire. But his verdant hat got stuck against the sides and when the colonel tried to wriggle out, he found he couldn't. Not an inch. 'Shoot!' said Colonel Craven, his voice muffled inside the barrel. Of course, what he meant by that was, 'Oh no!'

But when Cook Fracas heard 'Shoot!' his ears perked up. To him, 'Shoot!' could mean only one thing. If there was any hesitation at all, it was because he was a logical man. And it was plain that the colonel was inside the cannon back to front. If you were going to fly out of a cannon and soar across the sky, you had best not do it in reverse!

Now the pigeon chose this opportune moment to make a generous dropping—a thick, gluey one. And with commendable aim, it dropped the dropping clean into the barrel of the cannon. Till it met the back of the colonel's neck with a satisfying *plutt*!

Now, you must remember that the colonel was stuffed into the barrel head first and tethered there by his hat. Imagine his disappointment when the pigeon's dinner trickled up his neck!

'Shoot!' he shouted, this time louder, shutting his mouth promptly and pursing his lips for fear of tasting pigeon poo. He waved his legs frantically in an effort to pull himself back out.

From the outside, things looked very different. Cook Fracas heard the colonel say 'Shoot!' clear enough. For the second time. Now he was waving his legs about like he couldn't wait to be off. Maybe the glitch in the cannon had been fixed and the colonel wanted to test it?

With a howl of excitement, Cook Fracas lit a new fuse. This time, it worked. The children had barely covered their ears when it went 'BOOM!'

It was an unforgettable sight, worthy of the finest circuses in the world. Colonel Craven shot out of the cannon, feet first, ramrod straight, soaring across the sky—a human cannonball reinvented! Over the gate he went, over the grass, too, screaming something that sounded like 'YOOOOOOOUUUUUUUUU IDDDDDDIOT!' though one can never be sure.

And then, as is the way with all things on our planet that go up in the air, Colonel Craven came down.

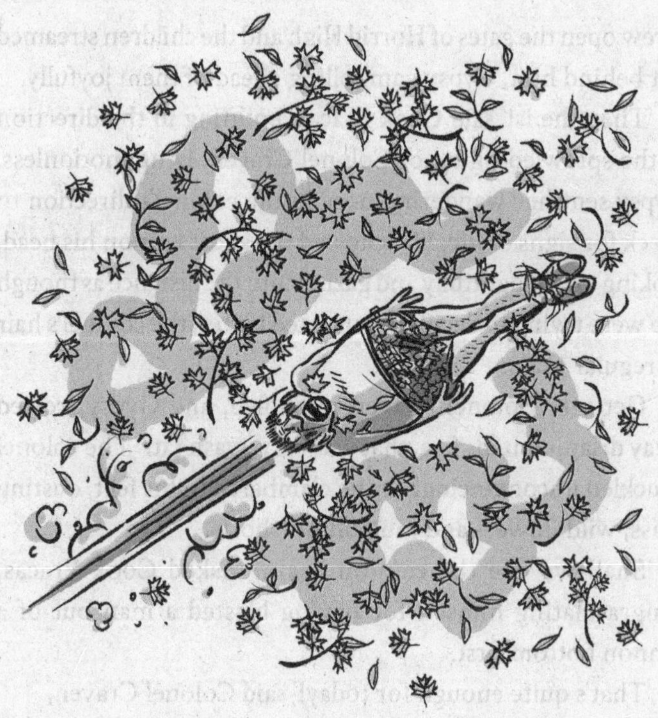

Down, down, down like a bird that had been shot, or a parachute that wouldn't open, Colonel Craven fell. The grass and the wild flowers in some field beyond Horrid High rushed up to meet him. The children prepared to hear a sickening thud, even though the colonel was landing well out of earshot. Bones would crack, something softer would go *squish.* They tensed.

But the colonel bounced upon a mound of springy grass. A soft landing! A frightened bee whizzed away. Cook Fracas threw open the gates of Horrid High and the children streamed out behind him, Gypsy gambolling ahead of them joyfully.

'There he is!' said Cook Fracas, pointing in the direction of the sprawled figure of Colonel Craven, lying motionless. Gypsy sent her wandering nose in the colonel's direction to check for signs of life. She chewed the short hair on his head, looking up thoughtfully and gazing into the distance as though she were trying to decide what tasted better, the colonel's hair or regular grass.

'Get off!' Colonel Craven mumbled, and Gypsy trotted away disappointed. 'See, that was easy, wasn't it?' The colonel chuckled unconvincingly as he clambered to his feet, dusting grass, wild flowers and mud off his shorts.

'Shall we fire the cannon again?' asked Cook Fracas, congratulating himself for having blasted a man out of a cannon bottom first.

'That's quite enough for today!' said Colonel Craven, swaying a little as he tottered back to school. 'I think we might need a better evacuation plan!'

The children trooped back into Horrid High, the gates making a hideous creaking sound as they were closed again. They'd narrowly escaped being shot out of a cannon—but hadn't the colonel talked about a 'better evacuation plan'? What enterprise would he come up with next?

CHAPTER 13

The large gates of Horrid High stood closed for the first time since Principal Perverse's reign. The children were cut off from the outside world again. Four days had passed since Granny had left. Her absence weighed on the children's spirits heavier than the rucksacks Colonel Craven made them lug around everywhere.

Volumina was up to no good, and although Ferg was convinced that the twins knew more than they were letting on, they didn't leave her side for even a minute.

Poor Fermina was having a terrible time of it. She had had such hopes for the twins. She'd imagined reading books with them up in the Tower Library; passing notes to them in class; dancing to the radio in the common room with them after school was done. She just couldn't understand why the twins had seemed so friendly on that first day and why they were so remote now. On two occasions, she tried to engage them in conversation, even though it was getting harder and harder for her to make friendly advances when they were so clearly unwelcome.

What added to Fermina's misery was the loss of library time. 'Can't have the lot of you sitting around *reading books* when the enemy attacks!' Colonel Craven cried. 'Instead, we'll have a double sports class!'

That wouldn't have been so bad if they'd played volleyball or basketball. But what Colonel Craven had in mind was war games. He divided them house-wise and made them dig trenches around the school grounds. These were long, narrow ditches so deep that if the children fell in, they couldn't be seen at all from the outside. 'Four trenches, one for each house!' the colonel proclaimed. 'They'll make perfect hideouts!'

The children had just finished shooting at each other with water guns the guns were filled with tomato ketchup. Then someone suggested a ball game and Colonel Craven relented. But every time the ball was thrown in his direction, his eyes widened in horror. 'Bombs away!' he screamed, or 'Grenades!' or 'Sniper fire!' and dived into a trench, or worse, threw himself down upon the children to protect them.

Fermina had the worst time of all. As she clambered out of a trench for the second time that day, dusting off a strange and clumpy mixture of tomato ketchup and mud, an idea struck her. It should have struck her a long time ago, but Fermina had been without family for so long, she'd quite forgotten that she *did* have family now, even if that meant just one uncle. Uncle Max! He was a special uncle and equal to a dozen ordinary ones.

Hadn't he come to her rescue at the Grand Party when the children had been discovered by Principal Perverse and marched up to the tower? When it seemed all was lost? After retiring from his job as school inspector, Uncle Max was travelling the world, as he'd always dreamed of doing. He was in South India now, at a yoga camp, lost in meditation. Fermina's heart felt lighter at the very thought of him.

Hadn't he said that there were no telephones at the yoga retreat? Surely, a letter would be allowed in? Saturdays were no longer library day at Horrid High, but Mondays were most certainly post day! Fermina's heart did a little cartwheel. There was nothing that stopped her from sending a help note to that address in South India that her Uncle Max had given her! And then Uncle Max would swoop down on Horrid High, knock sense into the colonel's head and set Volumina right too. The twins would go back to being their normal, friendly selves. Granny Grit would return and be astonished to learn that the school had turned horrid in her absence. And all would be well again! But, Fermina realized even at her optimistic best, that everything hinged on the letter making its way to her uncle. A small voice in her head whispered, *What if he doesn't get it?*

Staunchly, she put that thought out of her mind as she wrote to him later that night. Her hands trembled with exhaustion. The children had mopped the floors. And washed their clothes. And scrubbed their shoes. After all, ketchup and mud leave a nasty trail. The only thing more stubborn than the stains was the children's determination to get them out. They couldn't risk upsetting Colonel Craven again. Fermina soldiered on, even though she was dropping off to sleep now:

Dear Uncle M,

This is a cry for help! Granny Grit has been called away to the Amazon, the school is in the hands of a new principal called Colonel Craven, and Horrid High is back to being horrid! It started with a few harmless pranks but now the colonel is losing his mind and there is no one else we can turn to! Please come quick because if anyone can help us, it's you!

Your loving niece,
Fermina.

The children felt comforted after Fermina had slipped her letter into an envelope and licked it shut. The letter was a long shot but it gave them the sense that they were doing *something* about their predicament.

'Granny would be proud of us,' said Ferg before they retired for the night. 'At least we're fighting back.'

'Somehow . . .' broke in Phil, sounding unconvinced.

'And if this letter reaches my uncle,' said Fermina, freeing her braids as she always did at bedtime, 'he'll be here in a jiffy!'

As it turns out, the children were wrong. The letter never made it to South India. Did it get lost in the mail? Did it get misdirected? Was it even put in the post box at all? We will never know. But the letter filled the children with hope, even if was only false hope. And that hope kept them going when things got worse. And things did.

That night, Colonel Craven decided to patrol. He marched

from the front gate to the back gate, his torch guiding him around the trenches. He rubbed sleep out of his eyes; this was no time for complacency. Horrid High was becoming horrid again; every cell in his body was sure of it, just as he'd been certain that his camp would be attacked by the enemy, all those years ago. And he'd been right then.

The colonel's left arm flew up of its own accord as old memories returned. That night, so many years ago, had been as dark as this one. Loud gunshots, bright flashes of light, the startled cries of men woken from sleep. They should never have been sleeping—he'd warned them that the enemy was coming. He'd put up a struggle but the enemy had dragged him away, blindfolded, into the thick grass, and they'd set the camp on fire. He could feel the heat of those flames on his face . . .

Wait! What was that? A movement in the bushes yanked Colonel Craven's thoughts back to the present. *Two* movements. His razor-sharp eyes were dependable yet! The circle of light made by his torch bobbed up and down, barely cutting through the utter darkness. 'Anyone out there?' he called and, although Colonel Craven was a brave man, there was a tremor in his voice.

A third movement. He could swear it! He drew closer to the back gate now. His torch lit up the strip of ground beyond the gate that led into the woods—a hotchpotch of footprints! Colonel Craven swung his torch in a wild arc. More footprints from the back gate to the school building. *Intruders!* Colonel Craven felt his blood go cold. The hair at the back of his neck stood on end. His imagination swung in wild arcs like his torch. The lock on the back gate was intact. *Trained and nimble intruders have walked out of the Get Lost Forever Woods, scaled the back gate and slipped into school!*

And then, something hit him in the eye. Hard. The colonel dropped his flashlight. The darkness was thick now, and it closed around him like a hangman's noose. Something hit him again in the small of his back and he dived to the ground. Bullets! No, not bullets for there was no blood. But some sort of artillery, that much was certain.

'RED ALERT!' he screamed at the top of his voice, leaping up and running to the school building as fast as his legs could carry him. This time, he would warn everyone. 'SOUND THE SIREN!'

A wailing sound jangled the tired children from their hard-won dreams. Fermina sat up groggily, Ferg rubbed his eyes. Phil rolled over and mumbled, 'Is the wailing bell back?'

The children assembled in their common rooms, confused, the air abuzz with rumours: 'Principal Perverse is back!' said one frightened boy in Pegasus House. 'Or maybe we only imagined that things had got better!' suggested a fanciful girl in Sphinx House. 'Or maybe,' said a nervous boy in Centaur House, 'we're being attacked by enemy planes and Colonel Craven was right all along!'

There were also cries of 'Don't be daft!' when Dr Bloom popped her head into the dorms: 'Evacuation alert, children! Assemble outside!'

Gasping with fright, stumbling over their pyjama bottoms, the children clattered down the stairs, out into the damp, cold night.

Mallus and Malo looked sweaty and flushed. 'They're terrified,' said Immy. 'New to such horridness, poor things!'

Ferg's ears were tingling hard. It was a cool night. Surely, the scamper down the stairs and out into the playground wasn't enough to get the twins this sweaty? And why were their pyjamas muddy? The same half-formed thought was eluding him. It was playing hide-and—

'Seek!' shouted Colonel Craven. 'Seek out the intruders!'

Miss Nottynuf had staggered out in her dressing gown, her hair dishevelled. She leaned in to tell the colonel something but he waved her away. 'Years of army experience, Miss Nottynuf, I'm dead certain that three intruders have come out of the woods! Centaur and Pegasus, search the back of the school with Cook Fracas! Come with me, Sphinx and Dragon, we'll take the front!'

Immy stayed close behind Volumina and the twins as they jogged around the school building. 'If those intruders dare to shoot at me,' Cook Fracas said, wearing his most menacing expression and clenching his fists, 'I'll throw chopsticks at them, I'll tie them up with noodles, I'll . . .'

But Immy was more interested in what the twins were saying to Volumina. 'It isn't right of you to . . .'

Volumina glowered at them and they shrank back. Immy's blood froze. Right of you to *what?* What did the twins mean?

Was Volumina playing one of her pranks again?

'Look sharp!' Cook Fracas yelled, sprinting towards the swimming pool.

Volumina's legs were struggling to keep up. The twins slowed down, too, and as Immy ran past them, she strained to listen.

'He won't . . . find anything on his own . . . and you know . . . why!' Volumina was saying, her breath ragged now. Immy gasped. Volumina was wicked beyond belief! She'd done something to spook the colonel and now she was gloating about burying the evidence.

'What did you do tonight to set off the colonel's panic?' Immy blurted out. 'Please, Volumina, you've got everyone into enough trouble already!'

There was an angry splutter from Volumina but the twins cut her off, aghast. 'Not now!' they said, pushing Immy away. 'If Cook Fracas catches us falling behind, we'll be in trouble!'

Immy bit her lip and fell away to join her friends. Had she picked the wrong time to confront Volumina? Why were the twins protecting her so much?

'Our friend feels faint!' the twins shouted. Volumina looked winded from the run. With a cry of alarm, Miss Nottynuf whipped out her little handkerchief and wiped Volumina's face with it. 'Let's go inside!'

'Is it safe?' asked Dr Bloom. She dropped her voice a little. 'After all, we haven't searched the building yet!'

Ferg frowned. Dr Bloom had a knack for saying exactly the

sort of things that would agitate the colonel. Only yesterday, she'd exclaimed 'Blood!' more than once after the children's ketchup-gun fight, at the red–brown footprints all the way from the main door of the school building to the showers. The colonel had jumped out of his skin at her suggestion and asked, 'Enemy blood or ours?' Her words had the same effect now. The colonel snapped to attention like a flag had been hoisted somewhere. 'No one goes in, not until we've made sure the intruders have left! We'll keep watch in the trenches! We'll run patrols! We'll booby-trap the gates!'

Miss Nottynuf tried to reason with him but his face was set hard like cement.

'The rest of you,' and he turned to the others, 'into the trenches and sleep with one eye open! The enemy is with us!'

CHAPTER 14

The children were up with the sun the next morning. After all, no child can sleep with one eye open in a wet, muddy trench!

'The school building is clear!' said the colonel. He looked like he hadn't slept a wink either. 'Inside, everyone, catch up on classes while we chart out a plan for tonight!'

Ferg hung back, staring at the back gate and tugging at his ears.

'What's the matter?' Phil asked.

'I retrieved the colonel's flashlight where he'd dropped it. I found that the footprints leading from the woods to the back gate were also leading back out into the woods!'

'That's good news!' piped up Immy. 'It means the intruders have gone, doesn't it?'

Ferg furrowed his forehead. 'Unless . . .'

'Unless what?' the others chorused.

Ferg shook his head. 'Unless there were no intruders at all? Look, the footprints go both ways. What if someone from school went into the woods and returned—'

'Only to get mistaken for an intruder by the colonel!' cut in Immy.

Fermina twirled her braid thoughtfully. 'The question is,

why would *anyone* want to go into the woods?'

The children fell silent. That question had no answer. Meanwhile, Phil knelt down. He held something yellow between his fingers, sniffing at it and squeezing it thoughtfully before popping it in his mouth. 'It's funny, could the colonel have mistaken these for bullets last night?'

'Phil, what are you doing?' cried Fermina in horror, watching his jaws move up and down.

'Popcorn!' Phil grinned. 'It was flying popcorn that set the colonel off!'

'So someone went into the woods last night and took a *snack* along?' said Immy, shaking her head. 'I can't believe it!'

'Volumina sounds like the sort of person who'd want a ready snack at all times!' retorted Fermina, feeling a little mean as she said it.

Immy's expression was grave now. 'You might just be right, Ferm!' She filled the others in on the conversation she'd overheard the twins having with Volumina.

'That's it! The twins were reproaching her for sending the colonel into a manic panic!' shouted Phil.

A manic panic? It was the sort of phrase that would have made them fall down laughing if they'd had any mirth left in them.

'She sounded like she'd covered her tracks,' recalled Immy. 'She told the twins that he would never find out on his own.'

Fermina straightened up. 'No more buts about it, I'm telling on Butt!'

'Wait, let's not alarm the colonel any more for now!' cried Phil.

Ferg was lost in his own thoughts. The intruder had climbed over the back gate but Volumina was scarcely that nimble! And hadn't Colonel Craven sworn that he'd heard *three* intruders moving in the darkness? Only one set of footprints led in and out of the school. Where were the others?

As the day passed, it was no longer clear to the children how many of Colonel Craven's enemies were real and how many imagined. 'The intruders will be back tonight,' he said ominously. 'This time, we'll be ready!'

Classes were a blur. It was more tempting to steal glances at Cook Fracas rigging a trap over the front gates. Or at Colonel Craven wheeling the cannon out in full view.

'Must perfect my aim!' giggled Cook Fracas, even more on edge as darkness fell. At dinnertime, his aim was impeccable, which was rather unfortunate for the children. Ferg's nose was hit by a dollop of yoghurt; Fermina had ketchup in her braids; and Immy ducked a flying cupcake, which would have been a good thing if Phil hadn't been standing directly behind her.

'Reflexes! Reflexes!' said Cook Fracas, his eyes twinkling as he caught Volumina at the back of her head with a soggy slice of bread. 'Good soldiers dodge bullets and you can't even sidestep a sausage!'

The only thing to do was crawl into bed and be thankful that the day was over but even those plans were scuttled. 'To the trenches, don't forget!' Colonel Craven shouted. 'No one sleeps in!'

Immy carted Ferg's and Fermina's blankets, rucksacks and pillows to the Sphinx trench. The two of them were on clean-up duty and wouldn't be out till much later.

'Fat help you are, Phil!' she panted when she found him in the trench, head and arms thrown back in a lounging pose.

'Shh, I'm in the throes of death by boredom right now!' he said, pulling a morbid face and ducking as Immy tossed a rucksack at his head. 'Hey, watch it!'

Immy made a mental note to drop her own things off and join Phil. If anyone could cheer her up, it was him! As she neared the Centaur trench, however, her eyes passed over all her dorm-mates. She was looking for two in particular.

Darting a quick look about her, Immy slipped around the corner of the school building. Where were the twins? She needed to ask them about Volumina.

It was a no-moon night and, as Immy scurried past the kitchen window, she heard the clatter of dishes being washed. The light from the kitchen streamed out upon the grass, making it glow a luminous green.

In the kitchen, Ferg and Fermina were elbow-deep in soap suds and neck-deep in a fight.

'The twins can't be trusted, Ferm!'

'Just because one of them is right-handed and one isn't?'

'Come on, Ferm, you know there's more to it than that! It's all the pretending that bothers me.'

'Remember how they told us, that first night up in the Sphinx common room, that their mother loved identical pairs?' said Fermina.

Ferg gave her a blank stare. 'Yes, but they also said something about how their mother found them a little disappointing.'

'Our mothers found us disappointing, too, or have you *forgotten,* Ferg Gottin?'

There was a stung silence, except for the sound of running water. 'I'm just saying that this explains why they pretend so much to be identical. Have you forgotten what it's like when you'll do anything for your parents to accept you?'

'Their parents aren't here any more,' said Ferg, his mouth set in a stubborn line. 'And I'm not sure that pretending to be identical is the only thing they're deceiving us about!'

'Deceiving?' scoffed Fermina. 'What do you mean?'

Ferg hesitated. Fermina would certainly not receive this well. 'What if all that kindness they've been showing Volumina is a pretence too?'

Fermina turned up the water and twisted away from him. Her voice was cold when she spoke. 'If you ask me, you can't see kindness for what it is any more! You're as mistrustful and suspicious as Colonel Craven!'

Meanwhile, underneath the kitchen window, the sudden cawing of a crow made Immy cry out. There'd been a flurry of movement near the Tower Library. Immy cast a quick glance up at the kitchen window. Should she call out to Ferg and Fermina? With a half shake of her head, she decided against it. All this talk of intruders was making her jumpy for nothing.

Voices! Immy took care to stay in the shadows and listened.

'This won't work!' said one of the twins.

'The colonel won't believe you!' said the other.

'You can't stop me!' That was Volumina! 'Not any more!'

Immy gritted her teeth. *What was Volumina going to do now?* Balling her hands into fists, she inched closer. She could make out their figures in the darkness now. Volumina, large and menacing, was dragging the twins somewhere. 'I've had enough!' Volumina was saying. Her voice was trembling with rage.

Immy shuddered. Hadn't she rescued Ferg once from Volumina's clutches a year ago, in the days when Horrid High was truly horrid? She prepared herself to speak like Colonel Craven: *Unhand the boys!* she would say. 'WHAT'S—'

'—HAPPENING THERE?' Immy shook her head in utter puzzlement. That was Colonel Craven's voice, but it hadn't come out of her! She spun around and cried out, startled. Colonel Craven was standing directly behind her.

'Can't have kids floating about like ghosts in the dark!' he said, hustling Immy back to the Centaur trench. She craned her neck to get one last look but the shadows near the tower had dissolved into the darkness. 'Dead silence now!'

Immy waited up for the twins; they would return to the

trench sooner or later. But the minutes melted into one another, and she had no idea when her eyes closed and the world went black. She dreamed of the twins. They were standing in front of the Get Lost Forever Woods. 'Follow us!' they said together. They stretched out an arm to her. One left arm, one right arm. Which one should she take?

Help! The twins were shaking her awake. 'Wha . . . what's happening?' Immy rubbed her eyes open, her eyelashes caked with mud. It took her a minute to realize that the dream had ended. She sat up, wide awake. It was still dark and a light rain was falling.

'Volumina's gone!' said one of the Brace boys. Which one? Mallus or Malo? Did it even matter?

'Gone? Gone where?' said Immy, as she staggered out of the trench behind the twins. They both pointed in the same direction and Immy's heart sank like a stone. The Get Lost Forever Woods!

In a few minutes, the children were standing at the back gate, staring into the dark woods in disbelief.

'Colonel Craven dragged her into the woods, we saw it ourselves!' the twins chorused. 'Said he would teach her not to play any more pranks!'

The children were horrified. Colonel Craven was clearly in the grip of one of his manic panics!

'I can't imagine it being easy for the colonel to drag Volumina into the woods without waking up the whole school,' said Ferg, still sounding doubtful.

'When Ferg and I came back from clean-up, we heard nothing,' said Fermina.

'It might have been because we were busy arg . . .' Ferg broke off. Fermina and he had been having an argument and there was no point in raking up old matters.

'We tried to stop him,' said one twin.

'You can't reason with him when he's in that mood of his.'

Ferg's thoughts were milling about. What if the colonel and Volumina were both wandering around in the woods now, lost beyond hope? *And was that such a bad thing?*

Ferg stopped himself and flushed red. That last thought of his had been a horrid one. It jarred him. Was the horridness around him *changing* him, the way it had changed the colonel? He shuddered—if you didn't keep horridness under control, it wormed its way inside you. And then a more powerful thought jolted him—he sounded paranoid! Wasn't that what Fermina had said to him in anger last night? That he was becoming more like Colonel Craven?

'I'll go after them!' he said, shaking himself out of his fearful mood.

'What?' Phil did a double take. 'You can't be serious!'

But the look on Ferg's face said it all.

'Oh, all right then, we'll all go!' said Phil, fidgeting with the straps of his rucksack to hide his terror.

'Count us in too!' said Immy, speaking for both the girls.

Fermina turned to the twins. 'You'll come with us, right?'

Mallus and Malo looked a bit taken aback. 'We'd only get

in your way. Volumina had gotten a bit tired of us tagging along behind her!'

Fermina felt a rush of affection for them. 'You won't be tagging along, don't be silly! You'll both be a great help! Right, Ferg?'

But Ferg's expression had changed. He was staring intently past Ferm now, at the back gate. 'Ferm, you should stay here too,' he said slowly. 'With the twins.'

'I don't understand.'

'It's—' and then he broke off as though he didn't want to say any more. 'We'll be back before daybreak. I doubt the colonel will get too far dragging Volumina with him!'

Fermina felt a flash of irritation. Ferg was getting back at her for being so hung up on the twins but what did she care? Besides, she told herself, it was the first time she'd have the twins all to herself. They'd sit up all night and wait for Ferg to return. Without Volumina around, the twins would open up to her. They'd tell her all about their favourite ice cream, their favourite kind of music and why they pretended to be identical. By the time Ferg, Phil and Immy returned with Volumina in tow, the Brace boys and Fermina would be thick as thieves.

'It's three hours to morning,' she said, glancing at her watch. 'We'll stay up and wait . . .' and her voice trailed off. She felt a little guilty now.

Her shoulders dropped as she watched her friends walk

past the back gate, down the mud path and towards the woods.

Ferg, Phil and Immy tried not to look back at Fermina's tiny figure growing tinier still behind them. Their feet were heavy and the army boots they had on would feel heavier in a few hours. Fermina had given them her rucksack and Phil had offered to carry it, being by far the tallest and strongest of the three.

'The woods can frighten anyone—even the moon has gone into hiding,' muttered Phil, his heart hammering.

'It's plain that Ferm and you haven't been getting along at all,' said Immy as they trudged down the mud path, slower than they had to. 'But you should have let her come along!'

'I didn't want to leave Fermina behind either,' said Ferg. 'I wasn't trying to punish her. It's the lock on the back gate that got me thinking. It was broken!'

Immy looked confused. 'So what? The colonel and Volumina went out that way, didn't they?'

Ferg took a deep breath. 'The thing is, didn't the colonel have a key to the back gate?'

'I don't rem . . .' Immy started because she really didn't remember. Or did she? A memory sprang up out of nowhere. Colonel Craven on his haunches in the mud, drawing an escape map and fumbling about in his pocket. A key flying out.

'You're right!' she gasped. 'Why would he break the lock if he had a key?'

'Maybe he was in a hurry to drag Volumina out and teach her a lesson—' started Phil, grasping at straws.

'Or maybe the colonel didn't go into the woods at all,' Ferg broke in.

'He *didn't*?' echoed Phil and Immy in unison, making Ferg cry out, 'Hush, you two!'

A loud flutter of wings beat the air, an angry rustle of leaves, and all three of them shivered. The forest rose up in front of them, a dark, shadowy presence. Ferg gulped. The woods threatened to swallow them up now. The air smelt dank here, like sweat.

'Great deduction, and on that note, I say we turn back and head to school ourselves!' said Phil, eager to be off. 'Maybe Volumina didn't go into the woods either!'

'Wait!' said Immy. 'If neither of them went into the woods, why did the twins tell us that they did? Surely you're not suggesting that the twins are lying?'

'They've not exactly been honest so far!' said Ferg, shining his torchlight ahead of him.

'Well, let's turn back and confront them!' Phil said.

'Don't forget, there was no sign of Volumina in the trenches,' Ferg said. 'Where else would she be?'

'Don't really feel like helping her,' muttered Immy.

'Especially if she sallied off into the woods on her own just to cause trouble!'

'Shush!' said Ferg, cringing. Immy's voice sounded unnaturally loud now. Ferg couldn't shake off the certain feeling that they were not welcome here and their presence was disturbing the forest. The inky darkness got noticeably denser, thicker. *Like blood.*

Phil shook his head as if to dislodge that thought. And although there was no light here other than the light from their torches, the leafless branches of the trees glowed in silhouette. Like witch fingers. Or skeletons. It was funny how many of these trees never sprouted leaves, even in summer.

Immy watched the three circles of light made by their torches bob ahead of them merrily in spite of the gloom.

'We'll keep the school directly behind us,' said Ferg resolutely, 'and proceed in a straight line through here!'

But that was easier said than done. There were dark clumps of roots waiting to trip them up. A sudden rivulet to cross. Gnarled creepers to watch out for. Ancient tree stumps to pick their way around. The children had hardly taken a few steps into the woods when Immy whirled around and gasped, 'Which direction did we come from?'

It was as if the tall trees of the Get Lost Forever Woods had closed in around them. If Phil stood on tiptoe and craned his neck, he could see just a glimmer of the tower above the trees but that was all. Everywhere looked familiar—*and* unfamiliar. Immy's gaze spun a full circle. Which way had they come?

Which way should they go? Indecision turned to confusion and confusion, to panic.

There was a breeze blowing, as unsettling as a ghostly breath. The forest floor bristled with resentment beneath them, as if it were alive and couldn't tolerate their stepping upon it. And the dead silence of the night was replaced by the deafening sound of hundreds of crickets chirping together. There were other strange, unidentifiable sounds—was that the hoot of an owl? And that odd chirrup there, what was that? But most unnerving of all were the whispers everywhere. *Go, go, go*—was that what they were saying? Or *come, come, come*? Maybe *never, never, never*? The children huddled close together and wondered which was more terrifying—the sense of being alone or the sense of *not* being alone.

'Let's use two torches and keep mine for later!' said Phil, switching his off. Immy cried out in fear as something grazed her forehead. Only a creeper of some sort. She hated the idea of moving with one torch less but she knew Phil was right.

'Wait!' said Ferg, who was two steps ahead and had planted his foot in squelchy mud. Immy and Phil froze as Ferg retraced his steps slowly. 'I think the ground ahead gives way to swamp,' he said. What was it that had been said about the Get Lost Forever Woods? That there were mud pools here that swallowed you up in seconds, that sucked you in and closed in above your head like nothing had happened?

'This place gives me the creeps,' said Phil, who rarely missed seeing the humour in things.

'You're right, these woods are filling our minds with horrid thoughts,' said Immy, rubbing her arms.

It made no sense to soldier on in such utter darkness.

'We need a fire to keep us warm till daybreak,' Ferg said.

'Till daybreak!' exclaimed Phil, dismayed. 'I thought we'd be in and out of here in a jiffy—who said anything about setting up camp? How long will we be here?'

'Let's look for kindling,' said Ferg, sidestepping a question that he had no reply to.

The darkness seemed to recede, if only a little, once the fire had taken hold. As the children crouched close, they felt thankful for the matchboxes in their rucksacks and for Colonel Craven's lessons on fire-building. What was it the colonel had once said? *If you know how to build a fire, you can survive anything, I promise!* Those words rang more true now than ever.

The children decided to take turns sleeping but sleep overwhelmed them all. Hours passed and it was close to noon when a few shafts of light managed to penetrate the spindly tangle of branches overhead. Ferg woke with a start and squinted at Phil's old wristwatch—'Midday!'

'Midday?' said Phil, taking off his spectacles and wiping them with the edge of his T-shirt. 'Wha . . . what happened?'

'We've overslept!' said Immy, rising slowly. 'It's something about these woods. I've never felt so drowsy . . .'

'We must get out . . . think clearly . . . find our bearings!' said Ferg, his mind feeling cloudy and his words coming out garbled. They avoided the spot that Ferg's shoe had squelched in the night before, heading instead in a new direction.

The forest floor was littered with dead leaves in myriad shades of brown as though the trees had shed all their foliage, once and for all. A snake slithered across the decaying muck. Another hung from a large-leafed shrub like a forest creeper, glittering green, till it slid to the floor and slithered away. Leeches as thick as a man's finger glistened black in the undergrowth. How far could Volumina have gone in these hostile woods? And why?

The children kept going and emerged in a small clearing. Light! The children looked up hungrily at the sky. 'Should we keep going?' asked Immy, feeling more awake now.

'Or turn back?' said Phil, still hopeful. 'Volumina might have returned to school. She might even be eating *breakfast*.'

Immy nodded. 'Ferm will worry about us! Let's turn back!'

'What about Volumina?' asked Ferg, even though he wanted to turn back just as much as the others did.

Immy shot him an anguished look. 'I don't know, we can only hope that Phil's right and she's safely back at school!'

'This way, then?' asked Phil, eager to get going.

Immy shook her head. 'No, I'm sure it's that way!'

'Listen!' Ferg said. His ears were tingling now. Listen? There was certainly enough to listen to: the cicadas who had joined in with the crickets; the deep-throated croaking of a frog somewhere; and the steady whispering of the woods. *Go, go, go. Come, come, come.*

Phil jiggled his spectacles with his nose. Immy frowned. They'd heard it too.

The soft crunch of twigs breaking underfoot. A rustle of leaves being parted. The sound of something lightly brushing against shrub and grass.

The children crouched down in puzzlement. Should they keep still or . . . 'Move!' hissed Ferg, 'Ahead together!' And just as Ferg set foot on the patch of moss in front of him, someone shouted, 'Stop!'

It wasn't Phil or Immy. It was someone else from behind them—a girl. Or a boy. 'A witch of the woods!' Immy screamed, so loudly, it felt like the forest would come crashing down on them. Phil turned and froze. A witch! Did witches even exist? And then a pair of hands, or jaws, clamped around Ferg's foot. When he spun around again, his foot was gone!

CHAPTER 15

While Ferg, Immy and Phil were still asleep in the woods, Fermina awoke at dawn, feeling awful. She'd crawled into the Sphinx trench the night before, her stomach fluttering, and she'd sworn she wouldn't sleep a wink till her friends returned. Besides, she'd hoped that the twins would trade secrets and swap stories with her. Instead, they'd trotted off to the Centaur trench without so much as a glance in her direction and she'd fallen asleep!

'To class, troops!' a familiar voice bellowed and Fermina's heart lurched. Colonel Craven! If he was back from the Get Lost Forever Woods, her friends were probably back too. She ran to the twins who were rolling up their blankets. 'Ferg, Phil and Immy are back, right?'

'Haven't seen them!' said one, rubbing the back of his neck with his right hand. A voice in Fermina's head whispered unbidden. *Why is he so unconcerned? Is this Malo, the right-handed one?* When he caught her staring at him, he flushed and rubbed the back of his neck with his left hand, as if to make a point of it.

'We'll see you in class?' said his brother, scratching his left cheek. *Left hand, left cheek. Mallus!*

'Where's Volumina?' shouted Fermina behind them.

But the bell had gone and the twins had run ahead. Perhaps they hadn't heard her.

Fermina walked to the back gate slowly. She would be late for class but she needed to clear her head. Ferg was right, the twins clearly preferred different hands though they did their best to hide it. Were the twins hiding something else? She cringed as she thought of how she'd had a row with Ferg the night before. Perhaps he had been on to something after all.

Her eyes fell upon the woods, as though she half expected her friends to emerge from the trees at that very moment. She traced the path from the woods with her eyes. Last night's rain had left no footprints, unlike the hotchpotch of footprints that had been there the day the intruders came. Her eyes travelled to the back gate—it would have taken a nimble intruder to climb over it the night the colonel sounded the alarm. It had been locked that day, as it was . . . wait, what was this? Fermina's feet gave way beneath her as she noticed something for the first time. The lock on the gate was broken!

Her shoulders tensed. She was thinking so hard now, she felt her head would cave in. Had Ferg noticed the broken lock last night? Just as he'd noticed that the twins used different hands? Just as he'd noticed *everything*? Had he wondered, as she was wondering right now, why Colonel Craven broke that lock when he had a key?

The next thought came like a slap in the face. What if Colonel Craven didn't go into the woods at all . . . What if this was a set-up? What if Volumina had broken the lock because she hoped that Ferg, Phil and Immy would go out into the woods at night, alone?

Fermina felt sick to the stomach. A groan escaped her—surely, Volumina had hoped that Fermina would go into the woods with her friends! Yes, that was it. She wasn't meant to stay behind at all. But why were the twins lying?

And then there was another ghostly groan . . . but not her own. Fermina looked around. Her gaze fell upon a half-dug trench close to the school wall—perhaps Colonel Craven had had the kids start on it and then changed his mind. The groan was coming from there. 'Help!'

'*You!*' she hissed, glaring at the 'ghost' in the trenches. 'What are you doing here?'

Volumina's face was twisted in pain. 'I fell in last night! My foot feels like I've twisted it!'

'Well, what did you expect, sneaking into the Get Lost Forever Woods and sneaking back again! For the second time this week too!' fumed Fermina, feeling no pity whatsoever for the school bully curled up at the bottom of a ditch. That was exactly where she belonged!

Volumina's face grew more puzzled than pained. 'I've never been in the woods. Why would I go there?' she cried.

Fermina placed her hands on her hips. 'Ah, so now you'll claim you didn't break the lock either! That's just too far fetched, even for you!'

Volumina shifted gingerly and the movement made her

groan again. 'Well, I'm sorry to dash whatever theories you've been forming in your head but I didn't.'

Fermina felt a wave of nausea. She would throw up, she most certainly would! 'If this is another one of your silly tricks, I'll make you pay for it this time, I will! The twins told us that Colonel Craven dragged you into the woods last night. What really happened?'

Her question was met with silence. She persisted in spite of the fact that she'd always been a little scared of Volumina. Who wasn't? 'Don't you see what you've gone and done? Ferg, Phil and Immy went off into the woods looking for you! You've sent them off on a wild goose chase!'

'*Your* friends went off into the woods looking for *me*? Why would anyone do anything for me?'

'I have no clue why—you don't deserve it, that's for sure!' Fermina's eyes flashed with anger, an anger she'd been feeling for weeks. 'You're the school bully and you've caused nothing but trouble this last week! We'd all be better off if you went into the woods and didn't come back!'

There! It had been said and could never be unsaid now. All this horridness was getting to everyone.

Volumina winced like she'd been punched in the stomach. 'You have every right to hate me,' she said presently, in a way that made Fermina's heart tug. Just a little. 'The twins told me that everyone did. Especially you.'

Fermina could think of a hundred hurtful things to say but she bit back her anger.

'I'd made up my mind last night,' sniffed Volumina, 'to tell you everything—well, not you, but Ferg, Phil and Immy! You wouldn't listen anyway; you've been shutting me up every time I try to speak.'

Fermina's words came through gritted teeth. 'Well, then, what stopped you?'

'The twins. I was on my way to the Sphinx trench, they were trying to pull me back, I fell and that's all I remember.'

All of a sudden, Fermina felt very tired. Nothing made sense. She sank down beside the trench. She needed to think. If Volumina hadn't gone into the woods, why did the twins say she had? Who broke the lock on the back gate? And why did the twins leave Volumina in the trench after she fell in?

Volumina's eyes were wet now. 'The twins were trouble from the word go! Sneaking into Dr Bloom's room because they wanted to steal one of her spiders! Keeping Saltpetre prisoner and then releasing him that day in Miss Nottynuf's class! Throwing apples at Cook Fracas and poor Gypsy. All of it!'

Fermina felt like the air had been knocked out of her. 'It doesn't seem like them, Volumina, the twins were always so good to you! And you barely cared for them, that day they came down with the rash—'

'A rash they brought upon themselves!' shouted Volumina, her eyes flashing now. 'Serves them right! Touched something they shouldn't have in Dr Bloom's room when they went up snooping for spiders. The teachers were in a meeting and—'

'And we were in the Tower Library,' recalled Fermina, frowning. 'I did wonder where the three of you had disappeared!'

'Well, it wasn't the *three* of us! I had no part in it! Told them they had no business going up into a teacher's room but you can't reason with them when they're together like that, snickering and smirking. I ran into school to stop them as soon as that first apple hit Cook Fracas but they were faster than me! They ran out the back and Colonel Craven found me instead . . .' Volumina choked back a sob.

Fermina teetered between belief and disbelief. Could she have been wrong about Volumina all this time? 'But why?'

Volumina shrugged. 'The twins have been making trouble at every school they've been to since their mother gave up on them!'

'But why did she?' said Fermina slowly. 'Was it because she found out that Malo is right-handed and Mallus is left-handed?'

'They grew up pretending to be identical,' Volumina nodded. 'Flatly denied it when I first noticed they weren't. I figure their mother left them feeling that being different was bad. Maybe they thought she would love them again, who knows?'

'I don't think it worked,' said Fermina wryly, remembering that first day the twins came to school. Their parents were only too eager to be rid of them.

'I think they're still angry about that,' said Volumina. 'They're mean because they're miserable.'

Fermina met her gaze and held it. It would not be easy to say this but it had to be said. 'You've been pretty mean too.'

Volumina burst into tears. 'I've been bullied at every school I've been to, called "fatty", "butterball" and "chubby"! And *no one* put a stop to it, no one! So when I got to Horrid High, I decided that I'd use my size as a weapon, put fear into everyone, and what's wrong with that? No one dares call me a fatty here, not to my face anyway!'

The school bully fell silent after this outburst and wiped her tears with the back of her hand.

'But you have no friends, everyone is scared of you,' said Fermina, unable to hold herself back.

'Granny Grit said the twins would be a fresh start for me, they hadn't been at Horrid High long enough to fear me,' and now Volumina's voice dropped. 'Or to hate me, I guess!'

Fermina drew a deep, long breath. So *that* was why Granny had chosen Volumina to show the twins around! No one had wanted to do this more than Fermina but no one had *needed* it more than Volumina!

'She made me promise her that I would be good to the twins, no matter what!' Volumina went on. 'That I'd look after them. So at first, I didn't care that they were up to mischief. I'd made a promise and they were my friends, the only friends I've ever had!'

Fermina's face softened. 'But they weren't really your friends, were they? They played all sorts of pranks and they made you take the fall!'

Volumina sniffed a little. 'When they're together, pretending to be identical, they finish each other's sentences; they read each other's minds. They were always a step ahead of me, getting me into all sorts of trouble!' She shuddered. 'But when they were apart, which wasn't very often, they were different. *Kinder.* I found it hard to stay angry with them for long. I feel so silly now!'

'We've all been fooled, Volumina, you're not the only one!' Fermina held her head. Ferg had started waking up to the idea that the twins were not as innocent as they seemed and she had accused him of being distrustful.

'Immy overheard you speaking to the twins the night the intruders came,' pressed Fermina. 'You were saying something about how the colonel would not find anything on his own.'

'Well, he deserved to know the truth, didn't he?' cried Volumina. 'The twins had been skulking around near the back gate that night, I have no clue why, and the colonel mistook them for intruders!'

Fermina's head reeled. Volumina's story matched Immy's, but at that time, they'd all supposed that the twins were reproaching Volumina for causing mischief. It had been the other way around all along! It was the twins who'd been causing mischief and they'd been reproaching Volumina for threatening to tell on them! How different things looked now!

'Immy wanted to talk to me that night but the twins brushed her off!'

Fermina felt positively sick now. Of course it made sense!

The truth had been staring them in the face, only, they'd been looking at it all wrong. It had been too easy to assume the worst about Volumina but hadn't she sat apart from the twins at breakfast to show her displeasure, glowered and scowled at them? And they'd seen all these things as a sign that *she* was guilty!

'So the day Dr Bloom was attacked by crows,' said Fermina, still trying to piece together the puzzle, 'it wasn't you who'd troubled a fledgling that morning?' She still wanted to believe that the Brace boys were innocent.

'What fledgling?' whispered Volumina, blinking her eyes in confusion. 'Don't remember anyone being mean to a crow, not even the twins! But yes, the twins can be cruel to animals. I begged them to let Saltpetre go but they wouldn't! So imagine my surprise when I saw him spring out of their hands that day in Miss Nottynuf's class! And then Mallus shouted "A mouse!" knowing full well that Malo had released the mouse! In all the confusion, one of them slipped the cake under me, and then—'

Like sediment sinking to the bottom of a lake, Fermina's thoughts were settling. 'Oh Volumina, do you think they still have Saltpetre?'

Volumina's silence said it all.

'Here, give me your hand.' She cried out in pain as Fermina helped her scramble out of the trench.

'Everything is such a horrid, horrid mess!' cried Fermina. 'Ferg had his hunches but I was blinded by the idea of making two new friends!'

'Everyone wants friends!' Volumina said. 'I wasn't that different, was I, wanting to hold on to the only friends I've ever had?'

Fermina curled her tiny hands around Volumina's large ones. 'No, you weren't. But your *friends* are in class now and they haven't spared a thought for you! Who knows, maybe they pushed you into the trench on purpose so that they could tell us you'd gone missing! Now Ferg, Immy and Phil are in the woods somewhere, looking for you, and they're not back!'

Her words provoked a fresh bout of tears. 'It was really decent of them to go out there and look for me,' said Volumina.

Fermina felt her heart wrench at what horrors her friends might have encountered in the woods. 'And it was mighty decent of you to think of telling us the truth, even if it meant losing the only friends you've known!'

As they hobbled into the school building together, they made a strange pair. A large girl resting her weight, ever so lightly, on the smaller girl walking beside her.

Volumina cast one more look in the direction of the Get Lost Forever Woods. 'What do we do now?'

Fermina looked grim. 'We can't risk alarming the colonel, we'll go to Miss Nottynuf.'

'The twins will deny everything. You can't outsmart the pair of them, you can't!'

Fermina paused. 'But what if they weren't a pair?' And she shifted her braids from back to front. As she always did when a plan was forming. A good plan.

CHAPTER 16

The moss parted like a curtain under Ferg's foot. What had appeared to be solid ground was liquid mulch! And what Ferg had mistaken for a pair of hands or jaws was heavy, wet mud pulling him down into its murky depths.

'It's a peat bog,' said the strange girl, settling down on her haunches at the edge of it.

Ferg tottered uncertainly on one leg and watched the mud swallow up his other foot. 'He-e-elllp!' he cried and to his dismay, both his legs surrendered to the muck and it yanked him right in.

Phil and Immy grabbed his arms and pulled, grunting with the effort. The mud made loud, gurgling sounds and fought back. This was not a tug of war they were going to win!

'Help!' cried Immy, turning to the scraggly-haired child who looked like she'd sprung out of the bog herself. 'Didn't you hear us? Help!'

'Nothing wrong with my hearing,' said the witch, although she sounded more like a girl their age than a wicked creature from some fairy tale. 'Tell the muddy one to stop heaving and hauling so much. Struggling only makes things worse.' Her voice was calm, even mildly amused.

Ferg's chest clenched with panic as the mud crawled up his calves now. 'Well, I'm not about to stop trying to get myself out!' he gasped. But as he pulled his right leg out a little, his left leg sank in deeper. There was a squelching sound and Ferg felt something give way. 'My boot!' he gasped. 'It's getting prised off!'

The scraggly-haired girl cupped her chin in her hands. 'Which is most unfortunate, because you won't get too far without your boots in such a place! Now will you stop struggling like this?'

'STOPPULLINGANDTHENHE'LLGODOWNAND BELOSTFOREVERWHAT'SWRONGWITHYOU AREYOUINSANE?' shouted Phil, not stopping to breathe.

'The two of you should really step back,' said the girl, unmoved by all the drama. 'And you, muddy one, get on all fours, will you?'

Phil and Immy stepped back, breathing raggedly. 'On all fours?' he cried.

'And your friends think something's wrong with *my* hearing!' was the girl's annoying reply.

Without further delay, Ferg threw himself forward, bracing for the impact. His body made a dull, gloopy sound as he landed, and now his arms were in the bog too. Thick mud congealed across his face now, like molten chocolate, only less tasty. How could flailing on all fours in this muck make any sense? The girl was out of her mind!

The strange girl got to her feet. 'Crawl like a lizard!' she urged Ferg. 'Slither like a snake! Stop struggling!'

Ferg crawled on his stomach just as Colonel Craven had taught them to. And as he stopped struggling, he found that he was still sinking but slower than before!

The girl was standing at the edge of the bog. 'Grab the grass!' Ferg reached for the yellow tussock in front and closed his fingers around it. With a rush of release, his right leg slid out, almost free now! The girl threw him a stick. 'Grab it!' And then she pulled—she was strong! With a slavering, slobbering sound, his left leg came free, and the bog spat the rest of Ferg out on to solid ground—black as tar.

'Glad you're out of there!' said the girl in a steady voice. 'These bogs have a way of devouring everything, animals, plants, people! It was mighty stupid of you to step in, you know!'

'Wethoughtyouwereawildanimalandthenwesupposedwe shouldmakearunforitbeforeyougetus!' rushed Immy this time, in a mad garble.

The girl cocked her head to one side and listened. 'Does the muddy one talk as funny as you do?' She surveyed Ferg's face and chuckled. 'On second thoughts, he'd better keep his mouth shut for now, at least until we've got all that muck off him!'

Immy bristled. 'He's Ferg. You should know that we have names!'

'Well, in that case, mine's Bat!' said the strange girl. 'Now keep the small talk for later and follow me!'

This was easier said than done. It was as if half the bog were still stuck to Ferg. Bat showed no intention of slowing down. They skirted two mud pools just like the one Ferg had been rescued from but this time, they had ample warning. Bat knew her way, winding around mazes of roots and dodging thorny stems with practised ease. The others were not as lucky. They were scratched and scraped sore.

By daylight, it was clear that the woods were a treasure trove of strange trees and plants that the children had never seen before. Humongous flowers whose petals gaped open like cavernous chambers; prickly cacti enormous as giants' clubs; leaves that danced in response to their footsteps; even a pitcher plant like the one Dr Bloom had brought to class, only ten times larger. They had so many questions that they were bursting to ask Bat but it was hard enough keeping up with her.

'I feel watched!' said Immy, stopping for breath and pointing at the most peculiar plant she had ever seen. Thick, red stalks with a large, white berry at the end of each one. A white berry with a single black dot on it that made it look uncannily like . . . 'Eyes!'

Bat sniffed at the air, not unlike a dog. 'It has an odd smell too!' she said. 'I call it the eyeball plant! Don't worry, it can't see you. It's poisonous, though.'

Immy snatched her hand back, feeling silly. She'd been tempted to touch those berries!

'I'd steer clear of *that* one too!' said Bat but the children didn't need telling. Bat was pointing at a plant with razor-sharp, orange thorns sticking out of its leaves, like rows of large teeth.

'Watch out for sleepy grass as well!' said Bat, 'Knocked me out clean once!'

'That might explain why we didn't wake up till noon!' muttered Phil but the others said nothing. The long trudge through the woods had left them winded.

Hours later, the children emerged in a clearing large enough for them to note that the sky had turned bright red and the sun was setting.

'Home sweet home!' cried Bat, pointing proudly at what appeared to be an igloo crafted out of branches. 'My twigloo!'

The children flopped down on the ground, grateful for the rest. 'Wow, the colonel would have approved of this!' panted Immy, wiping the sweat off her face with the back of her hand.

'He taught us to survive in the wild,' explained Phil, who could barely feel his legs any more. 'Gave us these rucksacks too.' Ferg's had been lost in the bog but Immy gladly emptied out the dry food from the other rucksacks for all to share.

'Haven't had these in a while!' said Bat, biting into a biscuit with grimy hands. 'Here, want one?'

Immy shook her head. 'Shouldn't we wash up first?'

Bat hooted with laughter. 'Are we going to be afraid of germs in a place like this?' she said, even as she led them around the back of the hut to a pool of clear water.

'So it was some sort of test, to send you here into these

woods?' she asked, speaking with her mouth full.

'Oh, no, Colonel Craven had his share of crazy tests but this wasn't one of them,' said Phil. 'We were searching for a friend of ours who might have come this way.'

'Barely a friend!' muttered Immy.

Bat raised an eyebrow. 'No one's come this way in *years*, I can assure you! Unless you mean that giant of a woman who came crashing through the forest in the dead of the night a year ago.'

Nurse Malady! The children exchanged looks. The nurse they had driven away last year had never been seen again.

'Now, I don't really get to look after my appearance around here, which suits me just fine because I never get to see how ugly I look anyway! But she took one look at me and screamed, "Spirits!"'

Bat threw her head back and laughed. Immy couldn't help giggling too. Bat was truly a sight, with an unruly thatch of hair that came down over her eyes, black elbows and knees, scratched legs and grimy cheeks. She must have frightened the living daylights out of Nurse Malady!

'The woods spook everyone, I guess! But if you ask me, these woods aren't half as fearsome or forbidding as . . .' and here, Bat's voice dropped away so that what she said next was inaudible to everyone. Everyone but Ferg.

'Did you say Horrid High? Did you just say these woods aren't half as fearsome as—'

'D'you know the school?' Bat shrieked. She was building a

fire now. 'Ah, it makes sense! The only children who'd take their chances in these woods are the sort that have nothing left to lose, right? I'd been to my fair share of horrid schools but this one took the cake!' She grinned, flashing two rows of broken, black teeth and dimples. 'Running away always came easy to me! I guess I've run from everything—foster families and orphanages.'

So she was an orphan. Immy felt closer to her already, even though her parents weren't dead, only missing.

Bat shrugged. 'I've been on the move all my life, riding on the tops of trains, hitchhiking, stowing away on a boat! Life is one grand adventure, don't you think? But my last foster family saw it differently. They got fed up of my running away and sent me to Horrid High. I found the back gate open one morning and couldn't believe my luck! This time, no one came looking. I mean, why bother looking for a twelve-year-old who's always running away, right?'

Bat smiled again and her dimples flashed. 'Your disappearance has become the stuff of legend at Horrid High,' said Phil, nodding in approval.

'You vanished into the woods a week before I arrived,' recalled Immy. 'Phil's right, the kids couldn't stop talking about what might have happened to you.'

'I'm notorious, aren't I?' grinned Bat. Immy grinned too.

'Perhaps Immy turned up at just the right time,' said Phil slowly, 'a week after the school had an orphan missing.'

Ferg couldn't stop staring at both girls, seated beside each other. Dimples. Uneven teeth. Frizzy brown hair—although Immy's had been teased into cornrows. 'Immy looks a lot like Bat, doesn't she, Phil?'

Phil emitted a low whistle of discovery. 'So she does! That's why Principal Perverse was so eager to take Immy in. She could stand in for Bat!'

Immy looked at the dirty little girl sitting beside her—did she look like *that*? Suddenly, she gave her a tight hug.

'Do we really look alike?' Bat sounded quite pleased herself, reaching out to touch Immy's hair. 'We'll make quite a pair in the woods, won't we?'

There was an awkward silence. Ferg cleared his throat. How should he put this? Phil and Immy cleared their throats too.

Bat sniffed. 'Either all of you are coming down with a sudden throat itch, or you're trying to tell me that you're not staying.'

The children could not meet her eyes. 'You can come back with us,' said Immy in a small voice. It wasn't a great offer and she knew it.

'I won't go anywhere near Horrid High,' Bat said. 'I'm just fine here.'

Immy squeezed Bat's hand. 'These woods are hardly the sort of place for anyone. Last night, I could swear I heard voices.'

'This place makes you feel most unwelcome,' agreed Ferg, shuddering at the thought of the peat bog.

'Cut the claptrap, will you?' said Bat. 'You might just kill each other with your scary stories. Now, eat! Fern fronds, go on, they're delicious. I boiled them first.'

They tasted surprisingly good and Phil was working on a second helping when the children began to speak again. 'So, are the woods as terrible as all the stories say they are?' asked Immy.

Bat had put a metal can on the fire now. Something slopped about in it and it smelt delicious. 'There are strange things afoot here, I'll grant you that! I learned about the woods the hard way.' She shivered as she remembered the unexplained drowsiness, the oozing rashes, the painful gashes.

'But I also think our imaginations make things appear worse than they really are. I'd gotten quite used to being here alone,' she bit her lip, 'and then you turned up! Soup, anyone?'

Immy rose and started to clear up. 'We have a friend back at school who'll worry about us if we're gone too long.' She slapped her forehead. She'd meant to bring it up with Ferg and Phil last night but the fearfulness of the woods made it hard to think about anything else! She recounted how she'd stumbled upon Volumina and the twins near the tower last night, how she'd overheard them whispering urgently.

'We won't let you!' one of them had said. 'You can't stop me!' Volumina had replied. 'Not any more.'

'Volumina broke the lock to take us on a wild goose chase through the woods!' concluded Immy.

Phil nodded, 'The twins probably made up that story about

Colonel Craven so that we'd go after Volumina to bring her back. We'd have never come out this far if we'd known she was up to one of her pranks again!'

Ferg's thoughts were flying in circles like dry leaves on a windy day. He put them into words as carefully as he could. 'There was something fishy about that lock being broken but I don't think Volumina was responsible.'

Bat, who had been listening intently until now, cut in. As an outsider, it was easier for Bat to see things for what they really were. 'Of course! It was the twins!'

Phil and Immy looked stumped.

'Well, just play back what Immy overheard that night. Go on!' urged Bat.

So they did, each one pondering over the words in silence. *'We won't let you!' one of the twins had said. 'You can't stop me!' Volumina had replied. 'Not any more.'*

Bat broke the silence. 'Don't you see? While it's possible that Volumina's the troublemaker, it's equally likely that the twins were up to no good!'

Ferg felt a little dizzy now. 'All those pranks that have been played at school, didn't they start after the twins arrived?'

Phil exhaled forcefully. 'Volumina's never played any pranks before—she's a bully, not a practical joker!'

They sat still for a few minutes, mulling over this stupendous discovery. Ferg's ears were tingling so hard now, it was unbearable. 'I knew that the twins couldn't be trusted!' he groaned. 'Perhaps they wanted all of us out of the way!'

'But you threw a spanner in the works by leaving your friend behind, didn't you?' said Bat. 'To watch your backs while you were gone?'

Ferg's face darkened. If Fermina was alone with the twins, she was probably too neck-deep in trouble to watch anyone's back. He jumped up. 'Show us the way to Horrid High, Bat! Fast!'

Bat threw a baleful look at the fading light. 'Not fast enough, I'm afraid! Your friend will have to hold on just a little bit longer!'

CHAPTER 17

The Brace boys had worn identical clothes from the day they were born. It had been their mother's idea at first but after she found out *they* weren't identical, she couldn't have cared less how they dressed. If the twins insisted on wearing identical clothes, it was because they hoped to win back their mother's affections by looking exactly like each other.

Of course, the twins failed. Mr Brace started thinking of getting a dog and Mrs Brace got over her love for pairs altogether. The twins blamed themselves but it was their unlikeable parents who were really to blame. Ferg's parents had been no better, or Fermina's, or Phil's. Phil had run away. Fermina had drawn strength from her uncle. And Ferg had learned to draw as little attention to himself as possible. The twins made the poorest choice of all. They decided to cope with their unhappiness by spreading it around. They made trouble at school after school. And this is easier done when you have a sibling who gets mistaken for you.

When the Brace boys returned from their showers to find half their clothes missing, they went berserk, and understandably so. They looked desperately for anything the thief might have missed, but alas, the thief had been very meticulous. Of every identical set of T-shirts and trousers they owned, one had been nicked! Stolen! Filched!

There were only two children left at school who could have done this. One was groaning in a trench somewhere, so it had to be Fermina! How the twins railed against her! Why else had that two-braided devil stayed behind instead of following her friends into the woods? They'd plunge that puny thief so deep in trouble, she'd never climb out on her own! They'd teach that red-haired runt a lesson she wouldn't forget!

Meanwhile, Fermina was upstairs in Miss Nottynuf's room. The maths teacher had just finished bandaging Volumina's ankle and the girls had decided that this was the perfect opportunity to bring up the missing children. Fermina cleared her throat. 'Something awful has happened!'

'Don't worry, that ankle will be as good as new with a little rest,' said Miss Nottynuf, not quite understanding.

Fermina cleared her throat again. 'I'm afraid Volumina's ankle is the least of our problems, Miss Nottynuf!'

'What's wrong, girls?' said Miss Nottynuf, reaching for her handkerchief. Then, the girls began to talk. Everything they told Miss Nottynuf was punctuated by a gasp of disbelief from their teacher. They left out nothing, explaining how the Brace boys had deceived everyone (*gasp!*), how their pet mouse had been stolen (*gasp!*) and how poor Volumina had been left to take the blame (*gasp!*). When they got to the point where Ferg, Phil and Immy had gone into the woods, however, Miss Nottynuf let out a shrill cry of utter alarm. Her face lost its colour and her handkerchief flew up to her mouth like a butterfly fluttering in panic.

There could not have been a worse moment for Colonel Craven to be passing by. 'TROUBLE, MISS NOTTYNUF?' he boomed, making everyone jump. The children gulped. They hadn't planned for this at all!

'Er . . . uh . . .' stuttered Miss Nottynuf, taken by surprise. Fermina shook her head at her maths teacher. *Please, don't tell him!* But what the girls had told Miss Nottynuf was too much for her to take in. Her eyes flitted to the window, to the woods beyond, and back to the colonel. Her hands trembled and her legs felt weak. Things were a real pickle. She could hardly take care of this on her own!

'Don't panic,' she started but those words always have quite the opposite effect, don't they? The colonel's right eyebrow shot up in the air. This was the first symptom of a familiar disease but Miss Nottynuf was no doctor. She was a maths teacher facing her biggest problem yet. She hurtled heedless into her next sentence. 'Three of our children are wandering around in the woods!'

The effect was instantaneous. Colonel Craven shot out his left arm and rushed out, tumbling down the stairs, three at a time.

'Wait!' Fermina cried, although she knew that nothing would hold the colonel back now. Nothing.

'Wait!' cried Volumina, hobbling after the colonel on her bandaged ankle.

'I told you not to panic,' said Miss Nottynuf feebly as the girls pelted after the colonel, down the stairs and out the school building. The colonel raced into the playground as if his feet were on fire. 'Their names!' he bellowed, dashing to the back gate. 'Give me their names!'

In a small shrub nearby, a few leaves stirred. A goat raised its head. It looked intently at the man running towards it. Two girls were running behind him. The goat pricked up its ears—the situation was alarming and it was scared.

It had every reason to be. 'Giddyap!' cried the colonel, springing upon the poor goat's back with surprising precision. 'MMMMEHHEHEHEHHEHEH!' Gypsy cried, her legs crumpling beneath her. After all, the colonel was no lightweight. But he grabbed her horns. 'Giddyap, Gypsy, giddyap!'

And, perhaps because the colonel looked like he wouldn't be shaken off, Gypsy lurched forward with renewed energy and took off!

'Ferg, Phil and Immy, those are their names!' shouted Fermina after him. She watched helplessly as man and goat barrelled down the mud path into the woods, kicking up clouds of dust behind them.

As the heavy-hearted girls returned to school, Fermina cursed herself for confiding in Miss Nottynuf. Perhaps Dr Bloom would have been a better choice? It took every ounce of willpower not to chase after the colonel but what good would it do for everyone to disappear into the Get Lost Forever Woods, one after the other? What would become of

Horrid High if all her friends were lost forever? If the Brace boys were not stopped?

Miss Nottynuf was in the hallway, kneading her handkerchief like a wad of dough. 'He's gone, isn't he?' she sputtered, 'It's my fault!'

And then a voice as clear as a bell rang out.

'You mustn't blame yourself, Miss Nottynuf! It seems the girls have been pulling a fast one on all of us!'

Dr Bloom! Her hair was up in a long, twisted roll today, like a plump slug had been burrowing in it and gotten stuck there. She giggled, and although she had giggled scores of times before, there was something about that little laugh that seemed more menacing than a raised voice. 'The twins have just been telling me how you've kept the school pet prisoner all week! Cruelty to animals is a terrible, terrible thing!'

'We've done no such thing!' shouted Volumina and Fermina noted that she sounded more like her old self, not like the cowering girl in the trenches.

Dr Bloom cut her off with a raised hand. 'I've got proof and I'll take you right to it!'

Dr Bloom's pinched nostrils were trembling as she marched the girls up the stairs to the Sphinx dorm. The twins were at the door. Their gloating expressions gave Fermina the strength she needed.

'You must believe us, Dr Bloom,' she said, swallowing her fear. 'You've got it backwards. They're the ones to blame!'

Dr Bloom squawked like she'd choked on a chicken bone.

'Evidence!' cried Dr Bloom, 'Incontrovertible and irrefutable! Because every scientific theory needs its proof! There!'

The colour drained from the girls' faces. Sitting squat in the centre of Fermina's bed was a shoebox. With trembling hands, Fermina lifted the lid. Saltpetre! The white mouse sprang out into her hands.

Before she could stop herself, she lunged at the twins. 'You kept him in a shoebox, how could you?' She had one of the twins by the collar now. Which one? She no longer cared. She clawed at him now through the tears in her eyes. She would shake him so hard, his silly grin would fall right off!

'THAT'S ENOUGH!' said Dr Bloom, wresting them apart with such strength, Fermina was practically yanked up into the air.

A few beads of sweat glistened upon Dr Bloom's upper lip now. Her voice rose, thin and quavering:

'How conniving of you two, how utterly SICK,
All this time you've been SYMBIOTIC!'

Fermina felt she would explode at the injustice of it all! The finger of blame was pointing at her and it was a long, slim finger. It hovered an inch from Fermina's nose and it belonged to Dr Bloom. 'To the tower!' she said icily, and Fermina knew, with a sick feeling in her stomach, that the moment for explaining had long passed. 'Both of you!'

Both? Fermina's legs buckled beneath her. If both Volumina and she were sent up to the tower, what would happen to their friends in the woods? Would the colonel even find them? Would anyone else even care?

'No!' she burst out, only half thinking her way through things. 'I stole Saltpetre and Volumina had no hand in it!'

'That's not true—' Volumina cried, but Fermina silenced her with a look.

'Suits me just fine if you want to play the martyr!' said Dr Bloom. 'The fat girl can do kitchen clean-up, we all know how much she enjoys it! And you can stay in the tower! Come!'

With leaden feet, the two girls followed the science teacher down the stairs, feeling with every step like they were being lowered into a bottomless well of gloom.

'You see, Miss Nottynuf, I told you it wasn't your fault!' sighed Dr Bloom. 'There's been such a bout of horrid pranks, it makes me dizzy. But alas, I have no choice, do I? I have a school to run until Colonel Craven returns!'

'But why would the girls come to me, tell me otherwise?' protested Miss Nottynuf.

Dr Bloom threw Fermina a look of such disgust, it made her want to curl up in a corner and cry. 'They were probably up to another of their tricks, if you ask me! And now she says the fat one had nothing to do with it!'

'Yes, I stole Saltpetre,' Fermina exploded, feeling the weight of their eyes upon her. 'Would you punish me and be done with it!'

Now the class gasped. Fermina felt herself shrivel up like a leaf in the coldest winter. The whispers rose up like a bad smell. Some of the children were casting horrified looks at Fermina. Could she have done such a thing?

Fermina regretted her outburst as soon as she had spat out the words. But it angered her that people who pointed fingers at others were never above blame themselves.

Dr Bloom clucked her tongue. 'Are we raising a child whose only future is to become a thief?' There was a roaring sound in Fermina's ears. Dr Bloom's words had brought back terrible memories of what Fermina's parents had said the day they decided to send her to Horrid High. Hadn't Mr Filch raised his eyes up to heaven: *What will God say if we raise a child whose only future is to become a thief?*

Fermina tried to swallow the growing lump in her throat and the uneasy sense that she had hammered the last nail in her own coffin. She flung her braids from back to front. Not because she had a plan to get herself out of this mess, but because she didn't feel sorry for what she had done. Not one bit.

'I'll take the child to the tower,' said Miss Nottynuf hurriedly, giving Fermina's shoulder a small squeeze. 'You have a school to run, Dr Bloom!'

'Rightly said!' nodded Dr Bloom. 'And if the young lady is truly sorry and writes me an apology note, she can come back down in the morning!'

As Fermina hurried to the tower, she clenched her teeth to keep from crying. Miss Nottynuf was holding her hand now, and just the warmth of her fingers was enough to make Fermina crumble. 'Courage, my child,' whispered Miss Nottynuf. 'I know this isn't fair!'

Fermina nodded mutely. How bad could the tower be? There were books up there, newspapers, encyclopaedias. Fermina's heart lifted a little. She needed nothing more than to be away from all this horridness for a while, to forget this horrid school and everyone in it. Everyone but her friends . . . and as Fermina thought of Ferg, Phil and Immy, a sob escaped her.

'I should have stood up for you!' said Miss Nottynuf gently as they climbed the winding stairs up to the tower. 'But I can hardly expect Dr Bloom to listen to anything I have to say! I'm sorry, my child . . .'

Fermina rushed to the door as it swung shut and pulled on it with her tiny hands. The key was turning slowly on the outside, and then Miss Nottynuf's light steps could be heard growing fainter. As Miss Nottynuf left the building, Fermina allowed the giant sob inside her to break free at last. She sank down on her knees, finally free to cry for all the things in the world that made no sense. For harsh punishments, misunderstood children and misguided grown-ups. For lost children in a forest somewhere. And for an overweight school bully, much feared and much hated, who was also now her only friend at school.

The horrid head had kicked his lemur and thrown his tantrum but he still didn't feel any better. 'I'm getting tired of your excuses!' he said. 'I have half a mind to come out there myself and find the Grand Plan!'

The calm, collected voice on the other end was about to remind the horrid head to begin conversations with a 'hello' and then thought the better of it. The horrid head should have been taught his manners when he was still a child. 'I'm not exactly having a picnic here. There are so many *children*!'

True, children were hateful creatures but if they were *well-mannered*—ah, it made them a little easier to tolerate. Like sweet medicine. The calm, collected voice shuddered.

'How long?' demanded the horrid head.

'Not long now,' said the calm voice at its cajoling best. 'There were a few minor obstacles but they've been taken care of. The coast is clear and I can do as I please!'

'Do as *I* please, you mean?' said the horrid head. 'It's about time!' And the phone went dead.

The horrid head felt a tiny bit better now. He liked hanging up on people, and besides, hadn't the calm voice said the coast was clear now? At last! There had been too many do-gooders and nosy parkers who couldn't just let things be! Bleeding hearts who couldn't see the value of horrid schools!

Children had it too easy, fumed the horrid head and the thought made another hair burn and fall off. They needed horrid schools to harden them and build character. How else could you go after what you wanted and get it?

There was a soft sizzling sound like the sort that gets produced when you pour cold water in a hot pan. The horrid head suddenly felt a little cooler. He had been deep in thought, but his feet had led him to his happy place. Above his head a pair of songbirds from Hawaii twittered away on their stoop, the last two of their kind on the planet. At his elbow, a Sumatran tiger slunk through the grass in its large enclosure. In the pond at his feet, three Indian Humpback Mahseer flicked their tails and dove deep.

This was his private menagerie: rare animals and birds, reptiles and fish, flowers and trees. His face darkened briefly. A few empty cages were still waiting for their occupants. *Blue-tongue skink. Jamaican boa. Andean cat.* These cages would be full if his Grand Plan succeeded. Why, his menagerie would be twice its size!

The Grand Plan would be his ticket to track down every last rare living thing on the planet. Creatures that were on the brink of extinction, or believed to be extinct. Creatures that no one would ever see again. And what was wrong with that? Such beautiful things couldn't be free! He'd paid good money for them, they were his and his alone!

He gazed at the Tahiti Monarch in flight. This little bird, no larger than a sparrow, was named as if it were an emperor. It rather reminded him of himself—small and *important.* He smiled at the thought. There was nothing he couldn't track down eventually if he put mind and money to it. Not even the Grand Plan.

CHAPTER 18

Volumina's stomach lodged a hungry protest as she wiped eggy splotches off the kitchen counter. The menu for the day read: *Lemon rolls with a lemon-cream glaze.* Instead, Cook Fracas had made a messy batch of pancakes, putting salt in the batter instead of sugar. The lemon slices sat around forgotten.

'Gypsy, poor Gypsy!' Cook Fracas moaned. 'Do you suppose that the intruders who captured the colonel and dragged him away into the woods took Gypsy too?'

Why hadn't someone told poor Cook Fracas that a panicked Colonel Craven had ridden out on Gypsy himself? That there had been no intruders at all? Volumina straightened up and opened her mouth to respond, even though the question hadn't been aimed at anyone in particular. But the faintest flaring of Dr Bloom's long, thin nostrils silenced her. 'I'm sure your goat has just wandered off in search of something exciting to eat,' purred Dr Bloom, in the sort of placatory tone grown-ups use with a sulky child. 'We'll find her, don't you worry!'

As Dr Bloom ran her long fingers through her hair, teasing a knot out, Volumina caught herself staring at her science teacher and looked away quickly. It was the first time she'd seen the science teacher wearing her hair loose. It was always so securely fastened and now it ran down her back and across her shoulders like a cascade. Golden brown with dark roots.

'But the colonel . . .' muttered Cook Fracas, 'If the person who took the colonel laid one finger on my Gypsy, I'll . . . I'll . . .' and now Cook Fracas was wielding a pancake in his hand. The children ducked in anticipation but Dr Bloom curled one snake-like arm around the cook's thick wrist and eased the pancake out of his hand. 'I'll take that, hmmm?' she said, 'Save it for Gypsy, how's that?'

The cook's shoulders slumped but he nodded miserably. 'Yes, for Gypsy, she'll be hungry by now!'

'And speaking of hunger . . .' said Dr Bloom, her jaw twitching ever so slightly as she turned her gaze on Volumina.

'I won't eat till my friend in the tower does, I told you!' said Volumina but her stomach picked just that particular moment to play traitor and rumbled loudly. It had been hard enough missing dinner the night before. The thought of missing breakfast, too, even if it was just salty pancakes, was an unbearable one.

'As you please! I suppose that a little bit of starving will do you good!'

Volumina bit her lip. She had been called 'fat' so many times, in so many ways, it shouldn't have hurt her any more. But it did. It was the way her being fat always seemed to creep into everything, into every conversation, that bothered her.

It was as if the only thing people could see in Volumina was how fat she was.

'Loyal!' blurted out a small, thin voice, softly at first and then a little louder. 'I think the girl is being loyal to her friend!'

Miss Nottynuf was nibbling at her little finger as though it tasted better than the half-eaten pancake on her plate. 'That child in the tower must be starving, and Volumina needs to eat too!'

Dr Bloom's nostrils constricted till they were so pinched, it seemed barely possible to Volumina that any air would pass through them. 'What are you suggesting, Miss Nottynuf?' she said at last.

Miss Nottynuf rose slowly, even though she was at least two heads shorter than Dr Bloom. The plate in her hand trembled, making the pancake jump. 'Well, just that I can take some breakfast up to the child in the tower,' she said. And then she added, 'It's what Colonel Craven would have wanted if he were here, or Granny Grit—'

'Of course!' Dr Bloom said, a little too brightly. 'A meal might knock some sense into that stubborn girl, make her apologize! Prepare a tray, Volumina, and I'll have the new school prefects take it up to her!'

The new school prefects? When Mallus and Malo stood up, their mouths full of pancake, Volumina's heart sank. The twins' hearts sank too. They didn't like running errands. Then Mallus thought that perhaps the Filch girl would be grateful for their visit, that she'd tell them where she'd stashed their clothes. He felt nervous, dressed differently from his brother for the first time in years. And Malo thought of how they'd call the Filch girl names, maybe even make up a nasty ditty, the sort that their science teacher would appreciate.

Their mouths inched upward into lopsided grins, Malo's more to the right, of course. And as the boys smiled, Volumina's heart sank deeper. They had the science teacher fooled, just like they'd fooled everyone else! Why else would she have made them prefects?

'Ah, and don't press the girl for an apology,' added Dr Bloom. 'I'd much rather she stay up in the tower, think about what she's done. A simple "I'm sorry" won't do, not in these circumstances!'

Better and better. The twins smiled wider now. Of course a simple 'I'm sorry' would not do! They were already nursing visions of making that thief pay for nicking their clothes. They'd have her kneel on the floor and write out the apology note as they dictated it! It would be a long apology note, *begging* for forgiveness. How they'd relish making that Filch girl write every word of it!

'I'll clear that up while you eat,' said Miss Nottynuf, dabbing at her upper lip with her dainty handkerchief, the embroidered

'N' in the corner quivering with the effort. Cook Fracas had lurched out of the room, close on Dr Bloom's heels, groaning 'Gypsy, my Gypsy!'

Volumina watched the twins carry Fermina's tray out carelessly. How could she ever have mistaken these boys for friends? The lemon slices she'd thrown in bounced upon the tray. All the syrup she'd managed to squeeze into a tiny pot to take the salty edge off those pancakes had already dripped on the floor!

Miss Nottynuf squeezed her shoulder. 'Eat and you'll feel better,' she said softly.

'Thank you for speaking up for me,' said Volumina, feeling oddly grateful for the smallest of things all of a sudden.

Miss Nottynuf's handkerchief fluttered nervously. 'Oh, I'm not the sort of person who could stand up for anyone, really! And Dr Bloom knows better, I guess. It's probably best the boys take up that poor child's breakfast tray. If I were going upstairs, I couldn't bear to leave her there again and turn the key in the lock, why it broke my heart yesterday. I marched down and told Dr Bloom that I believed the two of you.'

And now Miss Nottynuf wrung her handkerchief like it was full of water. Volumina took a few bites of the cook's salty pancake to silence her stomach. 'And?'

Miss Nottynuf swept her hair back in an ineffective way. 'And nothing! Dr Bloom said I was easy to fool, that you needed to be strong to run a school, that I was too weak.'

Volumina sniffed. 'Funny!'

Miss Nottynuf looked up, a tiny, bird-like lift of her head, as she emptied the last of the pancake crumbs into the bin. 'Funny? Well, I guess so, Dr Bloom did *giggle* when she told me that.'

'Oh, no, that's not what I meant,' said Volumina, grabbing the dish-scrub and going at the dirty pans so hard, it made her feel better. 'I meant that the twins told me things about myself, that I wasn't the sort of girl anyone could like. And it's funny; the more I believed them, the smaller I felt.'

Miss Nottynuf looked away quickly, but it wasn't quick enough. 'Oh yes, I know that you think it's strange, how someone as huge as me could be made to feel small!' said Volumina. Miss Nottynuf flushed with guilt.

'I felt very small,' continued Volumina, 'but when I stood up to them, I felt larger again, and I felt glad for the first time in my life that I was larger. Does that even make sense?'

Her eyes fell on the twins, playing Frisbee with the pancakes outside the tower. A pancake fell on the ground and they dusted it off before slapping it back on the tray. As if in response, the pancake in Volumina's belly made her feel queasy. She should never have listened to Miss Nottynuf—this once, a full tummy was only making her feel worse.

Meanwhile, the Brace boys had clattered up the stairs, singing at the top of their voices, the walls of the tower echoing their last words in a way that thrilled them to bits.

'We're here to rule,
This horrid school,

And if you stay,
You must obey!'

Granted, it wasn't the cleverest of rhymes but given a little time, they would come up with something more sophisticated.

The three pancakes on their tray were looking all the worse for wear: The one that had been used as a Frisbee bore only a faint resemblance to a pancake now; the second had been rolled up and down the stairs; the third had been half eaten, even though the boys were so full, they burped all the way up.

'Fermina FILTH, we're here! We've got *pancakes* for you!' they shouted as they swung open her door, Mallus tittering so hard that one piece of pancake that had barely made it down his food pipe decided to climb back up again. Malo held up a tattered specimen of the day's breakfast, hardly minding that the syrup dripping off it was now on his shoes.

Now, you might not have noticed this but when you laugh very hard or you smile very wide, your eyes have a way of closing. Which probably explains why it took two minutes of heavy-duty hahahaha-ing before the twins realized that they weren't getting any reaction from their prisoner. When their laughter subsided and their eyes opened, they were in for a shock.

A shock is what you experience when there is a dramatic contrast between what you *expect* things to be and what they really are. What the Brace boys had expected to see was the

Filch girl in tears, on her knees, begging for food, probably half worn down to the bone already, gnawing at the door like a mouse. Of course, some of this was their imaginations at work because Fermina had only gone without one meal. She was thirsty and hungry but she was certainly not about to beg for food! Far from it.

Instead, she was reclining in the cosy corner that Granny Grit had set up, a couple of plump cushions under her head, one under her feet, too, and a stack of books by her side.

'Don't want any, thanks!' she said, the very picture of courtesy.

'What are you doing?' sputtered the boys, aghast. Their prisoner looked too comfortable!

'Reading,' she mumbled, her nose in a book. 'That's what people usually do in a library.'

'Well, then, come and get your breakfast!' and the boys resorted to a game of catch with the pancakes.

Fermina didn't so much as look up. 'I already told you.'

The game of catch paused. 'Told us what?' asked the boys.

'Don't want any, thanks!'

The boys were beside themselves with disappointment. 'How can you not want *any*?'

'Well, if it irks you so much, you can leave the tray here and go!' said Fermina. 'Now shush, I'm reading!'

The boys were slowly turning red with anger. Fermina didn't look up and see this for herself but she could sense it in every bone of her body. No one likes being shushed and

it is an established fact that school prefects do not like being shushed one bit. Especially by a girl in detention!

'And what about the sorry note?' the boys said. 'The one you're supposed to write out for Dr Bloom!'

'Will get to it when I have the time,' muttered Fermina. 'If you'd like to wait?'

It was all too much for the boys. *Wait! Why, the nerve!*

'You could play catch if you like!' Fermina added, wondering if she'd gone a bit too far. The temptation had been tremendous.

The loud slam of the door was her only response, then a rough turning of the key in the lock, two sets of feet drumming down the stairs noisily and two voices floating up in a last, parting shot: 'Rot in there, see if we care!'

The boys should have been at least a little pleased. They'd managed to add two more rhyming lines to their nasty ditty at last, Even if they hadn't meant to.

Fermina was certainly pleased. She permitted herself a slice of lemon from the breakfast tray and leaned back against her cushions, sucking upon it. *Of course they care.*

'We didn't ask her where our clothes were!' grumbled Mallus. 'Let's go back!'

'She won't tell us,' said Malo. 'It will only make us look silly!' An unsettling thought struck him. Did he really want his clothes back? Or was he beginning to enjoy looking less like a twin and more like himself?

Miss Nottynuf passed the boys in the hallway. She didn't

pay them much heed because she was thinking about what Volumina had said. *Why judge people based on how large or small they look? What about how large or small they feel?*

Miss Nottynuf needed to stretch her legs, clear her mind, take a walk and think. She walked out the school building as if in a trance. Hadn't the girls come to her for help? What could she do to set things right at Horrid High?

'Could I be enough?' Miss Nottynuf asked herself this for the first time in her life.

Volumina stood at the kitchen sink, quite unaware of the profound effect she had had on her maths teacher. She stared at her large hands, wishing she were smaller. On the other side of the school building, Miss Nottynuf wrung her tiny hands and wished just the opposite.

Above them all, Fermina stood at the window and followed the flight path of a crow that had swooped down from the top of the tower. It winged past her, bound for the one place where every crow had been stationed all morning. A windowsill on the third floor. Dr Bloom's window . . .

Fermina thought of how the crows had dive-bombed Dr Bloom. Volumina had denied troubling the crow fledglings. If the twins hadn't troubled them either, why had the crows attacked Dr Bloom that day? And why were they gathered at her window now, like mourners at a funeral? It was decidedly odd. Fermina curled up near the window and opened *The Company of Crows: A Definitive Guide.* It was time for her to read.

CHAPTER 19

Miss Nottynuf lingered near the back gate and one question raged in her head: *Could I be enough?*

All those years she'd been made to believe that she was only half as good as anyone else, Miss Nottynuf had never asked herself this question. But now, for the first time, she wondered: What if she was—dare she even think it—*whole?*

The thought made Miss Nottynuf tremble a little but it steered her feet towards the woods. 'I'll find those lost and helpless children!' she told herself.

As it turned out, the children weren't lost or helpless. They'd slept in Bat's twigloo, where they were warmer and safer than they had been in the woods on their first night. Bat had woken them up at the crack of dawn and she'd set a punishing pace for the three of them to follow. No one wasted time asking Bat if they were heading in the right direction; the certainty on her face said it all.

'We're almost there!' cried Bat at last, and the children cheered loudly.

Their raised voices reached Miss Nottynuf's ears. *Trouble,* she supposed, doubling her speed and falling upon the surprised children. 'There you are!' They were a sweaty, muddy mess, and to Miss Nottynuf, they were the very picture of 'lost and helpless children'.

'I found you! I found you!' she cried.

Behind Miss Nottynuf, there was the faintest cracking of twigs snapping underfoot, a barely visible parting of the branches.

'Come out, it's OK,' said Ferg quietly, marvelling at how easily Bat had blended into the woods.

'Miss Nottynuf can be trusted, Bat!' said Immy, nodding towards where the rustling was coming from.

Miss Nottynuf felt as if someone had lit a candle in her heart. *Miss Nottynuf can be trusted.* Isn't that what Immy had said? Finally, after all these years, someone trusted her . . . But whom were the children speaking to?

Miss Nottynuf peered through her thick glasses into the trees. 'Don't tell me you have a pet *bat* now!'

'I'm no one's pet!' exclaimed the little girl and stepped out from the thicket, making poor Miss Nottynuf cry out louder than a real bat might have! Miss Nottynuf had a glimpse of bright eyes and a grubby face peeping out from behind a thick thatch of unkempt hair.

'What, I mean, *who* are you? You're . . . Bat?'

'We found her in the woods, Miss Nottynuf,' said Ferg. 'She's the long-lost orphan of Horrid High!'

Bat was hopping mad and why wouldn't she be? First the lady with the giant spectacles had called her a pet, and now Ferg was declaring that she was some long-lost waif!

Ferg's words produced the very response he'd been hoping for. You see, orphans make most hearts soften and Miss Nottynuf's heart fell squarely in this category. With a cry of affection, she swooped down on Bat, clearing her hair away from her face and gazing at her lovingly. 'Oh you poor lost dear, what an awful time you must have had out here, all on your own!'

The long-lost orphan of Horrid High glowered at her new friends. *Awful time?* Hardly! Ferg had his most plaintive expression on, Phil was mouthing, 'Please, Bat, please!' and Immy was clasping her hands in a dramatic begging pose but Bat had no intention of going back to that horrid school!

Miss Nottynuf clasped Bat's hand, an odd catch in her voice: 'I hope that finding you is a sign that our luck is changing. I'm afraid we are all quite lost!'

Bat bit her lip. The lady seemed awfully kind. Miss Nottynuf shook her head sadly. 'If only I'd found all of you sooner, Colonel Craven would not have gone off into the woods!'

'Was he looking for us?' Phil snorted in disbelief. 'Well, *that's* something!'

'You mustn't judge the poor colonel harshly,' said Miss Nottynuf, who always thought people were better than they really were, even though her parents had never shown her the same kindness. 'Many years ago, during the war, the colonel saw an enemy attack coming. He turned out to be right.

Many lives could have been saved if they had only taken him seriously. The colonel was convinced that Horrid High was becoming horrid again; he didn't want history to—'

'Repeat itself?' There was a wistful note in Ferg's voice as he broke in. Granny Grit had been worried about the same thing. 'Perhaps we misunderstood the colonel because he was a little . . .'

'Overwrought?' said Miss Nottynuf even though Ferg had been looking for the word 'batty'. 'People never come back the same after they've been to war . . .'

There was a moment of silence as the children considered where the poor colonel might be now. Miss Nottynuf squared her shoulders, set her mouth in a thin line and sighed. 'Your friend Fermina came to me for help. It might have been best if I'd kept things to myself but I'm afraid I made things worse by telling the colonel.'

'You made things worse?' Ferg braced himself for bad news.

'Fermina has been locked up in the tower for stealing Saltpetre, for every horrid thing that's happened, really!' Miss Nottynuf batted her hands about in search of her handkerchief.

'Locked up!' the kids chorused. It was preposterous!

'She confessed,' spluttered Miss Nottynuf, looking all around, 'but somehow I feel responsible!'

'She couldn't have *confessed*!' cried Immy. 'She didn't do any of those things!'

Miss Nottynuf's face softened. 'I believed her when she

came to me but Dr Bloom is in charge now and she doesn't.'

'What about Volumina?' asked Ferg, although he suspected it by now. 'She's at school, isn't she?'

Miss Nottynuf looked baffled. 'Why, where else would she be? If she hadn't told me about how she stood up to the twins for making her feel small, I might never have found my courage . . .'

She broke off to stare at the school as it came into view again. Ferg, Phil and Immy followed her gaze. They were all thinking the same thing. Of that first day the newly painted school building had stood in front of them, with its bright red roof and its spanking white walls and they'd thought the monstrous old ways would never return. How terribly, terribly wrong they had been!

Now both Granny Grit and Colonel Craven were gone. Fermina, who could always set things right with a flick of her long braids, was holed up in the tower for things she had never done! How was this possible?

'I'm afraid that the school is still every bit as horrid as the day you wandered out the gates,' said Miss Nottynuf, reading Bat's mind.

'I never wandered . . .' Bat burst out and then stopped herself quickly.

Miss Nottynuf gave Bat's hand a small squeeze. 'I guess everything isn't lost. We found you, didn't we?'

In a sudden rush, Ferg understood why he'd wanted Bat to

come back to school with them so much, not to slip away into the woods and never be seen again. She had a way of making anyone feel that things would be all right in the end.

Miss Nottynuf was sniffling now. She believed she'd found the children, even though she hadn't, really, and it had done her a world of good. In that special way Ferg had of sensing the truth about people and things, he knew that Miss Nottynuf was crying not just from the relief of having found the children but also from the relief of having proved something to herself. How could he ever take that feeling away from her by telling her otherwise?

CHAPTER 20

Fermina had hammered her fists against the windowpane. The window was only slightly ajar and, although she tried to push it open, it wouldn't budge. 'No, Miss Nottynuf, don't go!' she cried at the top of her voice, squeezing her mouth near the small opening. Miss Nottynuf didn't hear her. She saw the maths teacher walk out the back gate as if in a trance, and Fermina's heart sank.

It was not clear how long she leaned her forehead against the cool glass, listening to her breath come and go. Imagine how her heart leapt when she looked up again and saw Miss Nottynuf emerge from the woods with her friends in tow! Ferg, Phil, Immy—they were all there, and as Fermina settled her eyes on their familiar heads, her heart felt close to bursting!

Wait, there was another child, too, but Fermina tore her eyes away from them and back to Dr Bloom's window. The science teacher had stepped out only once, early this morning. Fermina had barely recognized her. She'd been wearing a scarf that covered her face. She'd lingered at the back gate for what seemed like an eternity, gazing longingly at the woods. But when a gust of wind whipped her scarf off and away, she'd cast one alarmed look up at the tower.

Fermina had ducked, feeling as guilty as someone who has been caught spying.

But it was the crows that Dr Bloom had been looking up at, not Fermina. Dr Bloom had made a grab for her scarf, but it had danced out of reach. Every time Dr Bloom let her hair loose, realized Fermina with a start, the crows seemed to recognize her from somewhere. Sure enough, the crows had swooped down from the top of the tower as if on cue, cawing at the top of their voices, diving at her boldly. Dr Bloom had sprinted into the school building, her long hair streaming behind her. And the crows had been back at her window ever since.

'I'm sure Dr Bloom will be so relieved to see you that she'll forgive Fermina!' Miss Nottynuf told the children as they filed into the principal's office. She couldn't have been more wrong.

Mallus and Malo were flanking Dr Bloom like bodyguards. They looked dumbstruck but Dr Bloom's response was measured. 'You made it back!' she said, cocking her head to one side. 'Now *how* is that even possible?'

Ferg stared at the twins. Why were they dressed differently from each other? They looked ill at ease, as if they had drawn some comfort from being dressed alike all these days. On the other hand, Dr Bloom looked relaxed. She had set her long hair free, and it ran down her back in brown rivulets. Golden brown with dark roots. Where had he seen that reckless, long mane of hair before? An image of a horse sprang into his head, its nostrils flaring, its thundering hooves clearing everything in its path. His ears tingled.

'I found them—' Miss Nottynuf was saying, still glowing from her little triumph.

'Can't imagine they needed *finding*!' cut in Dr Bloom. 'They look like they've been on nothing worse than a picnic.'

Immy frowned. Ferg was covered in dried mud, and although Phil and she hadn't been in a bog, they didn't look much better. 'It certainly wasn't a picnic!' she protested. 'There were mud pools that could swallow you up whole! And whispering voices coming at you from all directions!'

Dr Bloom rolled her eyes as though she were listening to a child spin a yarn.

'Leaves that dance in response to your footsteps!' continued Immy, desperate to be believed.

Dr Bloom was in the middle of a yawn when she straightened up. 'Did you say *leaves that dance in response to your footsteps?*'

'And . . . and . . . and grass that makes you drowsy!'

The science teacher was clutching the table now. 'Go on . . .'

'Plants with eyeballs growing on them!'

There was the slightest ripple in Dr Bloom's jaw muscle. 'Are you sure? Are you *dead certain?*'

There was an urgency in the science teacher's voice that made Immy hesitate. 'Um, I'm not sure about the eyeballs, really . . .'

'Or the grass!' said Ferg hurriedly. Why was Dr Bloom so interested in these things?

'Or the mud bogs,' said Phil, pitching in. 'We might have imagined those too!'

The children were sinking into a wholly different type of bog, the sort that gets created when you say something you shouldn't and then try to take it back. All their floundering was not very convincing. Dr Bloom, after all, was a science teacher, trained to be sceptical.

She turned to the twins. 'Didn't you tell me that *three* of them were lost in the woods?' The twins nodded.

Dr Bloom stared at Bat pointedly. 'Well, I see four children. Did you miscount?'

The twins looked too jittery to answer and they moved their heads in an undecided way somewhere between a nod and a shake. Miss Nottynuf answered for them. 'She's the long-lost orphan of Horrid High, the one who wandered off into the woods!'

'*Long-lost*, you say?' murmured Dr Bloom now. 'How *long*, child?'

She drew closer to Bat, an intense glow in her eyes. 'Long enough to know the woods inside out?' Bat felt the tiny hairs at the back of her neck prickling in a way that nothing in the woods had ever made them. There was something off-putting about the science teacher but it was Dr Bloom who pulled back first. Holding her nose, she cried, 'Oooooh, what is that smell?'

Bat suppressed a grin. She would happily refrain from taking a bath forever if it kept Dr Bloom away from her!

'The poor child needs a hot shower and some food, as do the others!' cried Miss Nottynuf. 'The woods are no place for anyone, especially a child!'

'But there are things of scientific interest in those woods, things worth *saving*,' said Dr Bloom, a peculiar tremor in her voice now. She smiled at Bat now, in that way that made her cheekbones disappear. 'Why, I'd be grateful to be shown a safe way in. We still have to rescue Colonel Craven, don't we?'

That last suggestion provoked vigorous nodding from Miss Nottynuf. 'Go on, Bat, tell her if you know anything about the woods that might help us to find Colonel Craven!'

Dr Bloom clenched her chiselled jaw. Curious, thought Ferg, how that tiny movement reminded him of a shark in icy waters. He could see Immy and Phil relenting now. 'Go on, Bat!' they said. 'Tell her!'

But Bat did something most unexpected. She rolled her eyes back in her head and sank to the floor. 'I . . . I . . . I c-can't bear to think of those t-terrible woods,' she whimpered. 'My head h-h-hurts, I feel f-faint!'

Miss Nottynuf rushed to Bat's side: 'The poor darling, she's in utter shock!'

Dr Bloom knelt down and took Bat's pulse. Then she placed a long finger under Bat's chin and stared at her like a scientist would a wriggling specimen caught in her forceps. 'You're

right,' she said presently. 'She has enlarged pupils, her pulse is fluttery. Classic signs of shock! Take her to the clinic, Miss Nottynuf, and I'll pop in and check on her later.'

Bat gave a juddering, shuddering groan and exhaled on Dr Bloom. The science teacher grimaced. This child clearly hadn't brushed her teeth in months, possibly years!

The children were concerned. Their new friend didn't seem the fainting type. As Miss Nottynuf led her out, making cooing sounds, Bat's gaze met Ferg's worried one. She winked.

'Er, could the rest of us get cleaned up?' asked Ferg, recovering quickly.

'I should certainly hope so,' said Dr Bloom, still holding her nose. 'But you won't escape being punished for traipsing about in the woods on a whim! You can join that fat girl in the kitchen. I'm sure she'll be grateful for the extra help.'

'What about our friend, Fermina?' asked Immy bravely.

'She can stew in the tower,' said Dr Bloom. 'From what I hear, your feisty little friend isn't feeling very sorry yet.'

Fermina had no intention of apologizing. Not yet. After her friends had returned to school, she'd picked up *The Company of Crows* with renewed tenderness and finished the book. What an eye-opener it had been!

She ran her fingers over the words gently, as though they were in a prayer book:

Crows are certainly not birdbrains. Remember Aesop's fable about the crow and the pitcher?

Fermina's mind wandered—an old memory returned. Sitting on Uncle Max's lap as a child while he read her the story of the thirsty crow who couldn't reach the water at the bottom of the pitcher. The clever crow had dropped pebbles in, one after the other, to get the the water level to slowly rise. Fermina read on.

Did Aesop know, by instinct, what scientists are only discovering now, that crows are highly intelligent birds?

'Remember, Fermina,' Uncle Max had said, stroking her long hair. 'If you're clever enough, you can find a way out!'

Isn't that what Granny Grit had said too, that adversity could make you clever? What did the crows at the top of the tower know that Fermina didn't? What were they trying to tell her? Fermina's eyes returned to the page:

Crows can recognize people.

Two crows swept past Fermina's window, black shadows, flying wing to wing. Could crows remember a human face, even though humans couldn't tell one crow from the next? Her pulse quickened.

Crows can hold a grudge for years. They have been known to retaliate against human cruelty by dive-bombing their tormentors.

Fermina's breath fogged up the glass pane. Her eyes alighted on the very spot where the children had all stood, a few days ago, peering at the branch of poison ivy in Dr Bloom's hand. Only a few minutes before the crows attacked Dr Bloom and no one else. What if that attack had had nothing to do with Volumina or the twins?

> *That's not all. Crows can communicate their experiences to other crows. So it doesn't pay to trouble a crow. You might just find the entire murder of crows dive-bombing you.*

Fermina glanced up at the crow congregation on Dr Bloom's window. Her breath caught in her throat as one question led to the next like it was the most natural thing in the world. What score did the crows have to settle with Dr Bloom? Where did the crows recognize her from with her hair down?

With a start, Fermina realized that she'd stumbled upon the question that most needed asking! *Has Dr Bloom been here before?* The crows were cawing again. A murder of crows plotting their revenge together. If only she could understand what they were saying. Or send word to her friends to tell them what she'd discovered.

That single thought propelled her eyes towards the breakfast tray. Still untouched, except for the lemon slices! She'd sucked her way through most of them after she found that the pancakes were inedible, and they'd taken the edge off her hunger. But now she wished she hadn't!

She flew to the tray and, with trembling hands, picked up the leftover lemon slices and squeezed out the juice in a cup. Even a few drops would be enough, she hoped, for some invisible writing! She had found one ballpoint pen in the Tower Library, but dipping it in lemon juice would make it hard to do any visible writing with it later. And that needed to be done too!

She looked around for any other instrument to write with. She could always use her little finger, but a finer writing tool was needed when there was barely enough lemon juice. There had to be *something*!

The crows flew past her window again, and something long and black sailed upon a current of air and stuck to the windowpane. A crow feather! It was as if the crows had read her mind.

Fermina eased one tiny hand past the iron grill and out the window. The opening was barely large enough and she feared that if she extended her arm out any farther, it would get stuck. She grunted, and her fingers strained to reach the feather. It slid briefly as the wind died down. *Don't,* mouthed Fermina. Her hand was barely an inch away from it now. She stretched her fingers —there! She had it now! Slowly, slowly, she eased the feather back inside.

Sounds! Voices! The twins were walking across the playground towards the tower, a tray in one boy's hand. Lunch!

Fermina's heart was pounding now. A blank sheet of

paper, quick! The paper napkins on the breakfast tray would do.

If only Ferg were here to tell her how it was done. She could only hope that it was as simple as dipping a crow feather into lemon juice and writing with it.

What was that? A door slammed downstairs. As she'd feared, the letter fell short of its final sentence and she was all out of lemon juice! Now what?

Footsteps coming up the stairs. Two pairs. Fermina spun about, confused. Where would she get more invisible ink from? That was when she saw the toilet at the distant end of the Tower Library. The toilet!

It was a ghastly thought but Fermina wasn't the sort of girl to get squeamish about such things. Pee was a perfectly natural thing, she told herself as she raced across the room.

The twins were dancing upon the stairs now. A loud clattering noise could be heard. Malo had dropped the lunch tray. 'You're so clumsy!' growled Mallus, stooping down to pick up the mess and piling it back on the tray, willy-nilly. He'd been in a terrible mood ever since their clothes were nicked.

'It's your fault for making me carry the tray up in my left hand!' grumbled Malo. He couldn't understand why Mallus was so agitated over the loss of their clothes.

'You're just a klutz, plain and simple! You know you can't be right-handed when I'm not!'

Malo flinched. His brother always came down hard on him for forgetting to use his left hand but he couldn't help forgetting, could he? He was *born* right-handed—it was only natural for him to let down his guard from time to time! Besides, was it fair that Mallus got to decide that they should both be left-handed just because he was a measly minute older?

'Maybe you should try doing everything with your right hand!' Malo grumbled before changing the subject. 'Are you going to ask her where our clothes are?' He secretly wished his brother wouldn't.

'I would shake her till her teeth rattled if it helped,' said Mallus through gritted teeth. 'We look ridiculous dressed differently! Nothing identical about us now!'

Malo sighed. It mattered so much to Mallus that they appeared identical. It always had. Malo would never admit this to Mallus but he was beginning to enjoy being a separate person. Dressing differently was a good start. 'We should drop this charade of both being left-handed!'

Mallus stared at his brother in disbelief. 'You ninny! Don't you see, if we "drop the charade", as you've so nicely put it, they'll find out we're different!'

Malo didn't like being called a klutz or a ninny. 'So what if they do?'

Mallus raised his eyebrows. 'Don't you remember how Mom got once *she* found out?'

'I don't want to pretend any more,' said Malo, still smarting from the insults. 'Why can't I be me and you be you?'

Mallus had been poised to cut his twin brother off when he

faltered. There was, after all, nothing wrong with that idea . . . 'You're a fool!' he said all of a sudden, not because he meant it but because he wasn't ready to admit that his twin brother could be right. He galloped up the stairs, holding the tray deftly in his left hand. 'Fermina FILTH, lunch is here!'

Behind him, Malo rounded his shoulders and winced. That was another thing he'd started to dislike. What was the need to call her Fermina Filth?

Two sets of loud raps sounded on the door. The door swung open with a bang. 'Ye-es?' said the girl, curled up among the cushions, reading *The Mutiny on HMS Bounty*.

Malo straightened up. This was no time to second-guess his brother. 'You've gone through an awful lot of lemon slices!' he said. *I've always been more observant than Mallus,* he thought, before he could stop himself.

'Oh, yes, thanks for those!' said Fermina, sounding infuriatingly calm.

'And the written apology?' Malo pressed. He felt a little bad forcing an apology out of Fermina but it would not do to look sympathetic to her in front of Mallus.

'Been too tied up writing something else!' said Fermina, gesturing to the breakfast tray.

'What? A new novel, perhaps! Or a poem?' quipped Malo. He'd always been wittier than his twin brother, too, but he scolded himself now for thinking so.

'It's a note for Volumina!' and here, Fermina scowled as best she could.

'Mind if we read it?' said Mallus and, as she'd expected, the twins read it anyway.

Volumina,

Switch a light bulb on in that fat head of yours! Read between the lines, idiot! But no, you won't, will you? Because you're as dumb as you are fat! You're nothing but a coward, stuffing your face in the kitchen while I'm locked up in the tower! Now I know who the most horrid person is at Horrid High. The question is, do you? Shed light on what I've said, you lumbering loser! And you just might see the truth, even if you think you can't!

Fermina.

Just as Fermina had hoped, the twins fell for it right away.

'Can't wait to see her face when she gets this,' said Mallus.

'It's mean,' agreed Malo, trying to sound like he approved.

In a moment of weakness, Fermina's voice dropped. 'It is, isn't it?' Fermina felt terrible about all the things she'd written but that was the only way she could guarantee that the twins would deliver it to Volumina. They'd never pass up such a chance. Her eyes met Malo's and, for a brief instant, it was as if they understood each other. But then, Fermina looked away and forced some brightness into her voice. 'The meaner, the better!'

The boys charged down the stairs. 'I'll show it to her!'

'No, I'll show it to her!'

Fermina cheered up. She'd needed a messenger. Two would be even better!

CHAPTER 21

Bat had a visitor at her bedside who was loath to leave. In the last hour, Bat had gone through all the stages of The Undiagnosed Illness for the benefit of the science teacher. She'd rolled her eyes back so many times, her head hurt. She'd gasped for breath so hard, she felt a little light-headed now. She'd gnashed her teeth and chipped one in her enthusiasm. She'd blown her nose emphatically, summoning up wondrously large boogers.

She was an expert at The Undiagnosed Illness, after all. She'd enacted it at least a dozen times before, falling ill during morals class at every orphanage she'd been to. Or fooling foster families into thinking that she had a highly contagious disease that they would catch if they took her in.

But Bat felt sure that if she kept up the act any longer, she'd fall sick for real. Dr Bloom was staring at Bat fixedly, and there was no letting down her guard. If only Dr Bloom would go downstairs for science class, Bat could take an actor's break. A much-needed one.

'Let me comb out your hair, dear,' crooned Dr Bloom, teasing out the knots with her long fingers. Bat grimaced. How she hated doing her hair! 'There! Doesn't that look so much better?' She stuck a little mirror in Bat's face. 'Take a look.'

The tiny ponytail that her hair had been pulled into stuck out behind her head and made her look like a cockatoo. 'I look bee-yoo-ti-full!' Bat gushed without meaning it. Perhaps now the creepy lady would leave her be.

Dr Bloom shuddered. She had never seen an uglier child but if the child thought she was beautiful, it was best to let her believe it.

'I've brought a book to show you,' said Dr Bloom, drawing her chair closer to Bat's bed. 'The *Rare Plants Register* is one of my favourites. Read it over and over again as a child! Look at this one here!'

A long finger hovered over the picture of a humongous flower with red, mottled petals the size of beef steaks. 'The corpse flower,' said Dr Bloom breathlessly. 'Smells of decaying flesh. You didn't see any of these in the woods, did you, my darling?'

Bat nodded. Of course she had. You could smell that flower from a mile away. She resumed moaning. Grown-ups were such tedious company.

'And look at this one! It's beautiful, isn't it? Seen it before, dear?' Bat feigned interest and nodded again. If Dr Bloom was going to insist on keeping her company, she might have read Bat an adventure story instead! Why this?

'Good! Good! And that's the titan arum. Notorious for its

stench. Seen it, dear?' Bat cursed herself for nodding. Now Dr Bloom had sprung off her chair and perched herself on the side of Bat's bed—'Where did you see it, sweetheart? Could you find your way back there?'

Up close, grown-ups were even more ghastly! Bat decided that it was time for The Cough now. It always worked when The Undiagnosed Illness failed. The Cough was the sort of hideous hacking sound that a person might make before she passed on to the next world. Bat had perfected it with practice. She churned up enough spittle and phlegm and, with a retching sound, unleashed a few choice chunks. *Next time she'll wear a raincoat,* thought Bat as Dr Bloom recoiled and returned to her seat swiftly.

'Cover your mouth, dear!' she said. The child's breath smelt like she'd *eaten* a titan arum. She turned to page 151 of the *Rare Plants Register*. The green jade flower. 'This one is gorgeous! A navy blue centre, quite unusual! Seen this one, my dear?' The child shook her head and Dr Bloom tried hard to hide her irritation.

What caught Bat's eye was the picture on the opposite page. Dr Bloom noticed right away. 'You know *this one?*' Dr Bloom sprang back to Bat's side. 'It's the bat flower, named after you!' she continued in her most flattering voice. She'd risk the child coughing on her if she'd seen the bat flower!

Bat nodded. 'Large flowers!' she said, holding up two scrawny arms to indicate their size. 'With *long* whiskers!'

Dr Bloom's fingers were trembling now. They clawed at the pages—'This! What about this?' and 'Here! Look at this one!' It was a blur for Bat—a plant with only two leaves tangled into a mass six feet long; trumpet-shaped blooms that were packed with poison; white, cottony blossoms that would kill anyone who ate them. She'd seen most of them before in the Get Lost Forever Woods but what she couldn't quite fathom was why her nodding was sending the science teacher into a fever pitch of excitement.

'You're a lucky girl, my darling, you've beheld all these wonders!' Dr Bloom gushed as she flipped through the pages. 'Take me into the woods, won't you, my dear?'

There was nothing Bat wanted more than to leave Horrid High and to disappear into the woods. But certainly not with this creepy lady. Oh no, she wasn't taking her anywhere!

The creepy lady was too close for comfort now. 'Promise me?' she crooned.

It was time for The Fit. The Fit was a sure winner—the nuns at the orphanage she was once at went berserk, clucking their tongues and running about like hens in a farmyard. What Bat needed now was a seizure of the most violent sort. Deployed together, The Cough and The Fit never failed.

With a fierce jerk, Bat's legs convulsed. She batted her arms wildly and, just for good measure, she tore at her hair too. She deployed a series of coughs that made her sound like she was being throttled, and a single vile sneeze loud enough to bring down the roof. 'Arrrrrghhh! Arrrrrghhh! My head hurts! I won't go into the woods, not now, not ever!' There. A few more tugs and her hair would come undone again. Bat lay back and rolled about on the bed, moaning, feeling the rubber band slip off her ponytail.

'Maybe another time, then, my dear?' Dr Bloom said, ducking to avoid flying spittle before picking up her book and hurrying out. At long last! Bat's heart leapt with joy as she sat up. She wiped her nose with the back of her hand in a long green smear. She blinked at herself in the tiny mirror that Dr Bloom had left behind. Her hair had flopped over her eyes again. She tousled it back into its matted state and smiled as she flung the rubber band into the bin—she had never cared much for cockatoos anyway!

The twins had exchanged a few punches on their way down from the tower the day before. There had been a tense tussle to decide who would give Volumina the letter. Malo was fed up of following his brother's lead—he'd done it his whole life. Although he couldn't drum up the same wicked glee over the letter as Mallus, he wanted to deliver it only so that his brother couldn't. The spat ended in a tie and it was finally decided that they should hold on to the letter for a day longer and savour every word.

They tore into the dining room the next morning, sniggering hideously. The children were cleaning up the kitchen after Cook Fracas had prepared another messy breakfast, pining for Gypsy.

'There's a love note for yo-oo-oou!' sang Mallus.

'It's not really a love note,' mumbled Malo, feeling a little embarrassed all of a sudden about what was about to unfold.

Mallus stopped short and shot his brother a puzzled look. Why was his twin brother contradicting him? Hadn't they always spoken in unison? It was a disturbing thought but he banished it. They were about to deliver a letter that would bring untold misery to that fat girl who'd threatened so many times to tell on them! They could work on their dialogue delivery later.

Volumina was tying a garbage bag at the top. 'A letter from Fermina?' she cried eagerly, stepping forward.

'For us!' said Ferg with quiet certainty, setting down a wet bowl on the drying rack and nodding at Immy and Phil. If there was a letter from Fermina, it had to be for them. Right?

Mallus smirked. 'Fermina's quite forgotten her old friends. This letter is for Volumina!'

Volumina flushed. She had a new friend now and she could scarcely believe it! She smiled.

'Would you like us to read it aloud to you?' asked Mallus, snickering nonstop.

Malo hesitated. Volumina did have the most wonderful smile. It made her eyes sparkle.

Mallus cleared his throat as if to begin. Malo took a deep breath, he was getting soft! The twins brought their heads close and this time, they spoke together: *'Volumina, switch a light bulb on in that fat head of yours! Read between the lines, idiot! But no, you won't, will you? Because you're as dumb as you are fat! You're nothing but a coward, stuffing your face in the kitchen while I'm locked up in the tower!'*

Volumina sank down on the bench. Her legs felt all wobbly. Her face burned and there was a loud roaring in her ears.

'Should we continue?' inquired Mallus, looking innocent. Volumina didn't answer but Mallus needed no encouragement. Malo joined in reluctantly. *'Now I know who the most horrid person is at Horrid High. The question is, do you? Shed light on what I've said, you lumbering loser! And you just might see the truth, even if you think you can't!'*

Mallus hadn't gotten beyond reading 'lumbering' because he'd collapsed into laughter. Malo read bravely till the end, but as Volumina's face fell, his did too.

'Give me that!' cried Phil, lunging for the letter and snatching it from Malo.

'Now I know who the most horrid person is at Horrid High!' screamed Mallus, pointing at Volumina, hooting with laughter. He still found it terribly funny. 'I told you, everyone here hates you, and now we do too!'

'Let's go!' hissed Malo, who was not having half as much fun as his twin brother.

'What's gotten into you?'

'I said let's go!'

'You're spoiling all my fun!'

'I'm . . .'

'I'm sorry that you had to hear these things,' Ferg told Volumina as soon as the twins had left the dining room, still arguing. She blinked back her tears and said nothing.

'There's no way on earth that Fermina would write such cruel things!' cried Immy.

Phil's expression was grave as he studied the letter. He sucked in his cheeks. This wasn't going to be easy but it had to be said. 'It's definitely Fermina's handwriting.'

'The twins must have *forced* her to write this!' said Immy, drawing as close to Volumina as she dared.

Volumina shook her head. 'I think Fermina wrote this on purpose.'

'You're just saying that because you're upset,' said Ferg in his kindest voice.

Volumina sniffed. 'Well, I *am* upset. Although I've been called fat so many times, it shouldn't bother me any more!'

The others looked at their feet guiltily.

'But it isn't that.' Volumina paused for effect. 'I know she's my friend and she wouldn't write me such a hurtful letter, no matter how much anyone tried to force her to, unless . . . unless . . .'

A heavy silence fell upon the children. Volumina was grasping at straws to make herself feel better, but it was understandable. 'Unless she was trying to send me a message,' Volumina finished.

Ferg looked up and a smile spread across his face slowly. 'Now *that* sounds more like the Fermina I know!'

He traced the letter with his forefinger, mouthing the words. '*Switch a light bulb on in that fat head of yours . . .* What an odd thing to say! And this bit is strangely worded too: *Read between the lines, idiot!*'

Phil was feeling very sorry for the school bully. She was still clinging on to the hope that Fermina and she were friends, and he couldn't bear it any more. 'Will the two of you stop?' he said, springing up and snatching the letter. 'There's nothing here, just some silliness about shedding light and seeing the truth! Whoever says things like that?'

'Shedding light!' cried Ferg, jumping up. 'Why, that might be it! Quick! Give me the letter!'

Phil looked lost. 'What are you doing now?' But Volumina had dragged a chair over and Ferg had climbed up on it. 'I'm shedding light, Phil!' he shouted, grinning like a monkey and holding the letter close to the light bulb.

As if by magic, the letters appeared, brown and squiggly:

I'm awfully sorry that I had to say such horrid things to you, Volumina! I meant none of them, but how else could I make certain that the twins would give you my letter? Ferg,

Phil and Immy, my time in the tower has been very useful. I've found out that there's more to Dr Bloom than meets the eye. Find a way to search her room. Hurry!

'I told you from the very start,' said Volumina, choking on her words. 'Fermina wrote this on purpose!'

Phil felt fierce admiration well up inside him for the school bully. There had been so much bad blood between Fermina and her, how had Volumina still managed to trust her?

'I'm glad you're right!' said Immy, as she slipped her hand into Volumina's.

'Why is everyone holding hands?' came a voice from behind. 'Are we having a séance or something?'

Bat! She looked unrecognizable, in a pink nightdress, her hair pulled back in a—

'Cockatoo!' Bat grinned wryly. 'My ponytail makes me look like a cockatoo, I know! And a pink nightdress, for heaven's sake! Of all the available colours . . . *pink?*'

Ferg showed Bat the letter. 'She's a clever one!' said Bat, reading aloud. 'Now I know who the most horrid person is at Horrid High—She means Dr Bloom, doesn't she?'

Ferg uttered a sharp cry and slapped her on the back. Bat always had a way of getting to the heart of things.

'We'd never get away with searching her room,' cried Immy. 'If Dr Bloom or any of the twins were to see us . . .'

'We'd all be locked up in the tower and forgotten forever!' said Phil.

Then, Bat flashed a broken-toothed smile. 'I have just the perfect way to get all three of them out of here and me out of this hideous pink confection! Up for a picnic, anyone?'

CHAPTER 22

'Thank you for taking us to the Botanical Gardens, Dr Bloom!' said Bat two days later. It had been Bat's suggestion that they go on a picnic and Dr Bloom had come up with the perfect place for one. She would do anything to get the wretched child out of bed, and perhaps all the flowers at the gardens would stoke her memory.

A rattletrap bus carted the kids off on their first-ever field trip. Bat gazed up at Dr Bloom lovingly and rested her head on her science teacher's shoulder. Dr Bloom stifled a shudder and patted her head awkwardly. She could still feel the knots in her hair, large tangles that had almost wrenched the teeth clean off the comb. But that bird's nest of hers was in a ponytail now, if you could call that shrub sticking out the back of her head a ponytail!

A loose spring in the tattered seat dug into Dr Bloom's bottom and she cursed under her breath. Cook Fracas was driving the bus blithely over every bump in the road. They'd needed a driver to take them to the gardens, and Cook Fracas had agreed to come along. For his own reasons, of course. 'Keep an eye out for Gypsy, everyone!' he shouted.

The jungle child was chattering nonstop and her nose ran. 'I promised you, didn't I, Dr Bloom, that I'd jump out of my sickbed if you took us on a picnic! I feel as good as new now!' Dr Bloom flashed her a plastic grin, trying not to focus on the green gob clinging to the child's nostrils.

'Well, you and I could have had a picnic of our own in the woods,' said Dr Bloom in her most coaxing voice.

The rotten child burrowed her nose in her teacher's shoulder. When she looked up, the green gob was gone. With a sinking heart, Dr Bloom realized where the child had deposited it. 'What if I had had another fit in the woods?' the child shivered. 'What if I'd *coughed?*'

Dr Bloom edged away and wiped her face without realizing it.

'I promise we'll go, Dr Bloom, when I feel well again,' said the child.

Dr Bloom perked up. 'I'm sure the plants at the Botanical Gardens will seem familiar to you, my dear. You'll point to the ones you've seen before, won't you, my darling?'

The child snivelled. It was a rather threatening sort of snivel, promising more gob, more goo, more green gunk. Dr Bloom felt her insides heave.

'Here, take this!' she said, producing a dainty handkerchief with great reluctance.

'What shall I do with this?'

Of all the *idiotic* questions in the world! But Dr Bloom calmly said, 'Blow your nose, my darling!'

The darling blew her nose like a trumpet. 'Here!' she said now, holding out the wet rag.

'No, no, you keep it!' said Dr Bloom hastily. *Stuff it in your mouth and shut up*, she wanted to say.

'How can I keep what isn't mine?' said the child.

'It's yours now!'

The twins sat behind Dr Bloom and Bat, sullen. It was most unfair—they'd taken that Fermina Filch all her meals, they'd driven the fat girl to tears, they'd hatched the perfect plot to get Ferg and his nosy friends out of the way forever!

But now this savage from the woods had Dr Bloom wrapped around her grubby little finger! And everyone at school seemed to be able to tell them apart. Didn't that pipsqueak whose seat Mallus grabbed cry, 'Hey, Mallus, aren't school prefects supposed to be fair to everyone?'

Of course, that was before Mallus had hauled the boy up by the collar. 'Did you call me Mallus? How do you know I'm Mallus?'

The runt had chortled—the cheek of it! A sharp clip to the head had sorted that out. A sharp clip to the head was always an effective thing and Mallus would have been only be too glad to serve it to that woodling too!

'*Woodling*,' he chuckled, marvelling at his ability to coin new words. He nudged his brother. 'A creature from the woods with lice in her hair and mud under her fingernails.'

'Quit it!' came his brother's sharp reply. Mallus faltered but he recovered quickly. 'Why is your watch on your left hand?'

'It's my watch, it's my hand,' Malo whispered.

'But you can't wear your watch on a different hand from me!' said Mallus. 'We're identical, remember?'

'*Almost* identical,' muttered Malo, 'and I don't think you should have pushed that boy off his seat!'

'Remember what Mom said! That there's nothing such as *almost identical*! Being *almost identical* didn't do us much good then. It won't do us much good now!'

A shadow came over Malo's face. He slumped down in his seat and looked out of the window.

Phil had followed Bat's instructions to the T. He'd mixed three teaspoons of salt into a glass of warm water, given it a good stir and downed it in one go. He followed it up with the sickly sweet coriander milkshake Cook Fracas had served this morning. It was a sure shot to achieve what Bat simply called The Vomit!

Dr Bloom glared at him suspiciously at first—'You don't look too ill to go to the Botanical Gardens!' she said. 'Now buck up!'

A minute later, she was standing in a dark puddle. She lifted the sole of one shoe in disgust and stared at its sticky underside—'I didn't say *chuck up*!'

The short hand of the clock nudged ten. Phil still felt greener than the milkshake as he watched the bus swing out the school gates and careen down the road. Once he was certain that the others had left, he climbed out of bed. He plumped up the pillows and pulled the blanket over them, standing back to see if he'd achieved the desired effect. If Miss Nottynuf looked in from the doorway, she'd mistake the pillows for him sleeping.

He raced across the playground to the tower. He looked around guiltily as he slipped a pick into the lock. One twist of his wrist and he was in! Up the stairs he pelted, another twist of the wrist, and the door of the library flew open.

'Fermina!' 'Phil!' And although the two children would never be caught dead hugging each other, here they were, making an exception just this once.

'Got anything to eat, Phil?'

'I can't bear to look at food right now!' Phil groaned, rubbing his stomach.

'That's most unlike you!'

'It's a long story. Now keep an eye out for Nottynuf, she stayed behind to look after me!'

The Botanical Gardens were hosting a special exhibit: *Plant Collectors down the Ages.* Squads of schoolchildren filed past prickly cacti and purple crocuses in bloom, pointing at giant palms and gasping in surprise at the sight of a fat caterpillar curled up on a leaf.

Dr Bloom stopped at the statue of a female Pharaoh. 'Collecting plants is an ancient activity, going back as far as the Egyptians. That's Queen Hatshepsut, who sent ships out to East Africa to look for rare plants and flowers. Their illustrations can be found on Egyptian temple walls even today!'

'That's Christopher Columbus!' cried Ferg, pulling ahead. He'd read all about the explorer and his discovery of America.

'Quite right,' nodded Dr Bloom, stopping to read out loud from the information plaque. 'There are trees of a thousand sorts and all have their several fruits; and I feel the most unhappy man in the world not to know them, for I am well assured they are valuable.'

The children mouthed the words to themselves. 'I wonder why plants have fascinated people for so many thousands of years,' whispered Immy.

'I wonder if Fermina and Phil have found anything yet,' whispered Ferg before Immy kicked him on the shin.

Dr Bloom had stopped at the roses now. 'The mandarins of China, the emperors of India, there was no one who did not feel the lure of an exotic flower that they simply had to have for their own private garden!'

'Those are rhododendrons, aren't they?' said a skinny girl who'd loped ahead.

'Joseph Dalton Hooker carted them from the Himalayas to England, along with 7000 other plant species the world didn't know about!' said Dr Bloom.

The children couldn't help but be fascinated by these stories. They were as gripping as Granny's, throwing up many ideas all at once. 'I hope that Fermina's hunches about Dr Bloom are wrong,' muttered Immy. 'Her lessons are fascinating!'

'And she hasn't said anything strange or suspicious yet,' frowned Volumina.

As they wound past shining cycads and glistening creepers, Dr Bloom enthralled them with stories of plant hunters who'd fought off pirates, been caught in landslides, even been trapped in a pit meant for wild animals.

'The best scientists were also great collectors,' said Dr Bloom, picking her way around a cluster of lurid bulbs. 'Ah, what a life of adventure it was, trekking in distant jungles with just a cutlass!'

Ferg stopped at another plaque. 'It says here that a man called Henry Wickham smuggled thousands of rubber seeds out of the Amazon and planted them in Singapore and Malaysia.'

'Isn't it a form of robbery?' wondered Immy, 'all these collectors going to poor countries and plundering their plants—'

Dr Bloom practically snarled. 'Robbery? The entire history of plant exploration is about plant hunters trawling the world, discovering rare plants and taking them home! No one knew these plants existed, no one thought they were of any value or cared to conserve them till they were sketched and studied for the first time!'

Immy hadn't expected such a strong reaction from her teacher. 'What I meant was—'

'Never mind what you meant! Plant hunters risk their lives, and not for money or for fame! It's a scientific endeavour, don't you see, it's a *passion*—'

'I saw that in the woods,' cut in Bat, rushing to poor Immy's rescue.

'What? This one?' Dr Bloom lingered near a single pink flower, slender in appearance and her long fingers closed around Bat's skinny arm. Bat felt her teacher's grip harden and she wrenched free. 'I've seen that one too!'

'The Snowdonia hawkweed!' murmured Dr Bloom, drawing closer to the explosion of yellow flowers, entranced. 'Are you sure?'

'She's getting a little weird now,' crooned Volumina softly.

Bat thought so too, but she was quite enjoying the effect she was having on her science teacher. Dr Bloom spoke in a hushed tone:

'The Snowdonia hawkweed
Only two grow free,
That's sad indeed,
When once there were three.'

'What happened to the third?' asked Mallus, who was overhearing this and assumed that showing a little interest in plants couldn't hurt. 'It's none of your business, Malo!' snapped Dr Bloom.

The real Malo couldn't help chuckling. 'At least *she* can't tell us apart!' he whispered to his bristling twin brother.

Bat was trying her hardest to annoy Dr Bloom. She blew loudly into the handkerchief her teacher had given her. 'That one with the chocolatey smell sets off my cold each time!'

Dr Bloom whipped around. 'What did you say?'

Mallus saw another chance to be in his teacher's good books. 'The woodling says that the brown flowers there smell of chocolate and make her sneeze!' He laughed loudly to make his point.

'And she's right, you nitwit!' said Dr Bloom, putting a protective arm around Bat. 'They're known as chocolate cosmos, extremely rare too! Did you say you've seen them before, child . . .'

She broke off when something caught her eye. 'What's that?' asked Mallus, desperate to be noticed.

'Nothing,' snapped Dr Bloom. 'Let's move along!'

She ushered the children towards the orchid house but Bat noticed the teacher cast one last longing look at the bright pink flowers that anyone might have mistaken for roses. Bat strained her eyes to read the plate below: *Middlemist's Red.*

CHAPTER 23

It was child's play for Phil to break in but he hesitated in the doorway. They were in Dr Bloom's room without her permission and it made him jumpy.

Fermina had already set her feelings aside. 'We don't have time for second thoughts, Phil, we won't get another chance like this one!'

Her eye scanned the room, taking in the shelf where all the books had been meticulously arranged from the largest to the smallest; the neatly made bed; the desk on which a hundred things had been carefully balanced; the windowsill where a dozen plants were growing out of gleaming glass jars; the hiking boots, where you entered, lined up in perfect pairs. Their science teacher had even taken care to place the muddiest ones on a sheet of newspaper so that the floor would not get dirty.

Phil rummaged through a row of weather-worn knapsacks, pulling out pruners, trowels, notebooks full of pencil drawings, a few hand lenses, plant presses, empty collecting bags . . . 'It's clear that she loves plants, the odder the better, but there's nothing here to suggest that she's been at Horrid High before!'

Fermina was in the bathroom, turning bottles around to read the labels. Insect repellent, sunscreen, nothing out of the ordinary for a science teacher who loved being out in the open. She felt certain that Granny Grit's bathroom shelf wouldn't look much different.

Phil was at the desk now, peering through a microscope. 'There's a slide in place but I can't *see* anything, Ferm!'

Fermina snorted at Phil's ignorance. 'Try turning the focus knob! And careful, don't leave any fingerprints on the lens, or she'll know we've been here!'

Phil drew a sharp breath. The leaf on the slide looked so different under a microscope—the flat, shiny surface seemed to break up into little hexagonal compartments that fitted into each other perfectly . . .

'Wow!' gasped Phil. 'Come and see this!'

'Uhhh hmmmmm!' Fermina was poring over the bookshelf. It was where she felt most at home. She dropped down to her knees to read the spines aloud: '*The History of Plants* by Theophrastus, *Hippocrates & Plant Lore*, *Catalogus Plantarum*.'

'They sound like Greek and Latin to me,' Phil said.

'That's because a lot of them are.'

Fermina touched the books with reverence, leafing through their yellowed pages gently. Some were so old, their moth-eaten words crumbled beneath the pressure of her fingers.

'Look at this! The *Rare Plants Register* that sent Bat into a coughing fit! Phil chuckled. They leaned over the book, giggling together. 'Dr Bloom is obsessed with plants and she's got it into her head that Bat has seen some of these strange specimens in the woods—oh no!' His elbow had knocked over a pile of mounting cards and sent them flying.

'We'll have to put them back just as we found them!' Fermina fretted. Every card had a dried specimen stuck on it, a tiny flower, a leaf or a piece of bark. There was a label under the specimen, bearing its name and where it had been obtained.

'Don't see why the Get Lost Forever Woods matter so much to her,' said Phil as he read the cards. 'It seems she's travelled everywhere! China, the Himalayas, Sarawak, Hawaii—'

'She seems so much like Granny Grit, doesn't she?' said Fermina, a catch in her voice. 'I miss Granny.'

As Phil arranged the mounting cards upon the table, he felt morose. Their search had yielded nothing. Fermina leafed through the *Rare Plants Register* dolefully, skimming the pictures and words, something about a pitcher plant that could digest rats and frogs, another plant that smelt like poop. Fermina turned up her nose in disgust at the thought . . . and then she sat up ramrod straight. 'Phil, look at this.'

Phil stared at the picture of the world's smallest water lily. 'The one we saw in the newspaper up in the Tower Library, of course I remember! I wondered if it was edible!' He chuckled.

'Not the picture, Phil, look at *this*!'

Fermina held a ticket stub in her hand. 'It was on this page,' she said quietly. 'Stuck in like a bookmark.'

Phil looked confused. 'Maybe she doesn't believe in buying real bookmarks of the bookshop variety—'

'*Read it!*'

Phil threw up his hands in exasperation. 'It's for the Botanical Gardens they're visiting today, and yes, it means she's been there before. But so what?'

'The *date,* Phil!'

Phil's heart lurched. 'Fourteenth February!'

Fermina's expression was grave. 'Valentine's Day! The same day that the water lily was nicked!'

'D'you think she nicked it?'

The sharp cawing of a crow made them jump. Fermina lunged at the window—'Go away! Be quiet!'—when Phil seized her arm. 'WATCH OUT!'

He pointed at one of the plants on the windowsill. Its leaves were growing in sets of three, two branching off in opposite directions and a third leaf at the top. It looked disturbingly familiar.

'Poison ivy!' gasped Fermina. 'If it weren't for you, I'd be itching like the twins in Miss Nottynuf's class.' She broke off and stared at Phil when she realized what she'd just said.

Phil's eyes lit up. 'Is it possible the twins had a *poison-ivy* itch that day?'

Fermina scooted to the bookshelf, her fingers running along the spines, her eyes searching—she'd seen it, where was it now? *Plants & Their Toxins.* She ran her fingers down the contents until she found the right page:

Poison ivy, oak and sumac contain a resinous sap called urushiol that causes a rash when it comes in contact with the skin.

The pictures were horrid: dark red, oozy patches of skin covered with blisters. The twins' welts had looked no different!

Phil whistled under his breath. 'Pretty gruesome! That's what your arm would have looked like if I hadn't stopped you. Dr Bloom would have known straight off that you'd been here . . .'

'Like she knew straight off that the twins had been here!'

Phil straightened up to his full height. '*She knew?*'

'It makes sense, doesn't it? There's no poison ivy growing in the playground. Colonel Craven said so himself! And the twins were up here snooping for spiders, Volumina told me so.'

Phil adjusted his spectacles. 'When they broke into a rash in Miss Nottynuf's class that day, Dr Bloom must have had no trouble identifying what it was!'

'Why didn't she tell Colonel Craven about what the twins had done?' Fermina wondered, chewing her lip. 'And have them punished?'

The children had run out of answers.

'Didn't know the Botanical Gardens were so old . . .' mused Fermina, who had returned to the *Rare Plants Register*.

'What do you mean?'

'There are so many ticket stubs here, stuck on different pages . . .' Her voice trailed off as she did a silent count.

'Twenty-four in all, for the same Botanical Gardens. They go back twenty years, all of them but one!'

'The one that coincides with the disappearance of the water lily!' nodded Phil.

'They must be important, why else would she hold on to them?' wondered Fermina as she noted down the dates on the ticket stubs. She pocketed four of them and replaced the rest carefully on the same page she'd found them.

'Are they some sort of catalogue of all her visits to the gardens?' asked Phil, kneeling down on the floor beside Fermina. 'Or of all the plants she's stolen? The world's tiniest water lily is another thing but I can't imagine that she stole all these plants and hid them under her bed!'

Fermina gnawed at her fingernails. Phil was right—where were they? Plants were fragile, they needed light and air and the right soil . . . Fermina had nicked things before. It was time to think like a thief would. Where would Dr Bloom stow her precious plants so that they could thrive without being noticed? Her eyes fell upon the muddy hiking boots at the door. 'The Get Lost Forever Woods, Phil!' she exclaimed.

Phil turned the boots over. 'Look, fresh mud from a recent visit! Say, do you think Dr Bloom went into the woods the night the colonel thought we had intruders? Were those her footprints on the mud path?'

Fermina narrowed her eyes. 'She looks nimble enough to scale the back gate. And Volumina said that the twins were skulking about near the back gate that night too! Were they her lookout, perhaps?'

Phil shrugged. 'It does explain why the colonel swore that there were three intruders but we found only one set of footprints going in and out of the woods!'

'The question is, why would the twins do anything for Dr Bloom?'

Phil raised an eyebrow. 'Maybe they had a favour to return after she figured out they'd been snooping in her room?'

Fermina shivered. 'Who knows what favours we'll have to return if she finds us here!'

Just then, they heard footsteps. Hesitant, meek footsteps. 'Miss Nottynuf!' hissed Phil. 'She must have heard us in here!'

'Be still, she's probably returning to her own room, that's all!' hissed Fermina. 'It's the one next door, isn't it?'

The footsteps were drawing closer.

'We can't take any chances!' said Phil, pushing Fermina out into the hallway. His eyes darted around for an escape. The door marked PRINCIPAL! Miss Nottynuf would never come in there. He prayed that it was open as he gave Fermina a hard push towards it. They tumbled in, Phil landing upon Fermina with a thump that knocked the air out of her.

They crawled under the desk, his hand pressed to her mouth and a finger to his own lips. *Quiet!* The footsteps faded, just as he'd thought they would. They would have heaved a sigh of relief. If it weren't for the roaring sound of a heavy vehicle being driven rashly. Fermina shot up, her head hitting the desk—'Ouch! Are they back already?'

She stared out of the window in dismay. It was as Principal Perverse had always wanted—a window overlooking the front gates from where he could watch an unsuspecting child come to the school for the first time, or an unsuspecting child attempting to leave . . .

Now a certain rickety bus was making its way up the road, earlier than it should have.

Phil stated the obvious. 'We'll have to run again!'

Fermina lurched forward, stumbling over the mess on the floor. Why had Dr Bloom kept the principal's office in such a shambles? Books, papers, pencils with chewed ends—her own room had been neat enough! She followed a line of large ants with her eyes as they climbed over a black book. A familiar black book. The last surviving copy of the *Book of Rules*! Principal Perverse's own long-lost copy! 'Phil, look at this,' she began, but Phil's long arm snaked around the door and pulled her out.

Down the stairs they clattered now, hardly caring for what Miss Nottynuf might think. 'Around the back!' Phil shouted, and they were out the school building just as the first kids off the bus trickled in.

They skirted the swimming pool, crouching low to stay hidden. Cook Fracas was backing the bus out through the gates again. He would be dropping it off at the junkyard he'd picked it up from. Dr Bloom, a scarf wrapped about her face,

stole nervous glances towards the tower and scurried to the building.

At a window on the third floor, a pair of mousy eyes blinked through thick spectacles. 'Hurry, children!' whispered Miss Nottynuf, exhaling with relief as Phil and Fermina darted into the tower. In the nick of time. She hadn't meant to alarm them. At first, she'd visited the tower with some food, only to find Fermina gone. She'd peeked out of the window and seen shadows moving about in Dr Bloom's room. And then her eyes had fallen upon the well-thumbed book on the floor. *The Company of Crows*. She'd read the dog-eared pages and marvelled at the cleverness of the poor girl in the tower. How could she have missed it herself—how the crows had attacked Dr Bloom and no one else, how Dr Bloom had been wearing a scarf outdoors ever since.

And then Miss Nottynuf saw the bus winding its way back. So soon? She would have wrung her handkerchief but what good would that do anyone? Instead, she hurried back to the school building to warn the children but her footsteps drove them away. All the same.

She watched Phil sneak back to school. She only hoped that he had enough time to jump into bed in place of the pillows that he'd left there. They hadn't fooled her. She was certain they wouldn't fool Dr Bloom either.

CHAPTER 24

Mallus was hopping mad. He could have sworn that Dr Bloom had pushed him into the mud pond at the gardens on purpose! For certain, he'd leaned out a little too far over the railing, but he'd only meant to look as interested in all the boring weeds as that woodling! 'Look at that!' he'd shouted in the glasshouse, pointing to a bush of bright, fragrant flowers. 'Those are rare, aren't they?'

'They're only roses, you ninny!' Bat grinned and Mallus had decided, then and there, that that strong clip to the woodling's head was long overdue! He'd barely raised his hand and closed it into a fist when Dr Bloom cried, 'NO YOU DON'T!' and the next thing he knew, he'd tumbled head over heels into the mud.

Loud cries from the children, gasps of disbelief, Bat leaning over the railing now and saying, 'Come, give me your hand!'

'Not in a million years!' he snarled, blinking back tears of humiliation.

And then Malo, leaning over the railing and sticking out his *right* hand, for heaven's sake, in full view of the others! 'The *other* one,' Mallus insisted, flailing in the mud.

'Don't be a fool!' said Malo, who was done with all the

pretending. And that's when Mallus gave in to self-pity and sank back. He felt something go *squish* under him, not unlike the sound the chocolate cake had made under Volumina's bottom a few days ago! It was a priceless lotus, and as Mallus was not a Hindu goddess in the habit of sitting on one without crushing it, there was an irate shout from above his head.

'BOY, GET UP! TO YOUR FEET, YOU IMBECILE!'

Mallus had been called many things that day: a ninny, a fool, a nitwit and now an imbecile. *You're the imbecile!* he wanted to bellow back but a tiny detail stopped him: the irate man was in uniform. The man extended a pair of strong arms and lifted him out of the mud, his legs dangling below him. The man's face was so close to his now, Mallus could count every enlarged pore on his enlarged nose. Showing good sense for the first time that day, Mallus calculated that a strong clip to *this* man's head would only result in a broken fist. He decided to settle instead for some hard gulping and some heavy-duty gasping on the lines of, 'She pushed me!' 'Not my fault!' and 'Put me down, please, mister!'

The man whisked Mallus past the astonished children and through a glass door marked *Security* with a look of utter scorn on his face. Like he was carrying a specimen marked *World's Most Disgusting Child.*

'Where's your teacher?' he howled, replaying the disgraceful incident on his closed-circuit camera for other men and women in uniform, who all clucked their tongues in unison.

'There! Do you see? My teacher pushed me!' protested Mallus in vain, because all they had seen was Mallus picking a fight with Bat and then keeling over the railing.

Dr Bloom rushed in, red in the face. 'You fell over by yourself, you nasty boy. Whatever possessed you to lean so far out?'

There was much apologizing to be done—the rare lotus Mallus had fallen upon had certainly seen better days. 'We'll leave at once,' said Dr Bloom. 'This minute!' And all the way back, she sat in stony silence, her bag clutched close to her.

Malo was also furious. Mallus had refused to take his hand and ended up flattening a rare lotus instead. It wasn't fair of Mallus, making him pretend to be left-handed because their mother had been so hung up on the identical-pair business. Malo had learned how to write with his left hand, he'd learned to do everything with his left hand, really. But he slipped up. Once too often. Their plan to win back their mother's affection failed. And Mallus had never forgiven him for it. That was the whole trouble with keeping up a pretence. *Everyone* found out eventually.

He sat beside Mallus, who was all muddy and sulky. Malo tried not to care. He was tired of being one of a pair. Was it so wrong to want to be a *person* instead?

Mallus threw him a miserable look as if he could read his brother's thoughts. It made Malo squirm in his seat. He gave Mallus a reassuring pat on the shoulder, taking care to use his left hand this time. After all, he told himself, what sort of identical twins weren't totally identical?

Back in the tower, Fermina had her work cut out for her. She ran a finger down the list of dates that Phil and she had compiled from the ticket stubs in Dr Bloom's room. They went back twenty years. A theory was taking shape in Fermina's head but she needed to be certain.

She would never be able to find newspapers dating back twenty years, but she decided to read all four papers on the day the world's tiniest water lily was stolen. There was not a single story about the theft. It was decidedly odd! She unearthed the story dated 14 March, the one Ferg had found in the library and called all of them over to read. But that had been written a month later. Surely, there was a story written *right after* the theft occurred? Why couldn't she find it?

She paced the floor searching for an answer when it struck her. But of course! If the theft took place on 14 February, the story would only make it into the papers on 15 February. She'd been looking for the story on the wrong day! With renewed energy, she looked again. Nothing in the *Evening Gazette*; nothing in the *Herald* or the *Tribune* either. Nothing at all.

Her eyes fell on the *Daily Post*. It was buried deep in the paper, a news item so tiny, she might have missed it altogether if she hadn't been looking so hard. It was on page twenty-three:

What's the point?

Rumours are rife at the Botanical Gardens that the Valentine Thief is back.

She had barely read through the first line, but Fermina's hands were trembling already. Was Dr Bloom the Valentine Thief?

Twenty years ago, the gardens suffered a devastating spate of thefts that they have never quite recovered from. Rare horticultural species vanished, among them, the ibraltar campion and one of two Snowdonia hawkweeds that were the gardens' pride and joy.

'There were twenty-three thefts in all, over five years,' recalled manager Passiflora Patel, whose father worked here before her. 'And there was always a theft on Valentine's Day.'

Fermina's breath caught in her throat. Twenty-three thefts over five years. Fermina looked at the dates she had jotted down from the ticket stubs, counting again to be sure. Twenty-three visits to the gardens over five years—if you left out the most recent ticket stub from the day the water lily went missing. Did these twenty-three visits from twenty years ago coincide with the thefts that the manager in the news article was speaking of?

What riles the gardens more than the disappearance of the world's tiniest water lily is the indifference of the press and the

public. 'How can we be sure it's the only one of its kind in the world?' asked TV star Viktor Vapid. 'There might be others.'

'It's just an ordinary pink flower, who cares?' said a fashion stylist who doesn't want to be named.

The police don't care very much either. 'It's the first time in years that there's been a theft on Valentine's Day and they're already building theories about the Valentine Thief being back!' scoffed a highly placed officer. 'We've got real crimes to solve!'

'Like where some of the 1000 teachers from the Grand Party have disappeared to,' muttered Fermina absent-mindedly. She fidgeted with her braids, lost in thought. 'Or where the Grand Plan is.'

She shuffled through the four yellowed ticket stubs she'd snuck out of Dr Bloom's room. A set of half-faded numbers caught her eye. Not a date, but a price, *an entry charge*, and then the letters swam before her eyes. She looked at all four stubs carefully, her heart hammering in her chest. They said: *School Group Entry Charge.*

And then it struck her like a bolt of lightning. 'Did Dr Bloom take *school trips* to the Botanical Gardens twenty years ago?' Fermina whispered to herself. 'Was that school Horrid High?'

She staggered to the window. For a whole minute, she watched the congregation of crows at Dr Bloom's window and waited for her thoughts to settle.

Then she opened *The Company of Crows* to page seventy-two: *How long do crows live?*

Most crows die in the egg or as nestlings. But once they survive the first year of life, data indicates that they can live up to twenty years.

Long enough to remember a horrid teacher! Long enough to hold a grudge! She flipped her long braids from back to front. A plan was forming in her head. She grabbed a paper napkin from the day's lunch tray and started writing:

Dear Dr Bloom,

I am so sorry for what I did. Please forgive me.

Fermina

It was time to come down from the tower.

CHAPTER 25

The trip to the gardens had worn out the children. They were turning in early for the night when Fermina took them by surprise. 'I'm back!' she cried, flying into everyone's arms by turn. Everyone's but Bat's. After taking in Bat's runny nose and knotted hair, Fermina settled for a handshake instead.

The excitement of seeing Fermina again brought Volumina and Immy over from Centaur House. 'What took you so long to come downstairs?' they asked as the other children went to bed and the Sphinx common room emptied.

'Can't separate Ferm from her books!' joked Phil. 'We were on the brink of being discovered this afternoon, and yet, Ferm couldn't stop herself from grabbing a book in the principal's office!'

Fermina glowered at him. 'It wasn't *any* book, Phil! It was the principal's copy of the *Book of Rules*! And you didn't let me take it!'

Phil broke into a slow grin. 'That's because I took it for you!' He pointed to the loose floorboard. Back when the school was run by Principal Perverse, the loose floorboard had housed another treasure. There was a squeal of delight and loud protests from Phil as Ferm hugged him for the second time that day.

Ferg lifted the *Book of Rules* out gingerly as though it might bite him. He could still remember Principal Perverse dropping it into his hands when he first came to Horrid High . . .

'Look at this!' cried Phil, feeling oddly nostalgic. '*Rule number one: Children are not allowed to laugh!*'

'Remember this one?' said Fermina. '*Rule number thirty-eight: Children are not allowed to eat chocolates because chocolates cause tooth decay!*'

'We're still not allowed to eat chocolate,' muttered Immy, stroking Saltpetre on the head as though she understood how much he must miss it. 'Colonel Craven told Miss Nottynuf that children and cadets shouldn't eat any!'

'I can't bear to look at these horrid rules,' groaned Fermina, skimming all the way to the end and tossing the book back under the floorboard. 'Two hundred rules, as pointless then as they are now. I don't know why I even bothered retrieving this from that mess!'

The conversation turned to the events at the Botanical Gardens that day. Fermina teared up with laughter as they told her the full story of how Muddy Mallus had flailed about in the muck and been hauled out by a guard.

'I think Dr Bloom pushed him in,' said Ferg when the laughter subsided. 'But don't ask me why!'

'Perhaps she wanted to push Bat in for driving her nuts, but of course, she couldn't! Bat's her *favourite* person these days!' teased Phil.

'I'm not anyone's favourite person!' retorted Bat. 'But I do enjoy the effect that any talk about the woods has on her!'

'And I think I'm beginning to see why,' said Fermina. She lowered her voice and filled the others in about everything she'd discovered up in the Tower Library. The crows, the attack on Dr Bloom, the ticket stubs with a *School Group Entry Charge* on them, the Valentine Thief.

'So Dr Bloom is a notorious plant thief!' exclaimed Immy. 'And *that's* where she stashes her loot, her rare herbs and prized flowers!'

'In the Get Lost Forever Woods!' nodded Bat. 'Where no one will give them a second glance.'

'Don't forget, she's probably a horrid teacher too!' added Fermina. 'I think she taught here years ago and took class trips to the Botanical Gardens.'

'The perfect alibi for the perfect theft!' said Ferg. A strange look came over him now. 'Come to think of it, I now know where I've seen her before.'

Ferg recounted how the horrid teachers had swarmed into school the day of the Grand Party. Only one had come on horseback, his hair streaming loose behind him, almost trampling over the others.

'I mistook her for a man that day, she's tall enough!' said Ferg.

'But Dr Bloom wears her hair tied all the time,' said Fermina. 'And it's golden brown—'

'Golden brown with *dark roots*!' said Ferg. His voice had

the sort of certainty in it that had annoyed Fermina so much before he'd disappeared into the woods. Only, now it didn't. 'She's worn it loose ever since—'

'Ever since the colonel left,' Volumina broke in. 'Ever since she became principal and she could let down her guard!'

Phil snorted. 'She's hardly fit to be principal! The office has been turned upside down!' He thought of the papers and books lying askew. 'Granny would never have left it that way and Colonel Craven was too disciplined.'

Fermina shook her head. 'It's funny, her own room was so neat by comparison!'

Ferg straightened up. 'Wait a minute, do you think the principal's office was a mess because Dr Bloom was looking for something there? Something that she didn't mind turning everything upside down for?'

'It would explain why she's back,' agreed Phil, recalling the disarray. 'What do you think she could be looking for?'

'It certainly wasn't the *Book of Rules,*' cried Fermina. 'No one has any need for 200 pointless rules that should have been burnt with the other copies.'

Ferg's ears were tingling like they would fall right off. What had Principal Perverse told him that first day? 'There are 300 rules in here and rules, as you know, are EVERYTHING!'

He gripped Fermina's arm and tried to keep his voice calm. 'Did you say *200* pointless rules?'

Fermina had apologized to Dr Bloom but not even this could cheer up Muddy Mallus. His brother and he were the laughing stock of the school. 'We're freaks!' Mallus muttered. 'Identical twins who aren't identical!'

They're laughing because you fell into the lotus pond, Malo wanted to say but he bit his tongue. Mallus was overreacting but pointing this out wouldn't help him any. Not now, anyway.

'Cheer up!' Malo said. 'At least we have our things back! And we didn't have to ask for them. It's a victory for us, isn't it?' He pointed at the clothes. They were on their beds, folded in a neat pile. Courtesy the Filch girl, of course. Malo slipped into the same pyjamas as his brother, even though his heart was not in it. 'Wait, what's this?'

It was a newspaper cutting sitting at the bottom of the clothes pile. An article from a science journal titled: *Are you a mirror-image twin?* Malo started reading. '*Researchers have yet to explain why one in four sets of identical twins is asymmetrical.*'

But he couldn't get any further. 'I don't want to listen to that rubbish!' cried Mallus, burrowing inside his blanket. 'I'll tear it up if you don't stop!'

It didn't seem like rubbish to Malo, but this wasn't the time to make a point. 'You're right, who can trust anything left behind by that *Filth* girl?' said Malo. He hated calling her Fermina Filth, but he knew his brother would approve.

'Do you think even Dr Bloom can tell us apart now?' asked Mallus, his voice sounding small. 'Is that why she isn't interested in us any more?'

Mallus was right, they were no longer Dr Bloom's favourites. But it wasn't because she could tell them apart. It was because the woodling had made quite an impression on her. The more Malo thought about it, the less he cared about the tiresome business of pleasing Dr Bloom. If he could have his way, he'd refuse to carry out the job she'd just given them. But he wasn't doing it for her, he told himself, he was doing it for Mallus.

'If we do this tonight, we'll get back into Dr Bloom's good books, just you see!' Malo told his brother. He stuffed the news cutting under his pillow with his left hand. God knows, being right-handed had caused enough trouble already!

'I hope so!' Mallus whispered back as the lights went out. He sounded better already.

It was the middle of the night when Volumina slunk back to Centaur House, her head reeling with everything they'd discovered. A secret compartment inside the *Book of Rules!* They would never have found it if Ferg hadn't reminded everyone that there were 300 rules in all.

She started. She'd heard a sound. Maybe it was nothing but her own wakefulness. She would never be able to fall asleep, not after everything that had happened that night! Page 200 had been stuck to the back of the book but Phil had prised it up carefully with a pocket knife. Beneath, they'd found the last 100 pages pasted together in one solid block and a tiny cubbyhole cut out in the centre of it. It was no larger than the space required to store two pencils. Instead, it had a paper neatly folded inside it. A paper with 1000 names on it. *A thousand horrid names.*

Volumina scurried past the stairwell when a movement caught her eye. The glimmer of a hand sliding down the banister. A *second* hand. The twins! They were tiptoeing down the stairs to the ground floor. Where were they going in the dead of night? Nowhere good, she felt certain.

Volumina darted back towards Sphinx House to fetch the others and then she stopped herself. If she didn't follow the twins now, she'd lose them. She planted one foot on the top stair, undecided. Being near the twins always got her into trouble. But the next foot followed and before Volumina knew it, she was headed downstairs on the heels of the Brace boys, no matter where they took her.

Past the kitchen and the dining room they went, past the classrooms even, but just as Volumina felt certain that they were headed outside, they stopped. In front of two large double doors that had been shut ever since the Grand Party. For a moment, Volumina closed her eyes and floated back to that day. The churn of horrid teachers pouring in past those double doors, the noise, the rowdy merrymaking, Miss Lavina Loathsome doing the Beastly Boogie . . . the Great Hall. How many times had the children shuddered while passing the Great Hall at merely the thought of what lay on the other side?

An image of Principal Perverse's black whip and his ridiculous velvet chair rose up in Volumina's mind. The Throne. The double doors swung open and the twins went in. Volumina slipped in behind them as stealthily as she could, but it took every ounce of willpower not to cry out in fear. There they were, the whip and the Throne, as though they had sprung out of her worst nightmares and taken solid shape before her eyes. In a glass case.

Volumina's feet were stuck to the ground now, as if spellbound. The twins had no such fears. They hadn't been to Horrid High when it was at its most horrid. They knew nothing of the perils of Principal Perverse and the whip he wielded. Volumina's hand flew to her mouth as the twins produced a key and deftly opened the glass case. *How did they get their hands on the key?*

They had climbed inside the case now. Volumina had half a mind to spring up and lock them in. But the key was in Malo's hand as the boys crouched down beside the chair, patting it, running their fingers over the smooth cushioning, stroking the legs. *What are they doing?* wondered Volumina. Malo had crawled under the Throne now, he was knocking on the underside of it as if to check for a hollow space in it.

Volumina risked two steps forward. The Great Hall was dark. As long as she stayed out of the shaft of light spilling in from the hallway, she'd be fine. But she brushed against something and the boys stiffened. They'd heard her! Volumina cursed herself, she was simply too large to be stealthy.

In a trice, Mallus had grabbed the whip. Both boys jumped out of the case. Mallus was winding the whip around his hand now. Malo was swinging the door of the glass case shut and turning the key. They were stealing the whip! Without another thought, Volumina jumped out of the shadows shouting, 'NO YOU DON'T!'

She was upon Mallus now. Hands flying, legs flailing, a gasp as her elbow struck the floor, the clatter of a key falling as three figures grappled in the darkness.

'Give me that!'

'Take your hands off it!'

Volumina pitted her strength against both boys. The struggle turned into a tug of war. Volumina wrested the whip from the boys and curled her fingers about the handle; the boys grabbed the other end. Everyone pulled. Everyone grunted.

And the whip came apart! Volumina hurtled backward as the handle came free in her hands. Something white slipped out of the open end of the handle. The twins fell the other way, the whip-end closed inside their hands. They staggered to their feet. A shadow appeared in the door, small and frail against the light outside. 'What's happening here?'

Miss Nottynuf! The twins dropped the whip and rushed past her, out of the Great Hall and into the hallway, almost knocking her down. Volumina stayed, expecting what she had always come to expect when she was around the twins. Trouble.

'Give me that!' said Miss Nottynuf, her face stern. She bent down to pick up the whip and the key. Then she put her hand out for the handle. 'Now!'

'Is it broken?' asked Volumina. She was in so much trouble now!

'It is,' came Miss Nottynuf's quiet reply. 'Now, go!'

Go? Volumina could scarcely believe her ears. Why was Miss Nottynuf letting her off the hook? She shuffled to the door. There was no point telling Miss Nottynuf that the twins had led her here, that they were stealing the whip and that she had only tried to stop them.

'One more thing,' said Miss Nottynuf.

Ah, there it was! Volumina steeled herself for the punishment.

But Miss Nottynuf was staring at the rolled-up paper that had fallen out of the hollow handle of the whip.

'I think you should have this,' she said.

CHAPTER 26

Miss Nottynuf was surprised. The whip was not broken, as she'd first assumed. Instead, it seemed that the whip was *meant* to come apart and it was just as easily put back together. She returned it to the glass case and left the key in the keyhole. Then she walked upstairs to Dr Bloom's room in the dead of night and knocked.

The door was flung open in a trice. 'Have you got it? Oh!' Dr Bloom looked shocked to see Miss Nottynuf. 'It's-it's you!' she stuttered.

Were you expecting someone else? The question leapt into Miss Nottynuf's head, unbidden. 'It's l-late!' said Dr Bloom. 'I was sleeping!'

Miss Nottynuf tried not to stare at Dr Bloom. She looked like she'd been caught unawares but she certainly didn't look sleepy. Why, she wasn't even in her nightclothes! 'May we speak in private?' she whispered, gently squeezing past Dr Bloom into the room.

'Er, of course, but *now? Here?*'

Miss Nottynuf nodded, plonking herself down on Dr Bloom's bed and noting that the bed was still made.

'I heard noises from downstairs,' Miss Nottynuf said,

scanning Dr Bloom's face for a reaction. Nothing. 'The noises were coming from the Great Hall . . .' Miss Nottynuf paused on purpose. Nothing. 'I think someone was trying to steal the whip from its glass case.'

A barely perceptible clenching of Dr Bloom's jaw. 'Did you see who they were?'

They? Miss Nottynuf curled her fingers around her handkerchief and squeezed it hard. *She knew!*

Miss Nottynuf shook her head. 'I think I frightened them off. They left the key in the keyhole.'

Did Dr Bloom's shoulders relax just a little? 'Thank you for bringing this to my attention!' she said. 'I'll go down and take a look. We'll find out who's behind this tomorrow, don't worry.'

Miss Nottynuf got up to go. She had a fair sense of who was behind this. And she was certainly worried.

The twins were playing the blame game.

'*You* dropped the key!' said Mallus.

'And *you* dropped the whip!' said Malo.

'I couldn't hold on forever on my own with her tugging on the other side, could I?' grumbled Mallus. 'What were *you* doing?'

'Figuring out which hand to use!' retorted Malo. He'd sneaked a peek at the news cutting Fermina had left them. The words rang in his ears:

Researchers have yet to explain why one in four sets of identical twins is asymmetrical: one will be right-handed, the other left-handed . . .

'You're having no trouble figuring out which hand to use right now,' said Mallus, eyeing the way Malo was spooning porridge into his mouth with his right hand. Malo shifted the spoon to his left hand guiltily and put the news cutting out of his mind.

'What do we tell Dr Bloom?' asked Mallus.

'Speak of the devil,' said Malo, gulping hard. Dr Bloom's nostrils were pinched with displeasure as she towered above them. 'Upstairs, to my office!' she said, her voice a low growl.

The boys had never seen her this livid. Dr Bloom paced the room like a tiger in a cage. 'Have you forgotten that we had a deal? That we agreed to make trouble at Horrid High?' she spat out the words. 'Tell me, isn't that what you do best?'

Mallus and Malo nodded mutely. 'I protected you after I caught you snooping in my room! I appointed you school prefects! And this is how you repay me?'

The boys kept mum.

'It was an open-and-shut case of search the chair, bring the whip to me, blame the fat girl,' said Dr Bloom through clenched teeth. 'And what do you buffoons do? You go and bungle things!'

Mallus opened his mouth to speak but Dr Bloom raised her hand. 'Don't! Miss Nottynuf told me everything!'

Everything? The boys felt destroyed. 'You're lucky she didn't see you! Imagine how furious I was when I found the whip in its glass case and *this* dangling in the keyhole!'

The boys gasped as Dr Bloom held up the key. How on earth did this happen? They could swear that they'd dropped both the key and the whip, and the whip had been in two pieces!

Dr Bloom's fingers curled around the key as though she wanted to crush it.

'You've always played your pranks to perfection, so I asked you to play a few for me. What's different now? Wait!' She drew closer, peering at them through narrowed eyes. '*You're* different now. *Different from each other . . .*'

The boys squirmed. They were dressed in identical clothes again, but they'd been having disagreements all week. They'd never felt less like twins.

'If you're keeping something from me, there's only one way to find out.' Dr Bloom's voice was tight. 'Leave the room and shut the door behind you.'

The twins got up to go, relieved.

'No, not you,' said Dr Bloom, looking straight at Malo. 'You'll stay, your brother can wait outside. Let's see if your versions of what happened last night are *identical*, shall we?'

Malo's heart sank like an anchor. He heard his brother close the door softly behind him. Dr Bloom was determined to find out the truth and Malo was determined to keep the truth from her.

'It was dark,' he began, buying time to think. 'We went downstairs to do what you had told us to.'

'Hurry up!' Dr Bloom lashed out. Malo flinched as though he'd been touched by a real whip. His mind raced ahead. What should he say next?

'Then we heard footsteps!'

'Whose footsteps?'

'Miss Nottynuf's!' lied Malo. 'We panicked and ran back upstairs.'

'So I was right!' Dr Bloom's breath was hot on Malo's face. 'You didn't so much as *touch* the whip! You wimped out after making enough noise to wake up the school!' It was the perfect story. It was what Dr Bloom believed anyway. Malo hung his head, looking appropriately ashamed. 'If you're lying, your brother's account of things will be different, you know,' she said, her grip crushing him as she led him to the door. 'Send your twin in!'

Malo rubbed his arm where she'd held it. He could feel a bruise coming on. Mallus would give them all away, poor Volumina too. He would certainly tell Dr Bloom about how the whip had come apart as they struggled, how Volumina had dropped the handle and how they'd seen a slim scroll of paper inside it. The palms of his hands felt clammy. They were done for.

It wasn't long before the door had been yanked open and Mallus had been shoved out roughly in the same manner. 'Out!' screamed Dr Bloom. 'I'm done with the two of you!'

'Wha-what happened?' stuttered Malo as the door slammed shut behind them.

'I told her the truth,' said Mallus. Malo's heart sank. It was just as he'd feared. But Mallus broke into a slow, lopsided grin that inched up on the left. 'Up to the point where we went downstairs . . . And then I decided that I didn't need to tell her about Volumina, not when Miss Nottynuf hadn't. Or about the whip and what's inside it. If that's what she's looking for, let her go find it herself!'

Malo broke into a slow, lopsided grin that inched up on the right. 'And?'

'And there's nothing more to it, is there?' said Mallus. 'I jumped to the part where we heard footsteps. Told her what she believed anyway, that we lost our nerve and turned tail! She doesn't think too highly of us now that we've confirmed her worst hunch about us, that we're a pair of chicken-hearted wusses!'

'I guess we're on our own now!' said Malo, expecting his brother to whip himself into a panic. Didn't he always?

But twin brothers can be full of surprises sometimes. 'We have each other, don't we?' said Mallus. 'Now, do you still have it?'

For the first time in days, Malo understood what his brother meant right away. They had never felt more like twins as they walked down the stairs together to the Centaur dorm. Malo slid the news cutting out from under his pillow. 'Ready for this?' he asked Mallus.

Researchers have still to explain why one in four sets of identical twins is asymmetrical: one will be right-handed, the other left-handed; one will part her hair to the right, the other to the left; one will always stand on the right in family photos, the other on the left. When asymmetrical twins look at each other—

'It's like looking in a mirror,' both twins read aloud. They looked up and saw each other properly for the first time.

'Look what I have here!' cried Volumina and Fermina in unison, and they weren't even twins.

Miss Nottynuf had given the class the morning off. 'I don't think it'll hurt to take a break from decimals,' she'd said, looking pointedly at Volumina. 'Some of you might have other things on your *hands*!'

Volumina tightened her grip on the paper that had fallen out of the handle of the whip last night.

'You go first,' Volumina and Fermina both said together again. Volumina was only being gracious. She had taken a quick look at the scroll in her hand and she knew how important it was.

'No, you!' Also together.

'Aaaargh, you sound like the Brace boys now!' cried the others.

So Fermina went first. She'd nipped up to the Tower

Library earlier that morning on a hunch that paid off. There, the *Daily Post* headlines caught her eye: *Has the Valentine Thief struck again?*

> *This Thursday, not even two months after the Botanical Gardens lost the world's tiniest water lily to a theft, a rare flowering plant disappeared.*

'Yesterday!' gasped Volumina, 'all but forgetting that what she had to share was more important. 'We were probably at the gardens when this happened!'

The children were huddled in the half-dug trench that Volumina had fallen into a few days ago. No one would come looking for them here—they had no intention of getting called back to class halfway through such an important discussion.

> *It may seem like an ordinary rose bush with bright pink flowers, but it is one of the rarest plants in the world. Once feared extinct, it has no more of its kind in the wild now.*
>
> *'It's a terrible loss for us!' said Passiflora Patel, the manager of the gardens. 'The Middlemist's Red was one of our most prized plants!'*

'The Middlemist's Red!' gasped Bat, clutching Ferg's sleeve hard. 'I saw Dr Bloom staring at it before we entered the glasshouse. I made a mental note of its name!'

According to security guards at the gardens, Thursday was a busy day with many school groups . . .

The children gulped. That meant them. 'Wait, there's more,' said Fermina.

. . . and a minor mishap near the lotus pond had garden staff in a tizzy.

The children groaned. If only Muddy Mallus hadn't chosen that precise moment to fall into the pond!

'What if he didn't fall in by accident?' said Ferg. 'What if Dr Bloom pushed him in? It would be the perfect diversion!'

'It would certainly give her time to nick the Middlemist's Red,' agreed Bat, wiping her nose with the back of her hand. 'No wonder she was in such a tearing hurry to leave and clutched her bag close to her all the way here!'

'No wonder she was holed up in her room all evening after we got back too!' said Immy. 'Probably potted the plant for later, until she could take it into the woods!'

'Do you suppose that everything she ever stole from the gardens is in those woods?' whispered Phil.

'A cache of rare specimens, the last of their kind, left behind for safekeeping . . .' pondered Ferg. It was a staggering thought.

'If you'd left your life's treasures in those woods, they'd draw you back, wouldn't they?' said Bat. 'To Horrid High?'

'The woods,' nodded Volumina, who had waited long enough. 'But something else too. Something that she might have turned the principal's office upside down for, but not found.'

She straightened out the rolled-up paper she'd held on to so patiently. 'Miss Nottynuf said we should have this.'

'What is it?' cried the others, leaning forward to take a look.

Volumina flushed as she felt everyone's eyes upon her. 'The Grand Plan.'

CHAPTER 27

There were two pages to the Grand Plan. The trench was a tight fit for the children and they jostled each other for a better look. Page one was written by Principal Perverse. It bore all the marks of being his, and Immy decided to read aloud in the principal's own high-pitched, nasal voice.

'Horrid schools are the need of the hour. Too long have we been gulled into believing that education should be fun, that schools should be happy. This grand delusion needs a Grand Plan to correct it!'

More nonsense followed about how children were too happy these days for their own good, how a crackdown on horrid schools had forced horridness to go underground.

'The Grand Plan is revolutionary. It will transform Horrid High into Horrid High International, a chain of horrid schools in distant countries where schools of any sort are unheard of.'

'Horrid High *International*? Really?' marvelled Phil.

'Revolutionary!' scoffed Fermina, shaking her head in

disbelief. 'Principal Perverse never passes up an opportunity to pat himself on the back!'

'Hush!' said Immy. 'Listen!' She put on her Principal Perverse voice again.

'Horrid High International is a global vision of horridness, a selfless mission to set up horrid schools in the poorest, most remote corners of the planet where the wretched natives—'

'Natives!' erupted Phil. 'That's preposterous!'

'You mean pompous?' cut in Ferg.

'Shhhhh!' said the others.

'. . . where the wretched natives will wring their grimy hands in gratitude for a school where they can dump their children and forget about them! Where no school inspectors will come snooping around, where no school boards will need answering to!'

'I wish we had one of Miss Verbose's dictionaries here to look up all the possible synonyms for "conceited fool"!' muttered Ferg.

'He's no fool,' said Immy, who had read further while waiting for her friends to fall silent.

'This is our proudest moment! Twenty years after we embarked on our noble mission, we have trained 1000 horrid teachers on the

hallowed grounds of Horrid High in the fine art of being horrid! Now they are ready to become horrid principals at 1000 horrid schools, to inspire and lead more horrid teachers everywhere.'

'That's why they came flocking: Lavina Loathsome, Harvinder Heckle, Clammy Curmagin, the whole lot of them!' said Phil. 'They hoped that there was something in it for them and there was!'

'The chance to be horrid principals!' said Fermina. 'Although I wonder where they'd get the money from to build all these schools? Most of the kids here are orphans and runaways, and such children don't—'

'Cough up any fees,' Bat nodded.

'Is there a polite way for me to tell you both to shut up and let me read?' asked Immy.

'It will take money to build 1000 horrid schools in 1000 distant places, but not too much of it. Our horrid schools will come up in swamps and jungles, far from civilization, in inhospitable and uninhabitable places.'

'Oh, great!' muttered Phil. 'It looks like he wants to create a thousand copies of this wonderful establishment!'

'Shut up!' said Immy, dispensing with courtesy as she continued.

'There will be no need to splurge on all the facilities that happy

schools provide. No beds, no tables, no chairs, no blackboards, just four walls and a roof, although we can do away with the roof too.'

'Do away with the roof!' spluttered Volumina, even though they had all vowed to hold their tongues till Immy was done reading.

'Might as well send everyone into the Get Lost Forever Woods,' sniggered Bat. More shushing.

'Covetus Clutch, our most accomplished alumnus, has gallantly pledged all the funds we will need for this Grand Plan of ours.'

'Who is this gallant villain and where did he crawl out from?' cried Fermina.

'It says so here, doesn't it?' said Immy, a little exasperated. 'Some alumnus of the school! Now, please, no interruptions!'

The others stifled a laugh in spite of the sombre mood. Reading aloud brought out Immy's bossiest side.

'Mr Clutch came to Horrid High a penniless orphan and he is a multimillionaire today. Horrid High made him what he is and he is committed to the cause of preserving horrid schools for generations to come.'

'Sounds like a fun sort of guy,' muttered Ferg, earning a glare from Immy as she continued. 'The first horrid schools will come up where Mr Clutch already has business interests and enjoys substantial influence. (See map).'

There was a sharp intake of breath as the children turned to page two. The map of the world with 1000 black dots marked on it.

A gentle breeze blew but it made the children shiver. They were not identical like the twins but they all had an identical thought: *Thousands upon thousands of children, trudging to horrid schools everywhere.* It was all too much to take in!

'We have the list of 1000 horrid teachers and the Grand Plan, what do we do now?' asked Fermina, breaking the silence at last.

'Go to class!' said Volumina, who had just stood up to stretch her legs. Miss Nottynuf was walking towards them, no doubt, to call them back to class. But as she drew closer, it was clear that their teacher was in no shape to teach decimals. It was obvious she'd been crying. Her nose was pink, her spectacles were smudged.

'I saw you from the Tower Library,' she said, sniffling. She glanced at the newspaper in Fermina's hand. 'So you've seen the news?'

'We all have,' said Fermina, a little baffled. While the theft of the Middlemist's Red was a terrible thing, it certainly hadn't moved them to tears!

'Oh, my dear children!' cried Miss Nottynuf, sliding into the trench without any concern for her clothes. 'Come to me, all of you!' And she threw her arms around them, hugging them and sobbing without any sign of stopping. The children exchanged puzzled looks as they were being smothered by Miss Nottynuf. 'The last of her kind and she's gone!' she wailed.

'Maybe she really loved the Middlemist's Red,' whispered Bat.

But Ferg's ears were tingling so hard now, it was unbearable. He snatched the newspaper from Fermina and pointed at the front page. To the story headlined *Has the Valentine Thief struck again?*

'You mean this, don't you, Miss Nottynuf?'

But Miss Nottynuf was crying harder as she flipped the pages roughly to page twenty-two. Her fingers were trembling so hard, she could barely point at the tiny story at the bottom of the page. The children found it anyway: *Jungle-tromping conservationist disappears in the Amazon.*

Granny Grit was gone.

CHAPTER 28

Bat was in the principal's office and she was in a fix. The Cold, The Cough and The Fit were losing their sheen. She'd rolled her eyes back in her head but Dr Bloom had stopped her mid-roll with a 'No more of that, please!' She'd retched and snorted but there is only so much nose-goo that one tiny girl can produce at a time. She'd even gone for a new variation called The Tremor, but Dr Bloom was adamant. 'We go into the woods this afternoon, just you and me, no arguments!'

The more Dr Bloom wanted to go into the Get Lost Forever Woods, the less Bat wanted to take her.

Dr Bloom restrained a shudder as she watched the child slouch in a chair and sulk. When the child sulked, she was positively ugly. At least there was no green gob hanging off her nostrils today.

'Show up at the back gate at four, my dear,' said Dr Bloom, trying not to focus on how furiously the blasted child was digging her nose. And now the urchin was clasping her hand with those same, cursed, nose-digging fingers as Dr Bloom showed her out.

As soon as the wretched creature had left, Dr Bloom fished out a bottle of sanitizer and sloshed its contents all over her hands. She was weighing the idea of spraying the room with air freshener, when the phone rang. Not the phone on the principal's desk but the little cell phone that belonged to her. Only one person ever called on that cell phone. Dr Bloom grimaced in anticipation.

'Grandma's dead!' shrieked the horrid head, hooting with laughter.

'She is?' cried Dr Bloom, quite taken by surprise. Of course she'd known that Granny Grit had booked a one-way ticket to the Amazon, but even then, one had to be kind to the elderly. 'Was she annihilated by an anaconda? Wiped out by a waterfall? Consumed by a caiman?'

'Maybe she met a less spectacular end?' said the horrid voice. 'Dropped her glasses and tripped in the undergrowth, half blind, or dropped off to sleep too close to the river and rolled right in, or forgot which way to go after her fading memory betrayed her . . .'

'Poor old dear!' said Dr Bloom, sparing a thought for the aged.

'I'll get to know the delicious details in good time,' said the horrid voice, 'but for now, we'll have to satisfy ourselves with a small mention on page twenty-two of the *Daily Post*. I mean, who cares, grannies die all the time, don't they?' More loud hooting interspersed by the frightened yipping of a lemur in the background.

'Grannies belong in rocking chairs, nodding off to sleep with knitting needles in their hands,' said Dr Bloom. The horrid head was in a good mood and Dr Bloom relaxed a little. It felt wonderful to let her hair down, to pull out all the pins that had held it tightly in place and to savour the feeling that she ruled the roost now. She was queen bee and this was her domain. Dr Bloom leaned back in the chair at the thought.

'Have you found the Grand Plan?'

The question came out of nowhere and rattled Dr Bloom out of her reverie. She gritted her teeth in exasperation. Hadn't she looked for that blasted Grand Plan everywhere? In the principal's office, in the glass case, in that abysmally boring *Book of Rules*? 'I've looked everywhere, I've practically excavated the principal's office. I'm beginning to wonder, maybe Principal Perverse didn't put the Grand Plan into writing?'

'Of course it's in writing!' snapped the horrid head. 'It has my signature on it! I'm coming there myself to get it if you won't!'

'No!' Dr Bloom cried out in dismay, before quickly adding, 'What I mean is, there's no need for that!' Her voice took on a whining quality. 'It'll be hard to explain, really!'

'I'm sure you'll come up with the right story,' said the horrid voice, frighteningly calm now. 'I'll be there tomorrow.'

Tomorrow! Dr Bloom cursed modern air travel as she slumped against the desk.

'One last thing,' said the horrid voice and Dr Bloom snapped back to attention. 'You didn't take the last Middlemist's Red in the world, did you? Because *if you did* . . .'

'I didn't,' bluffed Dr Bloom, thinking of how much she'd have liked to pluck out every last hair on that horrid head.

'You *know* I've always wanted it . . .'

The horrid head sounded twenty years younger now, petulant, like the teenager he'd been all those years ago at Horrid High, the teenager with the legendary tantrums, the teenager who wanted everything.

'You know who gets to keep it, right?' The horrid voice was grating at her nerves now. If only she'd given him a good walloping when he was half her size, she thought wistfully. Well, he was still half her size but he had all the money in the world now.

'I don't have it,' said Dr Bloom. It wasn't entirely a lie. She'd planted it outside the woods last night, beside the mud path. She'd have liked to leave it inside the woods but without that ugly child's help, she didn't dare to venture in.

'I hope that's true!' said the horrid head before ringing off.

Dr Bloom sighed. She was certain she'd never find the Grand Plan, even if she bulldozed this place down. But if she didn't let him come and see for himself that the Grand Plan was lost beyond finding, he'd call off the deal.

For years, he'd threatened to tell on her after he'd found out that she was the Valentine Thief. Not found out. *Guessed.* She hadn't come to teach at Horrid High twenty years ago because she loved children. After all, who did? She'd come to Horrid High because of the school's location. Close enough to the Botanical Gardens to visit them again and again. She had the perfect crime planned out and the perfect alibi. No one thought anything of a science teacher bringing groups of excited children to the gardens on a field trip. Even if a few plants and rare flowers vanished after her visits, plants that she'd never have the money to go looking for in wild, far-off places.

No one thought too much of a science teacher lingering in a small patch of land behind the school, tending her little collection and watching it grow. No one but him. He was a horrid orphan in his teens then. He'd promised to keep her little secret. For a price.

A few years later, when he'd made his money, he sent her off to rove the planet. To find him every last known blossom, every last known shrub. Her travels took her far from Horrid High, far from her precious plants. She gave them up for dead. They would waste away without her.

And then she returned for the Grand Party, many years later, and found that the little plot behind the school had burgeoned into a dreaded wood! It even had a dreaded name now. No one dared go in. No one who went in came out. It drove her mad, the little niggling hope that her precious plants might have survived. She couldn't bear not knowing.

She began to want nothing more than to return to school, and now she was back. At last. Because of the deal. He'd promised her that if she found the Grand Plan, he would set her free. She would no longer be his errand girl. Instead, he'd let her be principal of Horrid High for as long as she lived.

She would never leave again. She would return to the woods and she would tend them to become her own private Botanical Gardens. And no, this time, he would not come to know of them. She could not have him clamouring at her heels, eager to take everything that was hers. Her precious woods were not for sale for all the money in the world! Which meant that that pleasant little afternoon excursion of hers would just have to wait till the horrid head had come and gone.

'This is the time for new beginnings!' proclaimed Dr Bloom, standing on the stage in the Great Hall and speaking to all the children. They were crying, and although it was mostly because Granny Grit was gone, it was also because of the way Dr Bloom had broken the news to them. 'She died of old age, I'm sure, nothing too painful or bloody!'

Miss Nottynuf was wringing her handkerchief. Even Cook Fracas was wiping away tears—'She was always kind to my Gypsy!'

'Now don't you worry, you're all in safe hands with me,' said Dr Bloom. 'We'll throw the gates of the school wide open! We'll fill up all the trenches the colonel had us dig! Why, we'll even get our poor cook a new goat!'

Cook Fracas bawled, 'Not a new goat!' he wailed. 'There can only be one Gypsy!'

Dr Bloom's face hardened. This was proving to be more

difficult than she'd thought. These wretched children were like leaky faucets, they would never stop crying! Ferg thought of how he'd met Granny Grit for the first time. Phil thought of how Granny always roared loudest at his jokes. Immy thought of Granny's four chihuahuas. And Volumina thought of how Granny had believed in her when no one else had.

Dr Bloom shifted impatiently on stage. 'Tomorrow, we have a visitor. A renowned conservationist, an educationist, a philanthropist.' She held up three fingers and paused to think—had she said it all? The horrid head did have an interest in conserving rare plants and animals, if only for himself. And he did believe in education—a horrid education. As for philanthropy, well, that was a bit of a stretch, but two out of three wasn't a bad score!

'THE GREAT, THE ESTEEMED, THE HONOURABLE COVETUS CLUTCH!' she said, trying to sound more excited than she really felt. Fermina gripped Ferg's arm tightly and howled. The man who had funded the Grand Plan was coming to Horrid High. Could things get any worse?

'He's an absolute delight, my dear children!' fibbed Dr Bloom. An absolute fright was more like it. 'He's a prominent alumnus of this great school and he's coming here to tell you how Horrid High made him who he is . . .'

She trailed off as she counted his many qualities in her head: selfish, greedy, calculating, bullying—what, were the children still crying? *Still?*

'His story will inspire you at this difficult time,' she

continued brightly. 'You, too, can study at Horrid High and grow up to be like him!'

The children broke into fresh bouts of sobbing. 'We can't forget Granny Grit!' wailed a child from behind. 'Never!' mewled another. 'We'll remember her always!' whined a third.

Dr Bloom nodded sympathetically. Of course she understood! Why, if Granny Grit had chosen a slightly more convenient time to die, Dr Bloom would be in the woods now.

Through her sniffles, Miss Nottynuf snuck a peek out of the principal's office window. Dr Bloom was downstairs, scarf tied firmly around her face, shouting instructions at the poor children. They were filling up the trenches with shovels that were too heavy for them. All in preparation for a dreadful man called Covetus Clutch!

She flopped against Dr Bloom's desk. *Granny Grit's desk,* she corrected herself. It would always be Granny's desk, even though she was gone. She choked back a sob. She'd tried everything, hadn't she? Found the lost children in the woods, left Phil and Fermina to snoop around Dr Bloom's office, given Volumina what she'd found inside the whip. Miss Nottynuf allowed herself to wallow one last time in self-pity, and then she squared her chin and straightened up.

The children had the Grand Plan and the horrid list now. There was enough proof to arrest Dr Bloom and Covetus

Clutch. Surely, there was nothing to worry about. Or was there? What if police squads descended on the school, sirens blaring, and Dr Bloom got away? She'd given them the slip before. Miss Nottynuf allowed herself to tremble at the thought. As for Covetus Clutch, he was a powerful man, and powerful men have a way of escaping the consequences of their actions.

There was nothing else to be done. Miss Nottynuf set her worries aside and resolved to call the police. But before she could pick up the phone, it rang.

'Well, hello!' A tremulous voice assaulted Miss Nottynuf's ears. It took off at a thousand words a minute without introducing itself. Something about how the dear girl was just tired of being on an endless book tour, and how she hungered to meet her friends at Horrid High and read from her book to them, and what a treat that would be!

Who was this? Miss Nottynuf might have asked, but she could not squeeze in a word edgeways. Her eyes fell upon the calendar on the desk. There! She had her answer. Today's date was circled in red. And what had Granny Grit scribbled in the margin there? *Mrs Telltale's next call! Avoid at all cost!*

So it was Mrs Telltale's voice on the other end! Why, Mrs Telltale was so much in the throes of her speech, she hadn't even realized that someone other than Granny Grit had answered her call!

'. . . and the *Daily Post* has proposed a special back-to-school story!' Mrs Telltale was saying now.

'*Daily Post*?' Miss Nottynuf's hand flew to her mouth. She hadn't meant to speak but Mrs Telltale had just given her an idea. A completely far-fetched idea, but an idea all the same.

'Well, yes, isn't that what I've been saying?' continued Mrs Telltale, a little irked at being interrupted. Miss Nottynuf said nothing but her mind was a cauldron of thoughts.

'They've proposed a special story, all about Tammy coming back to her old school and her joyful reunion with her friends.'

It was anyone's guess what would happen when Covetus Clutch came the next day but it couldn't hurt to have the press around. Could it?

'Tomorrow?' Miss Nottynuf risked a single word in her best Granny Grit voice, which wasn't very good at all.

That single word made Mrs Telltale whoop with delight. She couldn't believe her luck. It would be a terrific story for her Tammy! 'First thing tomorrow!' she trilled, ringing off before Granny Grit could change her mind.

Then, Miss Nottynuf punched out the number for the police station, keeping an eye out for Dr Bloom.

CHAPTER 29

Covetus Clutch was standing on the stage in the Great Hall. He was a good ten years younger than Dr Bloom, but there's something about chasing money that ages you. Clutch's temples shone where his hair had worn away and, apart from a few wiry sprigs sticking out of his ears, he was almost bald.

Almost, because the back of his head had its fair share of hair. But Covetus Clutch wasn't about to show the back of his head to anyone except his two giant bodyguards. (And they both agreed, in their private moments, that it was a truly horrid head.) When he got out of his flashy, gold limousine, he was careful to keep his back turned away from the others.

He bestowed a smile on the children, the fillings in his teeth glinting more golden than his car. 'I spent my most memorable years at this school as a young boy,' Covetus Clutch began, and there were gasps all around. It was difficult for the children to imagine that this wizened man had ever been young. It was even more difficult to understand how anyone's years at Horrid High could have been memorable. 'Dr Bloom was my wonderful science teacher!' He swept his hands in her direction, and Dr Bloom flashed an acknowledging smile that any reasonable person might mistake for a grimace.

Clutch looked at the unkempt girl standing next to Dr Bloom and cringed. Children were like weeds, cropping up with reckless abandon, getting caught underfoot, messing up the prettiest garden. This one was particularly ugly.

'I'm so glad we decided not to go into the woods yesterday evening,' said Bat, tugging on Dr Bloom's arm.

Dr Bloom had her eyes fixed on Clutch and although she appeared to be hanging on to his every word, her mind had been on the woods that very instant. 'Why is that, my dear?' She patted the child's head in a distracted sort of way and noted that the tiny ponytail had come undone. Again. She gulped as she felt the child's hand on hers. No, she would not think of where those sticky fingers had been last, in the child's nose or ears or mouth.

'Well, Covetus Clutch is here, and that's a momentous thing! We can go into the woods any time, can't we?'

Dr Bloom bent down and stared the child in the face. 'No talk of the woods, d'you hear me, not till he's gone!' she hissed. 'Not a word, now!'

Bat grabbed this opportune moment for The Cough. The hot blast of breath made Dr Bloom stagger back. 'Ahem, sorry,' said Bat, clearing her throat. 'I guess we'll talk about the ghostly flower later then!' She turned to go, counting to three in her head. *One. Two.* And on *three,* Dr Bloom's long, snake-like arm had curled itself around Bat: '*What ghostly flower?*'

'Maybe later,' said Bat, 'when he's come and gone, like you said? If it's still blossoming—'

'*What's still blossoming?*'

Dr Bloom dragged Bat into a corner. Her eyes darted to Clutch but the old bore was still talking.

'It's just that it smells like soap when it blossoms!' said the child, spraying drops of spittle as she spoke. Dr Bloom reached for her hanky but she had none! Hadn't she given this slovenly mess of a child all her hankies? Never mind the spittle now.

'Is it a white flower with three petals?' gasped Dr Bloom.

The child nodded.

'An *unusually long* third petal?'

Another nod.

'Grows on the bark of trees?'

More nodding.

Dr Bloom's breath caught in her throat. The demented child wasn't talking about any flower! This was a ghost orchid! But just to be sure . . .

'Looks like a flying frog!' said Bat, choosing her moment carefully as Miss Nottynuf had told her to. 'Close your eyes and imagine the most beautiful flower in bloom in the woods right now,' Miss Nottynuf had told her. 'Make her want it'.

Dr Bloom tore at her throat. Beads of sweat appeared on her forehead. She stole another look at Clutch.

'My principal was none other than the great Percival Perverse!' he was saying. The children exchanged looks of astonishment and disbelief but Clutch did not notice. He was busy daydreaming of what he would do to old Percy, when he got out of jail, for writing out the Grand Plan and hiding it in a place so secret that no one could find it. The horrid ideas seething inside Clutch's head burned a few more hairs to a crisp until they fell off. Of course, no one saw this but his bodyguards and they yawned. They'd seen it a million times before.

'This great school made me who I am!' Clutch said. He thought of how horrid his schooldays had been, how they'd made him want to grow up and get away and get rich even if he had to mow down everyone and everything in his path.

The children were getting restless. Nothing that Clutch said sounded very truthful. 'I want to build more schools like this one, where children can learn how to make pots of money and buy every dream!'

But now the children were stirring. There was the sound of a car driving into the school—more than one car, really. Although they didn't know it yet, there was a TV van and a make-up van too.

'The press is here!' cried an excited voice.

'Who told the press that I would be here?' Clutch tried not to sound too nervous. 'Dr Bloom, was it you?' But Dr Bloom was engaged in an intense conversation with that mess of a girl. Covetus Clutch tapped on the mike with one impatient finger. 'Dr Bloom, was it you?'

'It wasn't me!' she replied, pushing Bat away guiltily.

Clutch puffed up his little chest and tried to conceal his discomfort. If the press was here, he'd make the most of it, he would! He'd tone down the praise for Principal Perverse but he'd still give them an interview to remember! He'd tell them about the wonderful schools he was planning to build in the poorest parts of the world. They'd never go checking in swamps and jungles if any of those schools were as wonderful as he made them out to be!

He snapped his fingers, and perhaps this meant something because his bodyguards understood right away. One of them stepped outside to take a look.

'The press can't have enough of me,' he said to the children. 'They'll be here in a minute, beating down those doors. There'll be cameras going off, newspeople scrambling to get closer.'

The bodyguard who'd stepped outside had just returned. He leaned towards Clutch as if to whisper.

'Away, man!' cried Clutch, jumping back in alarm. He'd always kept his staff at a safe distance. He was mortally afraid of what infections people carried these days.

The bodyguard raised his voice to be heard. 'THERE'S A CHILD OUTSIDE, SIR!'

'Well, it's a *school*, you idiot!' said Clutch. 'In case you haven't noticed, there are children everywhere!'

'She's a little girl, sir.'

Clutch's gaze softened. His barrel-chested bodyguard was scared of children—of course that was it! 'Don't worry,' said Clutch under his breath. 'Children are a little creepy, I'll grant you that, but all you have to do is kick them if they get too close.'

Just then, the sea of children in front of Covetus Clutch

parted. A hush went through the crowd. A gasp started from the back and rippled its way to the front. It would not have been amiss here if a drumroll had sounded, the sort that is used to announce the arrival of a princess. For at the far end of the room, a small girl appeared, and although she was not really royalty, she was every bit a princess to her doting mother.

With an imperious gaze, she walked forward slowly. She was a pink-faced girl with a square jaw and narrow, mean eyes. Her narrow, mean eyes twitched. Who was that old geezer on stage, standing where she should be?

'Tammy Telltale!' the children shouted and the girl swelled with pride. She was famous now, and everyone knew her. 'Give her a big hand!' said the tremulous voice behind her, and Mrs Telltale put her plump hands together to get the clapping going. Behind Mrs Telltale, reporters from the *Daily Post* and a local TV station surged forward like leaves on a current, eager to capture this photo moment from every angle possible.

Covetus Clutch, true to his name, clutched the microphone. He had no intention of sharing the mike or stage with this miserable child. Why, he'd never shared anything with anyone and he wasn't about to start today! He would talk about the Grand Plan—well, the part of it that was meant for public consumption.

'Horrid High is going international, my dear children!' he soldiered on bravely, paying no attention to the little girl and the people who'd swarmed in with her. 'Imagine scores of poor, dirty children in scores of poor, dirty countries, their grubby little faces lighting up with joy as they set off not just for any school, but for *boarding* school—'

'Who's the old codger?' Tammy asked the grubby girl who'd sidled up next to her. *Snotty and grubby,* thought Tammy as the girl sniffed and a tiny, green booger hanging off her nose jiggled.

'Covetus Clutch!' said the grubby girl, wearing an awestruck expression on her face. Just as she'd promised Miss Nottynuf she would.

Tammy snorted. 'And who's she?'

'Dr Bloom, the science teacher,' said the grungy girl, and picked at a sliver of food between her teeth. 'Lovely lady! Invited Sir Clutch to inspire us!' She emitted a rapturous sigh. 'He's a *multimillionaire*!'

'Bah! He might be a multimillionaire but has he written a book?'

The girl scratched her mangy head. 'Don't think so, but I bet he'd have quite a story to tell!'

'Well, *I'm* the one with the story,' cried Tammy.

'Er, not any more, I'm afraid!' The messy girl smiled, revealing two rows of incredibly crooked teeth, and pointed at the stage.

Of all the nerve! The reporters from the *Daily Post* and the TV people were clamouring around the stage. They couldn't believe their luck. They'd bargained that the Telltale girl returning to her old school for a reunion would make a fabulous front-page story. But here was Covetus Clutch, reclusive tycoon, who had been interviewed by the press only once before and had never appeared on telly! Imagine their excitement at the thought of two front-page stories in place of one.

'. . . a place where their stomachs, their hearts and their minds will all be nourished!' Clutch was saying. He'd always avoided the media. This was not because he was a modest and humble man who wanted to do great things without hogging the credit for them. Rather, it was because Covetus Clutch had never done anything great. His methods of making money were dark and clandestine. The less people knew about them, the better.

But here, at Horrid High, he was standing in front of hundreds of children, talking about schools and education and changing lives. That sort of claptrap was always lapped up by the media. They were thrusting mikes in his face, shouting questions, snapping pictures. Long cables were being unspooled, camera tripods were being set up, a TV camera was zooming in for a close-up.

Tammy felt a little left out and more than a little outraged. The press had come for her, and now they were craning their silly little necks to catch a glimpse of that fossil! Tammy took this to heart. Which is unreasonable because press people are notoriously fickle. They'll run to anyone standing on a stage who is willing to talk to them.

'It's very large-hearted of you to share your moment of glory with Mr Clutch,' observed the grubby girl innocently.

She was playing her role to perfection. If Miss Nottynuf had briefed her correctly about this Telltale girl, she'd be like a pot of soup on slow boil by now.

Tammy felt her cheeks go hot. She wasn't large-hearted. In fact, her heart was the smallest size possible to sustain human life.

'Loved your book, by the way,' the scruffy girl said, although she'd never read Tammy's book and had no intention of ever doing so.

Tammy relaxed a little. Her ego needed a little massage right now. 'What did you like most about the book?'

'How you laid bare all the secrets of this place,' said the grungy girl, not batting an eyelid. And then she delivered her punchline. 'This place has too many secrets still, if you ask me . . .'

Secrets? There was nothing Tammy Telltale loved more than secrets! 'What secrets?' Her narrow, mean eyes narrowed some more.

'I couldn't possible tell!' said the shabby girl.

And then she told her anyway.

Cook Fracas was making custard pies in the kitchen. They were Gypsy's favourite and he missed her. His eyes swam when the pink-faced girl with the mean eyes asked him, 'Are you missing a goat?' And the tears practically rolled down his cheeks when the girl said, 'She's in the Get Lost Forever Woods. Dr Bloom knew all along.'

Why had Dr Bloom kept this from him? The mean-eyed girl shrugged. 'Dr Bloom says that goats are just dumb ruminants with nothing on their minds but food.' Now fancy that! How would the mean-eyed girl know this anyway? She was only visiting!

'You heard this?' he asked the girl, feeling his pulse gallop a little.

'I heard this,' she said with a smug nod.

It was only a rumour and Cook Fracas didn't set great store by rumours. He would ignore the pink-faced girl and her rumours. As he would ignore the rising heat in his cheeks and the quickening of his breath. Cook Fracas went back to slapping out pies, although this time, he slapped them harder.

After Tammy had told Cook Fracas what she'd learned from the snotty girl, she felt a little better. She always did. Of course, she'd sworn to keep it a secret but where was the fun in that? Keeping a secret was like finding a large and precious stone and sticking it in a hole in the ground. It had to be held up to the light—seen by everyone—that was when it truly sparkled.

She slipped into the Great Hall again, still annoyed that everyone was so hung up on the old-timer on stage that no one had noticed her leave or enter. But she knew something the old codger didn't and that thought cheered her up. It made her feel more powerful than Mr Covetus Clutch.

'I have a question, sir, just one question!' That tremulous voice made Tammy start. It was her mother, skittering to the stage in her ridiculous heels, giving that old geezer such a simpering look, Tammy practically exploded! All that new-found cheer, all that sense of power, was wiped out in one fell moment!

To the stage Tammy Telltale strode, fists clenched, and she glared at Clutch. 'Hey, Gramps, get off!'

Her rude request was drowned out in all the din. And then some half-brain reporter shouted, 'Let's have a photo of Miss Telltale and Mr Clutch together!'

Before Tammy could protest, she was hoisted up on stage by several ready hands. A flustered face in the crowd caught her eye. 'You won't tell, will you?' begged the grubby girl. Tammy gave her a telltale smile.

Covetus Clutch wanted to get away from the press, and if that meant having to take a picture with this pink-faced girl, so be it. He also thought of how posing with children made grown-ups look better than they really were. That's why cruel kings and ruthless dictators always had a child at hand when the cameras were rolling. A child was no different from a cat or a dog that way. Or a bamboo lemur.

He patted the girl on her head and prayed that the cameras had caught the tender moment. He could picture the headlines tomorrow: *Multimillionaire with a heart of gold.* He'd kick her on the shins when no one was looking. But what that vicious, pink-faced girl whispered to him made him want to kick her right then and there.

'See that teacher there with that grubby child?'

Covetus Clutch picked out Dr Bloom and the grubby girl in the crowd. They were making a beeline for the double doors.

'They're off to the woods behind the school!'

'What for?' he whispered back as the newspeople set up their cameras in new positions.

The girl gave him such a smug look, he wanted to turn her upside down and give her a good rattle but she was taller than him.

'They know where the Grand Plan is and they're going to get it!'

The hair on Covetus Clutch's horrid head sizzled dangerously. 'Did you say the Grand—'

But someone was holding Clutch by the chin now. *Of all the nerve!* 'I must go!' he said, but the make-up artist had other plans. A half-dozen cameras were trained on this man and making him look good was going to be a real challenge.

'I must—' Clutch persisted, but he was eating face powder now. The make-up artist was laying it on thick. Powder, blush, mascara, this man would need it all! And after Clutch had had his nose powdered, his eyebrows combed, his cheeks bronzed and his shiny temples concealed, the make-up artist stepped back and nodded. 'He's good!'

Or as good as he would ever be. And some idiotic photographer from behind the cameras shouted, 'Smile, Mr Clutch, smile!'

CHAPTER 30

Up on the tower, an old crow surveyed the scene with beady eyes. It was not an entirely unfamiliar one: cars thundering in through the gates, loud voices, bright flashes of light. People always brought mayhem with them and the old crow had seen it all before. He might have been preening his feathers or doing whatever it was that crows did to pass the time. But one particular figure slipping out of the school had the crow all attentive now. A statuesque figure with long hair flowing down her back.

The old crow knew her well. He had a weak wing but a strong memory. He had not forgotten how she'd thrown the stone that broke his wing when he was learning how to fly. He would never forget.

It took a single caw to issue the command. As the old crow flapped his wings and took flight, a murder of crows on a windowsill took to the air too. Up they rose, like a black cloak, and down they swooped.

Dr Bloom heard the first caw and cursed herself for forgetting her scarf. She'd never cared much for crows, or for any animals, really. There had been a horse once, but she'd tired of it . . . What she loved most were plants.

At the edge of the woods, she knelt down beside a small plant with bright pink flowers. The Middlemist's Red. It had been sloppily stuck into the ground, too much in plain sight, two nights ago. She carefully drew it out by the roots. It would soon be home. Deep inside the woods where it belonged.

'What are you doing?' asked Bat, although she well knew it. 'It doesn't concern you!' snarled Dr Bloom, wrenching at Bat's arm. She gripped the collection bag in her hand. She'd splashed a little water in it to keep its precious contents alive.

She was dragging Bat towards the first line of trees when the child tripped. Dr Bloom cast a nervous look up at the darkening sky, at the circle of crows swelling in number. 'Quick!' she said.

Bat was in no hurry to get going. She was waiting for Clutch to catch up. Wasn't that the plan? She dusted herself off as slowly as she could. Dr Bloom ducked behind a tree trunk. She was not stepping out in the open. The wretched child could save herself!

A black shadow swept the top of Bat's head, its wing skimming her thatch of hair. Bat ducked, surprised, but the old crow flew up again, beating the air. He had a score to settle with the long-haired figure cowering in the trees, not the tiny one who'd fallen (quite on purpose!) on the mud path. He issued one more command and the black-winged shadows fell back.

'Hurry!' shouted Dr Bloom over the cacophony of crows. But the silly girl had stopped again! She was tying a rope to a

tree as slowly as she could. 'It'll only take a minute,' lied Bat, taking much longer. 'It'll help us get back!'

The rope had been fished out of one of Colonel Craven's evac-kits for quite the opposite purpose. It would mark out a route, Bat hoped, for anyone who followed.

As they wound their way deeper into the woods, Bat unravelled the rope, from one tree to the next, charting the course they were taking. The bare branches overhead sliced the sunshine to bits, and it was as if a light had been switched off. Darkness fell upon the two figures—stillness too. Except for the whispers. *Go, go, go. Come, come, come.*

'What are those whispers?' Dr Bloom was clinging to Bat now. Bat shook her head and continued walking. Only those who were afraid heard whispers inside these woods. It was their own worst fears calling out to them. For Bat, the woods were home.

The woods were stirring old memories. Not for Bat, who'd never looked back in her life, but for Dr Bloom, who'd been looking back ever since she'd first left . . .

Twenty years ago, right after Granny Grit had gone off to save the planet, Principal Perverse had hired Dr Bloom to teach science at Horrid High. Dr Bloom turned to look back at the red roof, the white walls, receding from sight. The school had changed so much since those early days. She squinted up at the dark masses of tangled branches. The woods had changed so much too. This had been just a tiny grove of trees once. The perfect hiding place.

Dr Bloom watched Bat's little body wriggle under a mass of creepers. She despised children and this particular child was more awful than the general lot of them. If Dr Bloom could have her way, she'd be far away from any school, in a remote jungle somewhere, discovering plants and trees that no one knew existed. Like the botanical explorers of the nineteenth century. But exploring the planet took money. Lots and lots of it. The sort that Covetus Clutch had. The sort that he'd used to buy the world's tiniest water lily from her. Even though that should have been her Valentine's gift to herself. Her face darkened at the thought.

From the corner of her eye, Dr Bloom saw what one of the children had described to her as a plant with eyes. '*Actaea pachypoda*,' she murmured, as if under a spell. Her heart caught as she saw the delicate, white flowers of the bois dentelle tree. How had this tree, found only in a cloud forest in Mauritius, survived here without anybody tending to it? She reached out to touch the buds tenderly as they passed . . . 'Let's go this way!' she told Bat.

'The ghostly flower is that way!' Bat pointed, snagging the rope around two more trees. She would take Dr Bloom deep into the woods. That was the plan. She prayed that Tammy had told one last tale and that Clutch was close on their heels now. What next? No one knew for certain what would happen next, but Ferg had said, 'There's no honour among thieves! Let's make them doubt each other!' Bat hoped that the woods would play their part too.

Dr Bloom could smell the ghost orchid's soapy fragrance in the air and it filled her with anticipation. One last caress for the white buds of the bois dentelle, and she plunged deeper into the woods with Bat.

A little way farther, Dr Bloom stopped again. 'The *Welwitschia mirabilis*!' she gasped. 'You never told me!'

Bat shrugged. Who'd have thought this ugly plant with only two leaves that curled and tangled into a mass would be of interest to anyone?

Dr Bloom was dizzy with joy. She'd never imagined that the woods would thrive so much without her. Every plant here had a name, every flower had a face. The Parrot's Beak, the black bat flower and the green jade flower, she was certain that they were here too. Hadn't Dr Bloom planted them with her own two hands?

Bat's heart flip-flopped a little as the soapy smell grew stronger. No sign of Clutch yet. Could Tammy have decided not to tell Clutch what Bat had said? Could she have stopped being a telltale? Bat thought of Fermina's words the day before: 'A secret is as safe with Tammy as a bag of loot with a thief.' She prayed that Fermina was right.

Dr Bloom's heart lifted as something floated past. The giant sphinx moth! Such moths were rare and elusive, like the ghost orchids they sucked nectar out of with their five-inch tongues! If she was lucky, she would witness the giant sphinx moth paying the ghost orchid a visit!

'Are we there yet?' she panted, stumbling over a clump of

ferns. As if in reply, the woods fell so utterly silent, it was as if the very silence rang in their ears.

'We are!' said Bat, feeling suddenly tired as she gazed up at the white flower nestled in the bark of the tree. It didn't take a botanist to appreciate how utterly beautiful this flower was, shining like the moon in the dim light of the woods.

Dr Bloom approached it slowly, her face glowing like a devotee's in a temple. The ghost orchid in bloom! She'd seen hundreds of exotic plants but never yet a ghost orchid in bloom! And here it was, in what had once been her very backyard! She knew what that hideous Clutch would say if she told him about it. 'How much is it worth?'

For Clutch, everything had a price. A rare plant that was the last of its kind or an animal on the brink of extinction. *Even a science teacher.* He left school and amassed a fortune quickly, and then he came calling as he'd always planned to. He reminded her that he had a little secret about her that he could tell the world, and then he offered to pay for her travels . . . She found trees that no one had ever seen, flowers that the best explorers had given up on finding. But Dr Bloom's joy of discovery was always tinged by bitterness. Clutch kept everything she found for his private arboretum because he didn't want anyone else to enjoy these things for free. Because he could.

She gazed at the ghost orchid again. This was priceless, as was the Middlemist's Red in her hand. *Everything in these woods has the mark of my hands on it,* she thought, *all this is mine. My private arboretum.* She knelt down to plant the pink flowers, half withered already in the noonday heat. Now they would grow free where that cursed Clutch would never find them.

Covetus Clutch had no intention of smiling for a bunch of camera-toting goofs! Dr Bloom was trying to hoodwink him, the Grand Plan was slipping out of his reach, the smug girl next to him had an annoying face, and he could taste make-up on his teeth. What was there to smile about?

There was a moment of hesitation. After all, it's very hard to misbehave on camera. No sooner than the first camera flashed, Clutch sprang up like a jack-in-the-box and vaulted off stage. His charge to the double doors was almost sprightly. He had eyes only for what lay in front of him: the long hallway of the school building, the playground beyond, the mud path, the woods and the Grand Plan at last!

Clutch's sudden exit caught his bodyguards by surprise. They were supposed to throw themselves behind him and eclipse his horrid head with their large bulk. They couldn't really do that now, could they? Not when their boss was hurtling across the room, not when a half-a-dozen cameras stood between his horrid head and them, and not when Clutch was so small, his head could barely be seen bobbing above the others!

Clutch heard the cries of astonishment behind him as he

sprinted to the back gate. His breath came in short bursts now and someone else was panting at his back. He whipped about, mid-run, and found himself staring straight into a camera lens. One swipe and the camera was knocked off its owner's neck!

'Hey! Come back!' cried the angry owner of the camera, scuttling after it as it bounced upon the grass. Fat chance of that! 'He went that way!' the cameraman shouted to the thickset bodyguards, as they pelted past, pointing at the horrid head and shuddering. What a grotesque sight it was! A look of relief crossed his face as he checked his camera for damage. The photograph looked OK. *More than OK*. The horrid head wove down the mud path, bobbed under the branches of the first trees and was lost to sight.

'Paparazzi!' muttered Cook Fracas as a train of newspeople plunged into the woods, hot on the heels of the horrid head and his bodyguards. He didn't think too highly of the paparazzi, and who could blame him? 'Paparazzi' is an Italian word for the sort of photographers who climb trees and scale walls to shoot pictures of famous people. Such pictures are sold for lots of money to worthless newspapers known as tabloids. And these worthless newspapers known as tabloids are read by lots of bored people, the sort of people who hold autograph books and call themselves fans.

Now there is nothing that excites the paparazzi more than a shy subject and a good chase. The horrid head was giving them just that. Meanwhile, back in the Great Hall, Tammy

Telltale had settled down to read aloud from *The Tales of Horrid High.* She smiled at her captive audience. The people from the *Daily Post* had stayed back—they were a respectable newspaper, after all, and not a tabloid. And the poor children of Horrid High had nowhere else to go.

Apart from a few. Bat was with Dr Bloom in the woods, planting the Middlemist's Red. Volumina and Fermina were in the kitchen, helping with lunch. Ferg, Phil and Immy had slipped out beforehand into the woods, daring to go no farther than Bat had told them to and remembering the promise they'd made to Miss Nottynuf to be careful. And the twins were not part of the plan but they had decided to jump in. If there was trouble brewing, they wanted to be a part of it.

It was wrong to hate the messenger, Cook Fracas knew that. If Tammy Telltale's message had even a grain of truth in it, it was Dr Bloom he should hate. But he thought of the girl with her narrow, mean eyes, and he wanted to seal her mouth shut with dough. Plaster her pink face with pie. Her words were taking root in his head like weeds. They were crawling under his skin. *Dr Bloom said that goats are just dumb ruminants with nothing else on their minds but food!*

As Cook Fracas replayed Tammy Telltale's words, they took on the sheen of the truth. As a lie often does when it's repeated again and again, even inside your own head. Cook Fracas thought of how he'd rescued Gypsy from a bunch of lunatics in Spain who wanted to throw her off a church roof. He would have liked to punish them for hating goats so much but who knew where they were now? One such goat-hating lunatic was at school, though. Hadn't the girl told him so? Slowly, Cook Fracas curled his large hands into fists. Now, where was Dr Bloom?

CHAPTER 31

It was the rope that spoiled things for Dr Bloom. It marked a walking trail through the Get Lost Forever Woods, past all the plants that had meant so much to her. At first, all Clutch could think of as he followed the rope was the Grand Plan. He'd get his hands on it and he'd destroy it. Feed it to his lemur, perhaps.

But then he saw the *Actaea pachypoda* and the bois dentelle, the *Welwitschia mirabilis* and the black bat flower. Of course, he didn't know them by name, or even recognize them all. But from a lifetime of collecting things, he knew something rare and precious when he saw it. And all these rare and precious things were here, free for the picking!

He stopped to remind himself why he was here. The Grand Plan. Besides, these woods gave him goosebumps. All wild places did. He didn't have the stomach to go looking for rare plants and flowers where they grew untouched, on steep cliff-faces and in treacherous swamps. That was the sort of work he hired Dr Bloom for. He liked rare flowers growing, neat as soldiers in a line, in his own private gardens. And all these flowers would look perfect there.

But first, the Grand Plan. Dr Bloom had made him wait—

and oh, there was nothing Covetus Clutch detested more than waiting! All she'd given him was excuses, and now, when he was here to get the Grand Plan for himself, she was making him dance a merry jig for it. He was tired of playing games. If the Grand Plan was somewhere in these woods, he'd find it. He *needed* to.

He was on the verge of something big. Horrid High International would give him unfettered access to the remotest places on earth. He would fish all the fish out of the rivers. He would mine all the limestone out of the hills. He would cut all the trees out of the forests. It was incredible, what building one piddly school could buy you! He wasn't going to let anyone else get their hands on the Grand Plan and risk the whole world finding out what he was really up to.

He could hear the twin grunts of his bodyguards behind him. They were stocky men, far more comfortable lifting weights than running an obstacle course through a tangled wood, but they stayed close at his heels. If they let him out of their sight again, they would lose their jobs when all this was over.

Two pairs of eyes watched this strange procession unseen and decided to follow . . .

Deeper in the woods, Dr Bloom tossed the collection bag to one side and knelt down to pat the soil over the roots of the Middlemist's Red. She prayed that it would grow undisturbed now. She would have brought it here sooner but it was the whispers in the woods that had kept her away. Why, even this rotten child who'd spent so much time in the woods had been afraid to return!

Dr Bloom could come and go as she pleased now. Hadn't the child marked the route with the rope? The mangy child was clasping her hand but Dr Bloom didn't need her any more. And if she didn't need the child, she didn't have to be nice to her either. She didn't have to let those awful fingers that had been who-knows-where earlier touch her again!

But first things first. She would nip back to school before her absence was noted and convince Clutch that the Grand Plan was truly lost for ever. Now that she had beheld the ghost orchid, she could wait a few more days for him to be gone. Her spirits lifted. She shook herself free of the child. 'Let's go!'

Bat blanched. She could see she was of no more value to Dr Bloom. She had no more time to buy. Where was Clutch? 'You haven't seen the moth visit the flower. You wanted to, didn't you? It's very special—'

'We go back to school NOW!' screeched Dr Bloom, dusting her hands free of mud and whatever the child had touched last.

'No you DON'T!' snarled the horrid head, bounding out of the bushes and lunging for the freshly planted pink flowers. Two bodyguards bounded out behind him.

'Buried the Grand Plan here, did you?' leered Clutch, digging up large clumps of earth. He yanked the pink flowers out of the ground and flung them away.

'You'll destroy the Middlemist!' screamed Dr Bloom, before gasping in dismay. Clutch froze, his eyes on the pink bunch of flowers that he had tossed carelessly to one side. 'Middlemist? I thought you said you never took it!'

Dr Bloom's eyes were on the pink flowers too. She inched closer to them. 'So I lied! Can't you let me keep one teensy-weensy flower for myself?'

Clutch inched closer. 'I paid you to give me everything you found. Everything. You deceived me!' He made a quick mental calculation of how far he'd have to dive to get his hands on that flower before she did.

Dr Bloom watched Covetus at his sneaky best, creeping closer to the flowers as though she couldn't see it! She felt a twinge of regret. She should have trounced him all those years ago, when he was still a boy! And then it dawned on her that he was no larger than a boy even now. Why, she would trounce him right away! 'I'd rather destroy the Middlemist than let you have it!' she screamed, lunging for the horrid child who'd turned into a horrid grown-up.

A scrimmage! A scrum! A skirmish! A scuffle! A free-for-all wrestling match! The bodyguards exchanged looks. They weren't exactly sure whether their job included interrupting two grown-ups who were slugging it out like street dogs, but it probably fell within the description of 'watching Clutch's back'. His back was being pummelled by a very tall lady with a rather strong set of arms. With a howl that their martial-arts instructors would have been proud of, the bodyguards jumped in.

Bat watched the proceedings with a mixture of alarm and

glee. She tried to sidestep the mud fight and get to the flowers but four people, three of them rather large, were rolling about unpredictably. It was impossible!

Eight hands and eight legs were pounding the ground, pulling hair, pinching skin, poking at eyes, and one hand crept closer to the pink flowers. One *left* hand!

Bat's eyes popped out of her head. 'Mallus!' she yelled in disbelief. Where had he come from? The left-handed twin was dancing about now, holding up the flowers like a trophy. 'Stop fighting, you fools, I have it!'

Eight hands stopped flailing, eight legs stood up straight, but Mallus was gone.

'He has it!' shouted Clutch. Of course, by 'it', he meant the Grand Plan. Hadn't it been buried somewhere under here?

'He has it!' shouted Dr Bloom. Of course, by 'it', she meant the Middlemist's Red.

'Which way did he go?' they both cried together. The bodyguards shrugged and dusted themselves off—they weren't paid to figure out where some silly boy with a bunch of wilting flowers in his hand had taken off to.

'There! I see him!' said Clutch, breaking into a run. The boy was threading his way through the woods, snickering loudly, holding up the flowers.

'There! I see him too!' cried Dr Bloom, breaking into a run. Another boy was threading his way through the woods, snickering loudly, holding up the flowers. In the opposite direction.

'I've got him!' shouted Clutch, veering left.

'I've got him!' shouted Dr Bloom, veering right.

The twins chuckled. Mallus had deposited the Middlemist's Red in the collection bag that Dr Bloom had tossed aside, and he had stuffed the bag in his pocket. There was some water inside the bag; it would keep the precious flowers moist. Not that Mallus was the sort of boy to think about such things.

What was in his hand, then? A bunch of ordinary pink flowers that the twins had chanced upon while Dr Bloom and Covetus Clutch were having their little face-off. From a distance, these flowers looked no different than a bunch of Middlemist's Reds.

Dr Bloom was in hot pursuit of Malo. There was something in her trouser pocket too, something that should have been inside a collection bag but wasn't. Something that had persuaded a runaway goat to return to school when she wore these trousers last.

Malo ran towards a knot of low-hanging branches. Dr Bloom's heart filled with hope. Surely, the boy would run headlong into them! They'd scrape his cheeks, they'd poke his eyes. Perhaps they had *poison* in them! 'I have the boy!' she sniggered.

But when the low-hanging branches were almost upon them, Malo took a sharp right. Dr Bloom congratulated herself on her razor-sharp reflexes. She took a sharp right too. A goat nosing in the shrubs looked up, disturbed. It smelt something familiar. Something good. It broke into a trot behind Dr Bloom.

A man nosing in the bushes looked up, too, disturbed. He smelt something familiar. Something bad. He smelt trouble.

The man had trained for this all his life. For the last few days, he'd been quite lost. There was something about these woods that made you go about in circles. When it seemed impossible to find a way out, he'd built himself a shelter. He'd survived on herbs and roots. He'd prepared the perfect camouflage. He'd always had a sixth sense about enemy attacks and he'd sensed this one coming. He threw himself flat on his stomach and waited.

Clutch was in hot pursuit of Mallus. He could feel his bodyguards panting down his neck. 'I have the boy!' he sniggered. *What do I want more,* he asked himself as he ran, *the rare flowers or the Grand Plan? Why choose when I can have them both?* That thought gave him a fresh burst of energy.

Mallus was running directly at the low-hanging branches now. When they were almost upon him, he took a sharp left. Clutch took a sharp left too, but his barrel-chested bodyguards barrelled into those low-hanging branches. Which was a pity, because those low-hanging branches turned out to be booby-traps. Before they knew it, they were hanging upside down from a tree, trussed like chickens for the pot.

Clutch was catching up with the boy. They were only a few metres apart now. But the ground rose up in front of him.

No, not the ground! A creature in camouflage! A mud-man with black stripes on his cheeks! 'Help!' Clutch turned and shouted to his bodyguards. But his bodyguards were in need of a bit of help too.

Dr Bloom felt an itch begin in her right leg. The poison ivy she'd used to lure that stupid beast to school! She'd forgotten all about it! She stopped and fumbled in her pocket. There it was. She flung it as far as she could, but now her hand was burning too. A goat ambled up behind her and picked up the poison ivy gratefully. Gypsy? 'Away!' yelled Dr Bloom, but Gypsy wasn't going anywhere. All she'd had after trotting out this far was one small stem. Surely, there was more where this one came from?

When Dr Bloom looked up, the boy was gone. 'Nooooooo!' she screamed, mad with rage. That boy had no business nicking her Middlemist's Red. That greedy Clutch had no business asking for it either. It was hers! Hers! Like everything else in these woods!

But Dr Bloom was wrong. The woods didn't belong to anyone. They had a mind of their own. Just like the Brace boys did.

Three more heads watched the chase in consternation. 'Why are the two of them doing this?' puzzled Phil. 'I don't know but I love it!' said Ferg with ill-concealed glee. 'Change of plans, fellows!' said Immy before throwing her voice in her best Brace boys impersonation. 'OVER HERE!'

Dr Bloom staggered in the direction of the voice. Her

leg was burning with pain now. She could feel the red welts coming up. She felt something sticky under her hiking shoes. What was she standing on? A giant cabbage, a beautiful pink rosette, really. She gasped. Could this be the *Pinguicula* she'd planted with her own hands years ago? The one whose fat, succulent leaves were covered with sticky glands to trap insects? How did it ever grow so *enormous*?

She grunted as she tried to lift her feet, one by one, but the gummy bond between foot and leaf would not give. The itch in her leg and her hand was unbearable now. She crouched down. She would wrench her feet free, one after the other. But wait, now her hand was stuck! The gummy bonds were stretchier than mozzarella! 'Help!' wailed Dr Bloom.

Just then, Dr Bloom lost her balance and fell backward. Was it the suddenness of coming unstuck? Or the whispers growing louder in her head: *Go, go, go.* Or was it because a shattering thought had struck her? These woods had grown so much without her. Even the *Pinguicula* had become more gigantic than it was typically known to be. It was as if every flower here, every tree, were finally free to follow its own natural cycles. To grow as bumper-size as it liked. Could it be that the woods didn't need her? That they never had . . .

Clutch still had the boy in sight. The trouble was, the mud-man had *him* in sight. Clutch had caught but a single, terrifying glimpse of the mud-man's painted face and his grassy headgear. He didn't dare to look back at him again.

He would hide. Yes, that was it! Someone as small-built as

him would have no trouble hiding. He spun about looking for a perfect spot. There! A large flower, or was it a leaf? With two parts, like a half-open green oyster. A colossal, humongous oyster. With green, prickly thorns sticking out of its rim. Covetus Clutch couldn't tell one plant from another but alas, it would have been a useful thing to know at a time like this.

Without another thought, Covetus Clutch climbed into the flower. He felt as cozy as Thumbelina asleep on a lotus leaf—as a new pea in a pod. He snickered. He would lie still for a bit longer till he'd eluded the mud-man. Then he'd find the boy, snatch the Grand Plan and the flowers from him and finish things up with Dr Bloom.

The sound of heavy footsteps signalled that the mud-man was close. Clutch held his breath. A slight movement startled him. It was nothing, only the flower he was hiding in. Moving in the breeze. He relaxed a little. Another movement, equally slight. The breeze again. But what sort of breeze would ruffle such a huge flower, the sort that a small-sized man could fit into? Clutch's hair stood on end. Whatever was left of it.

The flower shut tight and refused to open. Like a bad clam. In that horrid moment, Clutch realized that he had discovered an unearthly version of a Venus flytrap. The world's only Venus childtrap. It was a rare find, worth a lot of money, but how little it mattered now that he was inside it!

The itch in Dr Bloom's arm and leg was unbearable now. 'The woods don't want me,' she said, barely coherent now. The thought of being spurned by the woods she'd made was destroying her. She lurched forward, a few metres at a time. She was feeling drowsy. Her eyes were fluttering shut. Her body felt hollow and loose. Sleep was good! It would ease the itch. There was tall grass beneath her now, glistening with dew. It would make a soft bed—ah!

But neither was this regular grass, nor was it glistening with regular dew. It was sleepy grass, and that dew was sleepy nectar. *Follow the rope,* Dr Bloom told herself, *follow the rope.*

How many hours later did Dr Bloom totter out of the woods? Or was it only minutes? She would never know. Her itchy leg burned red-hot. No more of this school, no more of these woods, Dr Bloom told herself. *Let Clutch find his Grand Plan on his own! Let Clutch find his rare plants on his own!* These thoughts made Dr Bloom smile—and then she heard a caw.

Cook Fracas saw all kinds of people emerge from the woods. The paparazzi. The twins. The grungy girl. A few other kids that he couldn't put a name to. There was enough custard pie for everyone.

The crows were milling in the sky. Like a storm cloud. 'No pie for you!' he said. But the crows weren't here for pie.

That's when Cook Fracas saw Dr Bloom hobbling out of the woods. What had that pink-faced girl told him? *Dr Bloom says that goats are just dumb ruminants with nothing on their minds but food.*

His eyes widened. Was Dr Bloom shaking her fist at a caramel-coloured goat? A caramel-coloured goat with deep brown eyes that was trotting behind her? Was that—

'GYPSY!' he yelled, loud enough to shake the school building.

If you're a goat, there are only a few things better than poison ivy. A loving master is one of them. Gypsy bounded to the cook, bleating with joy. She buried her face in the custard pies. She would never eat so many on her own, thought Cook Fracas. He carted the custard pies to the cannon standing in the playground. He whistled *Funiculi Funicula* as he loaded it. He took aim. And he fired.

It wasn't clear what Dr Bloom saw first: a flying crow coming at her or a flying pie. But does it really matter?

Tammy Telltale found it funnier than most but as she threw her head back and laughed, Cook Fracas realized where he'd seen her last. She was the girl in the newspaper, the one whose photograph he'd spilt a blob of egg yolk on. She looked better with egg on her face . . . Cook Fracas loaded the cannon again. There were enough custard pies to go around.

Ferg saw it first: a flash of pink near the main gate. Four dogs bounding up the grassy slope. *Four chihuahuas.* Fermina rubbed her eyes. Phil sobbed like a baby. Immy tumbled down the slope like an apple. It was impossible. Granny Grit, alive and well. But this was the sort of day on which impossible things happened.

CHAPTER 32

Cook Fracas could not stop singing *Funiculi Funicula* at the top of his voice but no one minded. He was in the throes of preparing crème brawlay, and Gypsy was at his heels, claiming the scraps. Granny Grit had agreed to bend the rule about goats in the kitchen—but principals have been known to bend rules. A certain French dessert that you can take a hammer to made it all worth it.

Nothing could wipe the smiles off the children's faces. Granny Grit was back.

'I think Gypsy is still cut up about Dr Bloom's departure,' said Granny, her eyes twinkling with laughter. Everyone chuckled at the shared memory. Gypsy had followed the police car a good way out as it whisked Dr Bloom off, babbling about *Actaea pachypoda, Welwitschia mirabilis* and other unpronounceable things. Oh, and itching uncontrollably.

'There was definitely no more poison ivy there!' said Phil, sending everyone into fresh gales of laughter.

'I say Gypsy needs a poison-ivy patch of her own,' said Granny Grit after the laughter had subsided.

'Her own slice of goat heaven,' said Immy, feeding Saltpetre a well-deserved nibble of chocolate. 'What do you say,

Saltpetre, to the idea of a second school pet?'

Granny Grit looked pointedly at the twins, who were sitting by themselves at the back of the dining room. 'It's decided then, a poison-ivy patch for our second school pet, just as long as the *rest of you* can promise to stay away from it.'

Malo and Mallus shivered when they remembered the oozy welts. With a poison-ivy itch, once was enough. Besides, they were certain they wouldn't be at Horrid High for long enough to visit the patch.

'I don't think any of us imagined that your final prank would be such a good thing,' started Granny. 'Not even you.'

The twins had to agree. They'd plunged into the woods because everyone was plunging into the woods. They didn't know what game was being played but they wanted to play anyway. And when they saw how much Dr Bloom wanted those flowers, they knew it was payback time.

'I wonder what we'll do with you now,' said Granny. The twins gulped.

'We'll pack our things,' said Mallus, trying to put on a brave face. Their parents would not be happy to have them back.

But wait, what was Granny saying now? 'You do remember the sign on the gates of our school, don't you?'

Mallus didn't but Malo did. *There will always be a home here.* 'You mean you're not throwing us out?' he whispered. He couldn't believe his ears. 'After everything we've done?'

'Well, the two of you have some sorting out to do, with each other and with your friends,' said Granny Grit. 'But if you ask me, the trouble you stirred up in the woods saved the day! What do you think, Miss Nottynuf?'

For the first time, Miss Nottynuf's voice was firm and unwavering. 'I think they deserve a second chance!' She knew about second chances, after all. She'd invited Tammy Telltale to visit. She'd masterminded the plan to bring Dr Bloom and Covetus Clutch to loggerheads in plain view of the press. And she'd given the police the perfect idea for a plain-clothes disguise.

'Having them dress up as paparazzi was a stroke of genius—' started Granny Grit.

'The ultimate CAMOUFLAGE!' broke in Colonel Craven, laughing louder than the others. He looked like his old self with the black paint off his face, except that his eyebrow had stopped twitching and his arm had stopped swinging. He'd been lost in the woods for days and he'd survived. He'd seen the enemy coming and this time, he'd been prepared.

'He looks like he's at peace at last,' Ferg said in a low voice.

'Like the crows,' said Fermina, glancing out of the window at the top of the tower. 'Oh, I almost forgot!' And she jumped up and waved the day's newspapers at the others.

The laughter was uncontrollable as everyone pored over the headlines. Contrary to Clutch's expectations, the newspapers did not carry a story that read *Multimillionaire with a heart of gold.* Instead, the headlines read *Telltale girl comes home to horrid reunion.*

The picture of a certain horrid head in close-up had made

it to the front page of every newspaper. Even the *Daily Post*, however respectable, made an exception this one time. 'Look at this!' the children exclaimed. After all, how many times do readers get to see a bright-red head with strips of hair across it, like a pepper that's been on the grill for too long?

'Poor Tammy must be so upset!' cried Fermina, recalling how Tammy had preened and posed for the cameras.

Granny Grit shrugged. 'Hardly. She left first thing this morning, saying something about writing another book.'

There were groans all around. 'I'll never forget the look on the police inspector's face when we gave him the horrid list and the Grand Plan,' said Fermina.

'Or the look on his face when the Venus childtrap finally opened and belched out a rather sticky Covetus Clutch!' said Bat. She had been uncharacteristically quiet so far.

There was a chorus of 'Gross!' and 'Yucky yuck!' all around. Bat grinned. 'I guess there are some things even a Venus childtrap won't eat!'

'Did you know there was a Venus childtrap in the woods, Bat?' asked Granny. 'I've travelled the world but I'd never have imagined something like that could even exist!'

Bat shrugged. 'The woods are full of surprises. I guess that's why I miss them . . .' And now she scratched her head. 'I guess that's why I'm leaving.'

There were loud protests from the others: 'You can't go, Bat, you can't!' and 'Granny, you won't let her, will you?'

Granny Grit might have objected but she knew that Bat

had her mind made up. Children didn't belong in the Get Lost Forever Woods but Bat was no ordinary child. She was done with school, horrid or not.

'You'll take your classwork into the woods as we discussed earlier this morning,' said Granny in her sternest voice. 'You'll visit once a week and turn up for every test! And one last thing.'

Bat stiffened. She knew what grown-ups were like. They were always laying down rules. Always springing surprises.

'The Middlemist's Red and some of the other plants that were stolen from the gardens are too fragile to be moved back right away. You'll make sure they're fine, won't you?'

Bat grinned from ear to ear, showing off two rows of gloriously uneven teeth.

'And don't you try skipping your dental visits!' finished Granny. Bat might have objected but she knew that Granny Grit had her mind made up too.

'I'd like you to have this to remember me by,' said Bat, feeling suddenly grateful.

Granny stared solemnly at the snot-soaked handkerchief Bat had just handed her. 'Would you mind if we washed it first?'

Bat didn't see the point of washing it but of course, she didn't mind.

Meanwhile, halfway across the world, the police raided Covetus Clutch's home. Many endangered plant and animal species were returned to their rightful homes. No one was happier than a certain bamboo lemur.

Or maybe one person was as happy. 'The manager of the

Botanical Gardens, a Ms Passiflora Patel, called this morning to thank us all for finding the Valentine Thief!' said Granny Grit. 'She's invited us to the gardens for a special private tour next week!'

The children cheered, Phil and Fermina loudest of all. After all, they'd missed the picnic the last time around.

'She even asked about you, Mallus!' said Granny, raising an eyebrow in his direction. 'She wondered if you'd like to see how the lotus you sat on is doing? Would you like that?'

Mallus flushed. He was surprised to find himself nodding. Yes, he would like that very much.

The aroma of vanilla wafted through the kitchen. Everyone inhaled. It made it impossible to talk any more.

'Shall we grab plates?' said Granny as Cook Fracas wheeled out the largest crème brawlay they had ever seen.

'Here, Volumina, next to us!' shouted Fermina, patting the seat next to hers. Ferg did a silent count as he picked up plates for all his friends. Fermina, Immy, Phil, Volumina and Bat. How was it possible, he marvelled as he set the plates out, that their gang had grown even larger?

Volumina looked around at her new friends. What was she forgetting? 'Wait, I'll be back!' she said. 'There's place for two more.'

She walked to the back of the room where a pair of boys were preparing to eat alone. As she once had.

'I'd like to make a toast,' said Ferg, standing up. 'To Granny Grit, alive and well.'

'It is a small miracle, isn't it?' giggled Granny Grit. 'After all, how many grannies do *you* know who wander about the largest rainforest on earth, untraceable for days, and then emerge *alive and well?*'

'You didn't tell us what happened!' said Fermina.

'Or why you took so long to return!' said Immy.

Granny Grit shook her head. 'I thought a Gritter of mine was in trouble, but instead, I was led on a wild goose chase. I ended up stumbling upon a plot to build horrid schools all over the Amazon. I didn't expect to be gone for so long. No one did, which is why I was presumed dead. And the news of my death brought Covetus Clutch crawling out of the woodwork like the insect he is.'

The children looked disappointed. 'We'd been expecting—' began Ferg.

'—a rollicking story,' continued Immy.

'In typical Granny style!' pitched in Phil.

'With caimans and anacondas in it,' said Fermina, her eyes shining.

Granny smiled with her eyes. 'That's a story for another day. Now may I make a toast too?'

She cut the crème brawlay as carefully as she could. No flying sugar shards this time. 'Now that everyone has got their just desserts,' and she paused to think about Covetus Clutch and Dr Bloom for the last time, 'let's tuck into ours!'

A NOTE TO THE WONDERING READER

What I've gained from this book is the treasure trove of fascinating things I discovered while writing it. Who would have thought that crows were so intelligent? Or that goats would make wonderful pets? Or even that there are leaves on a tree somewhere that respond to vibrations?

I feel deeply thankful for a world that is magical and mind-boggling beyond anything my imagination can conjure up. And for the play-dough ability of the English language to bend and twist and stretch itself to express anything.

All the incredibly extraordinary plants and flowers in this book are real. Go look for yourself. Except for the Venus childtrap, which I conjured up out of my own imagination. Of course, one can never be too sure.

Read More in Puffin

Horrid High

by Payal Kapadia

A riotous, rambunctious adventure in the world's most horrid school–the first instalment!

If eleven-year-old Ferg Gottin had been bought from a store, his parents would have returned him and demanded a refund. For Mr and Mrs Gottin, parenting is an experiment gone badly wrong. So they look for a school where you can dump your kids and forget about them. At Horrid High, everything is downright horrid, from Chef Gretta's cooking to Master Mynus's truly mental maths classes. But Ferg finds four friends with extraordinary skills, and they make a series of startling discoveries about their horrid school. Can they survive Horrid High together? And can they stop Principal Perverse's wicked plans before it's too late? Open the gates of *Horrid High* and find out!

Read More in Puffin

Wisha Wozzariter

by Payal Kapadia

A charming story about a little girl's dream of becoming a writer.

'I wish I was a writer,' sighed Wisha.

'Well, you are Wisha Wozzariter,' said the Bookworm.

'So I am! But I don't quite know where to begin.'

'At the beginning, of course,' said the Bookworm, rolling his eyes.

Ten-year-old Wisha wishes to be a writer. When she meets Bookworm, she stops wishing and starts writing. With him, she rides on the Thought Express to the Marketplace of Ideas, the Superhero Salon and the Bargain Bazaar, and encounters a motley crew of characters.

Along the way, she discovers the creative process by which anything beautiful and lasting is created, a process in which Faith, Luck and Destiny play no mean part.

Roger Dahl's zany illustrations bring Wisha's imaginative world to life. Join Wisha on this rollicking writer's adventure and find out how she finally fulfils her dream of becoming a writer!